UNVEILING A PERFECT LOVE:

A Convergence of Fiction and Poetry

by
Kimberly C. Huff

PublishAmerica
Baltimore

First printing

ISBN: 1-4137-6608-0
PUBLISHED BY PUBLISHAMERICA, LLLP
www.publishamerica.com
Baltimore

Printed in the United States of America

Table of Contents

INTRODUCTION

Truly, the Holy Bible is the number one authority on the subject of relationships, for it promotes relationship with an omnipotent, omniscient savior—the eternal and righteous advocate. He was found in fashion as a man, which proves His desire to relate to man, and His desire to experience and be touched with the feeling of man's imperfections. The Bible is the perfect love story, which unveils the perfect love of God. From beginning to ending, from Genesis to Revelation, God's perfect plan of becoming one with His people is exemplified.

I pray that you find yourself intertwined in these pages and that this fictitious publication will bring to life new insight into God's individual purpose for you. I pray that you will possess an insatiable yearning to have a lifelong covenant with the one whom your soul loves. I pray that your heart will once again become ready to receive love, and thus give it away. I pray that the plight of the main character proves that "Perfect Love" can exist, once the fear of not having love reciprocated is eradicated, for those whose love cohabits with fear have not reached the full maturity of love, neither can they experience the full benefit of love.

This book is dedicated to you because you have truly determined to leave your excuses in the past and are constantly seeking God and learning to apply His example of relational love and wisdom.

To my family, friends, and counselors of the Word of God, thanks so much for our endlessly sound conversations regarding relationships. You are a gift to me, and this is our gift to God's people!

Special thanks to the most awesome and talented editing crew—Elect Lady Bunny Greer, Minister Eric and Sister Tanya Williams, Bobbie Townsend, Sister Yolanda Wilson, Jennifer Brooks, Veroncia Daffin, Josavonna Davis, Concetta Lewis, Lucio Lewis, Minister Shaun Maloy, Rogjett Peterson, Maurice & Akecia Thompson and Minister Tabitha Williams.

KEEP YOUR HEART SOFT...

Chapter One
A Greater Appreciation

Wisdom urged me to be patient along this expedition.
The stipulations were simple, yet quite expensive.
I was told that the process of sanctification could not be rushed,
and that I should commit to waiting patiently.
I was urged to welcome opposition,
which would alleviate shamelessness,
and multiply experience and hope.
Knowing my struggle would not be in vain,
I could be steadfast, unmoveable, and always abounding.

Yet instead of resisting and enduring,
in my desperation for companionship, a decade had passed and
I had habitually walked a path that attached me to strays of my faith.
I justified the journeys by branding each companion as confidant and protector.
I thought I could not bear traveling alone.
No, I did not know the companion's history,
past curricula, nor the agenda to come.
But I soon discovered that this companion believed in nothingness.
Yet I was taught to believe in everything righteous,

until I was inevitably persuaded otherwise.
A whirlwind came, and the dirt road we encountered was dry.
It did not offer much support, nor did my companion.
So I chose a greener pasture, which brought another companion.
But as I purposed to go south,
my companion went north, and so we parted.
And I was again alone and in solitude,
when I realized my path had shifted,
and my destination was even further than I anticipated.
My mistakes originally brought
necessary chastening, which birthed anger and bitterness.
But I was cleansed with love,
and the replacement was wisdom, strength, and courage to endure.

Rehiring wisdom and love as my counselors,
I found safety in this multitude.
I walked away from simplicity,
and my secret prayer was rewarded openly.
I did not allow my mistakes to consume me,
but I took them by the reins
and learned to steer them in the direction of destiny
wherein I would meet my eternal companion.
Inexplicably, I ascended expeditiously as an eagle,
and as I waited, I found my strength was renewed.
And the companion sent by wisdom and love
was the beloved friend my soul yearned for!

This companion is the object of my faith.
This companion is the lover of my soul.
This companion is my salvation from myself,
because of this companion's willingness to give the ultimate sacrifice.
The fresh, winding road we trod is rocky, yet concrete,
because I was turned back toward wisdom.

I now have a great appreciation for this newly-found strength.
Thus, I will not bewail the past or the future.
Because I fought hard for the manifestation,
I have a greater appreciation for this companion.

My hope is that this is the unveiling of
the perfect companion and the perfect timing for a perfect love,
and our rendezvous will continue perfectly
forever and beyond eternity.

Chapter Two
You Know It All

Lisa sat in the intensive care unit waiting room of St. John's reflecting on the current events transpiring in her life. She was experiencing nausea, coupled with feelings of pain and guilt. These emotions had not surfaced overnight, but had become noticeably overbearing and seemingly beyond her control. Of late, she had many restless nights. Even her eating habits were changing.

It took all of her strength to stay focused. Outwardly, she was normal, but inwardly, the voice in her head was strong and she could not shake the nagging feeling that she was a failure. She was appalled that, yet again, she was at a point in life where she felt extremely distracted and confused.

Lisa had felt very uneasy the past Sunday as Pastor Lindsay preached about enduring as "a soldier in God's army." She remembered thinking of the many unresolved issues she had subconsciously put on hold for years. She needed to search herself and rid herself of her past, once and for all. *That's what we all say, huh, Lord?* she thought. "I'm so, so, sorry!" she whispered, with tears swelling up in her eyes.

Six months prior, Lisa promised herself to focus on being the virtuous and forgiving person she had always intended to become. Yet she became preoccupied with school and work. During that time, she also met her current beau, James. There was no animosity between them, nor was she blaming him for her anguish. However, their relationship was masking her greater issues. Originally, she figured that having him by her side would lessen her load but, it had only compounded things. Now she had to sever her ties with the man, with which she had purposed to spend the rest of her life.

Her mind battled back and forth between two extremes—the idea that things were going fairly smoothly, and the reality of the situation—which forced her to admit she always had second thoughts. However, James kept calling, so her feminine intuition responded. Also, Aunt Ellen, whose opinion she valued dearly, kept stressing that James would be a great choice. Lisa agreed that someday James would likely make a great husband—just not for her.

In the past year, Lisa had dated four guys. Things turned out the same—Man pursues woman. Woman enjoys man's pursuit. The glitz of the pursuit wears off. Woman feels something is missing and is forced to move on. This reality forced her to acknowledge that the bulk of her issues laid within her.

The announcement over the intercom brought her mind back to the present. James's grandfather was in the hospital and she was there providing moral support. But it seemed more like their relationship was one excuse after another.

Lisa took a deep breath, and fought back tears. *I'm so emotional today,* she laughed within herself, knowing that she was a very emotional person most days. Just then, James's 13-year-old sister laid her head on Lisa's shoulder. Lisa rustled her hair and kissed her on the cheek, hoping to make her feel better.

She knew it would be hard to sever her ties with James's family. She had become a part of their weekly routine and had developed a very close relationship with his mom and older sister, Bonnie. Lisa always prided herself on being a respectable young lady who guys took home to their mothers. Yet it backfired because the attachment caused her to still get invitations to their family functions long after the relationship ended. Most had eventually fizzled out, even with her ex-boyfriend Paul's mom, Ms. Jamison. She had even warned Lisa that Paul may not be what she "needed in a husband until he matured more." That was a nice way of saying that her son was a clown, and was wasting Lisa's time. Lisa decided that she would do whatever it took to begin the inevitable process of separation, which would lead to the necessary process of healing, even if it included cutting off people she had grown to love dearly. *Lord, Please help me! I can't do it myself. Change whatever you need to. I need to move to the next stage in life because I can't continue as I am,* she prayed silently.

Lisa felt such a sense of déjà vu. She thought about her relationship with John Davis, her first true love. Things had gotten complicated and distressing between them. Yet she had a weakness for him long after they parted. Even at that moment she wondered where life's circumstances had taken him. She could not help but wish that things had worked out perfectly between them. He had treated her like a queen. He had been so spiritually mature, so physically gorgeous, and so perfect in every way…

"Are you hungry?" James whispered, interrupting Lisa's daydreaming. "Let's go somewhere, and sit down and have a good meal. I think Mom and Dad are planning to stay here until Dr. Siebert hires them," he said, as he playfully grabbed her and hugged her tightly.

Lisa smiled, but arising within her was an urge to give him a few reasons why they should never do anything together again. She imagined herself with a serious look on her face saying, *Actually, the allotted time for me to be annoyed with this whole scene, and particularly with your presence has expired.* She wanted to blurt out her feelings no matter how offensive, but instead she voiced the soft-spoken words, "I am a little hungry, but I need to get home and work on my paper. Fast food will have to suffice."

The look on James's face was one of disbelief. "Okay," he said, "I'll tell Mom and Dad we're leaving."

They walked to his car, in silence. They hardly spoke in the drive-through. By the time they arrived at her home, she felt such an urgency to move on. She wanted and needed progress in that facet of her life. She was totally convinced that James did not possess what she was looking for in a mate.

"Good night, beautiful," he said, as he hugged her and kissed her.

"Good night, sweetie," she said, out of respect more than anything else.

Lisa was in a melancholy mood while at the hospital and on the ride home. However, as she locked the door, she was overcome with an urge to release her stress. When she felt exceptionally emotional, or hyper, she often got extremely silly. Most of the time she kept her urges inside. She never had to put forth any extra effort in those instances, her imagination just seemed to take over and run wild. This was one of the ways she let off steam.

Her stepfather got such a kick out of that side of her personality. He had labeled her outbursts as "joking spasms," and had jokingly told her that he was going to check her into an insane asylum. "Mona Lisa, I can't believe how goofy you can get. Usually, you're my calm, reserved, highly educated, and bourgeois child," he had said. "I see now that you're an undercover clown with two personalities—one for impressing the big shots, and one for us peons in the world."

This particular spasm brought to mind a bug repellant commercial that her cousin, Tonya, had told her about. Her 3-year-old son had gotten several time-outs the day he saw it and asked, "Mommy, does that work for teachers, too?"

In the commercial, a family was having dinner when an enormous bug crawled near the teenage daughter's foot. Her father called the exterminator, who showed up immediately. The next scene showed the young lady at school being approached by a nerdy-looking guy. When she opened her locker to show that she had her handy, travel-sized bug spray he immediately disappeared, fearing the power of the repellant. The caption at the end of the commercial read, "Zap it and forget it! Use it for anything that bugs you!"

The parallel of the situations was quite hilarious to Lisa. She imagined herself running to the cabinet and reaching for her bug repellant to spray James before he drove off. Maybe she would not have to spray him and he would just leave on his own once he saw it.

She chuckled aloud, "Lord, I need some James repellant, please! And I need it to work immediately! Well, I at least need the willpower to make it through another break-up season," she said sincerely. She shook her head in laughter. If only her real-life circumstances could be solved so simply.

As she went into the kitchen to pour herself some pineapple-orange juice, and find something to eat, the phone rang. Even though the Caller ID said that the caller's information was unavailable, she decided to answer, in case it was her cousin, Cliff, calling from his cell phone.

"Hello."

"Hi. Is Ms. Wilson available?"

"Speaking!" Lisa was aggravated. It was not Cliff. It was a bill collector.

"This is Kenneth calling from Community Credit Union. I'm sorry to call you so late, but we need you to make a payment and bring your account current."

"Actually, I don't have a calendar in front of me, so I'll have to call you back."

"Ms. Wilson, you've sent the last six payments in late. You need to pay this debt as promised," the representative said with a harsh tone.

"Yeah, I got behind, but I'll be able to catch up soon," Lisa said calmly.

"Ms. Wilson, your car payment is already 45 days overdue. It's imperative that you handle this situation or we'll be forced to take further action."

"Look! I said I'll call back! If that's not sufficient then I guess this conversation is over." Lisa was annoyed.

"Ms. Wilson, it is not acceptable..."

Lisa had had enough. She was already carrying enough stress, and did not need additional reminders that her life was a mess. She put the conversation in the back of her mind. She would deal with it in a few weeks when she got paid.

Per her nightly routine, she double-checked that her keys were on the staircase landing, so she would not forget them and lock herself out again. Then she started the dishwasher, cleaned up the kitchen, and went upstairs to prepare for bed. The phone had rung while she was cleaning, but she did not answer. Anger rose up inside of her when she saw that it had been Mandy Redding, her college roommate. They had not spoken in about a year. Lisa deleted her name and number from the Caller ID and got in bed.

As the phone rang 30 minutes later, she did not even bother looking at the Caller ID. "Hello," she managed to get out, preparing herself for aggravation.

"Hey, young one," came the voice from the other end.

"David?"

"That's right. I know we e-mail each other a lot, but I haven't heard your sweet voice in a while. Man, you got a boyfriend, now you don't have time for your friends no more. I still love you, though," he said laughingly.

She laughed. "Yeah, it's about time for your dose of the Mona Lisa, isn't it?"

"Yeah! I guess so," David said sarcastically. "How've you been?" he asked. "I mean the real you, not the side of you that thinks she's a stand-up comedian."

"I'm great, I guess. How are you?" Lisa had lots of issues she could have brought up, but she did not want to overburden David at such a late hour.

"Well, I'm great, too, just a little home sick. But I'll be home in a few weeks, and I wanted to make sure I'd get to see you. Tell your husband-to-be that we're just friends. I'm not trying to steal you away. We'll do something safe, like our usual dinner and bowling. Of course, he's welcome to come."

"I doubt if he'll want to be in the same vicinity with me by the time you get here, but we'll talk about that later. And don't act like I'm not always available for you. Maybe I'll even give you some bowling lessons this time, for a small fee, of course. And I'll get the chance to pry into your business for a change."

"Yeah right! My life is an open book. Ask whatever you want to know," David said. "I am the walking letter of recommendation to Christ, an epistle to be read by all men." He was mocking their old Sunday school teacher.

They both laughed.

David continued. "Well, if you're having problems with your knight in shining armor, then obviously we have a lot to talk about. What are you afraid of now, that Mr. Big Shot won't be able to afford you or something?"

"Ha. Ha. Ha. Very Funny!" Lisa's voice was shaky.

David tried to be supportive without prying. "Okay, Lisa. I always knew that you didn't have a poker face, but now I'm learning that you're not very good at hiding your feelings over the phone, either. Tell me what's really going on?"

"Well, since you begged me." She laughed, trying not to cry. "I feel stuck because I had what I wanted, and can't seem to get it back. I know you don't want to hear about John." She paused. "I think what hurt most was watching him go through woman after woman, trying to find with them what we already had."

"Ah, sweetie, I don't mind. And as I've told you before, you don't have to feel bad for loving John or for being blinded by love, but you need to be open-minded in order to receive love again. If you've attached your happiness to one person, then pray till God shows you how to detach it. All the promises He gave you concerning a mate are still good. They weren't attached to John."

"I know, and I know that I'll be okay. I've been thinking..."

"Don't hurt yourself!" David joked. He always found a way to make Lisa feel better, not allowing her to sulk in her misery.

"Whatever! Seriously, I've found it necessary for a woman to experience heartache in order to grow, and learn to encounter such deep hurt and survive. On the same token, it seems necessary for a man to hurt a woman he truly loves in order to have a greater appreciation for the one with whom he chooses to spend the rest of his life."

What Lisa said actually lined up with David's life's story. "Wow! Kudos! That actually makes a lot of sense."

"David, you know that I've been hurt, and of course, I've hurt others. And now I feel like I spend all of my time repenting and going through the same issues over and over. Do you ever get the feeling that something is missing and that you need a change in your life, once and for all?"

"Hey, we all feel as if we're wasting time or going in circles. We keep making the same mistakes because, frankly, our flesh is enjoying the ride.

Our flesh is our enemy which is why the Bible tells us to mortify it. And that can be a long process. Allowing our sensuous nature to guide us will jack us up! Simply having control over our flesh, or should I say, self-control isn't enough. That comes and goes depending on our feelings. But the way I see it, the more we mess up and learn from our mistakes, the more experience we chalk up and the closer we move to our target." David thought for a moment. "Geez, as much as you beat up on yourself, you don't need any enemies. Stop doing that, young one."

"Yes, sir." Lisa was sniffling.

David continued. "Hey, it's actually good to feel bad every now and then. It shows the Lord how desperately we need Him. David, the psalmist, my namesake..." He laughed. "Says in Psalm 51, '...a broken and a contrite heart, O God, thou wilt not despise.' God sees that you have a repentant heart. I love to read about David. I think that one reason he's referred to as a man after God's own heart is that he was constantly in fellowship with God. He had a constant focus on getting his act together. When that king jacked up, he did so royally. No pun intended. But he also kept a repentant heart. That's how you stay close to God. His heart was soft toward King Saul, who tried to kill him, and even toward his son, who tried to dethrone him. His heart was pure at all times. So, you're on the right track. Keep your heart soft, young one. Do you hear me?"

"Yes, I do. And, thank you, sir," Lisa managed to get out through her tears.

"God's Word is true and it's in you. He's not slack concerning any promise He's made. So walk boldly. You hear me, young one?"

Lisa felt a lot better. "Loud and clear, old one."

"I'm sorry. I wasn't trying to fuss or lecture. I know it's late, so we'll finish this later. I'll shoot you an e-mail tomorrow, around noonish, with my flight info. I know you're a busy, business woman. So that's the most feasible way to catch you."

Lisa could not deny that she was addicted to electronic mail and spent lots of time on instant messaging (IM) software.

"Hey, I've also been meaning to ask if you've talked to Heather lately?"

"Nope. I guess she wrote me off. Whenever you tell somebody about themselves, especially if a trifling man's involved, you should expect them to separate from you."

"True. Well, I'm sure you've had a long day and you're ready to tackle your bed. I just wanted to make sure that your schedule would be open for me."

"I'm here for you anytime, except Monday through Sunday," she joked.

"No. You know I'm always available for you."

"That's all I needed to hear. I love you, Lisa. You're always in my prayers."

"Thanks, David. I love you, too. Have a good night."

Lisa missed David. They attended the same church growing up, and went to the state university together. Lisa recalled the time they went to eat at a restaurant near campus. David went into the rest room. They were out of his original request of chicken breasts, so Lisa ordered him a steak sub and some fries. "It's a good thing you know your boyfriend so well. That way I can put your order in right now," the waitress told Lisa. Lisa had simply smiled. No need to try to correct her, or the others that had mistaken them for a couple.

It had been two years since David's job transferred him to Chicago. Their friendship had actually grown stronger. Initially, it had been hard, but neither of them wanted to be responsible for him missing out on such a great opportunity. Lisa was thankful that his girlfriend, Susan, did not mind sharing him with her.

Sometimes she felt that she used her friends as a crutch, but she realized that they needed one another for accountability sake. Having them around helped her maintain her sanity. David, and her cousins, Cliff and Tonya, along with her best friend, Krystal, had been there for her when she broke up with John, her beau of three and a half years. She would need their help with her current dilemma with James, as well.

Lisa wondered if she would ever find "the one" and live "happily ever after." She was tired of relationship horror. She prayed, although she felt so unworthy of God's attention or presence. She had failed Him many times. Yet her mom would always say, "Failure is giving up." And so she refused to give up without a fight. Her Pastor had recently taught them that pressing on was the only way to access their futures, in spite of their current struggles.

Lisa read Psalm 34:19. "Many are the afflictions of the righteous, but the Lord delivereth him out of them all." She grabbed hold of that attitude by faith. She told herself that additional afflictions were included in the package, but that additional deliverance was also included. "God will not let us go, if we do not let Him go," Pastor Lindsay had said. Lisa was so appreciative. She could not fathom why God would spend so much time on someone so undeserving, although she knew that no one could really deserve God's love and grace.

Her life was such a mess, yet she still felt in her spirit that God was dealing with her. Having the foreknowledge that she would botch things up pretty badly along the way, He had still called her to do great things and it amazed her that God would choose to use someone who was prone to fail.

Hebrews 5:2 came to mind. *Who can have compassion on the ignorant, and on them that are out of the way; for that he himself also is compassed with infirmity*. Lisa exclaimed aloud, "You called me because I'm such a mess, I'll have compassion on others and help lead them to you."

She realized that if God did ever run out of mercy, she would be the one He would use it up on. She constantly used her daily portion. Yet He kept on giving her time to get herself together and remained mercy-seated regarding her situation. She vowed to get it together before He was forced into the judgment seat. She would not stop seeking Him until she got it right.

"Lord, I'm going to be just like You when I grow up!" she said aloud.

As she dozed off, David's question rang in her head, *What are you afraid of now?* Lisa was too tired to think straight. She did not look at the Caller ID the next three times the phone rang, but she was certain that at least one of the callers had been James. She did not have the strength to deal with him.

She lay on her back a few more moments, talking to the Lord. She remembered that there was a time when they were not on the best of terms. She was happy that He had restored her with open arms. It was as if they had never parted. With God, she did not have to put up a front, or pretend. The more she trusted Him, the more she wanted to trust Him. She did not come to Him using fancy words or clichés, she approached Him as her most holy, understanding Friend. She knew that God was omniscient, but she still wanted to express her feelings, "Lord, you know the beginning of my story, and you know how it will end. God, You know it all. And I trust you to do right by me!"

You Know It All

Remember the deal we made, the vow I vowed?
You knew from the beginning that I would fail.
You know everything.
You Know it All!

You knew I would miss the mark, yet You still called me.
Then You loved me to repentance. And You gave me purpose.
Then You increased my faith.
Then, again, I missed the mark. Yet You loved me unconditionally.
And You reminded me of The Call and Your purpose.
And Your mercy—It strengthened me.
For godly sorrow does work repentance—a change of heart and mind!
My spirit longs for You so. My flesh is yet resisting.
But You know all that. You know everything.
You Know it All!

I thank You that You have forgiven me and washed me clean. I still have hope.
Your character entitles You to be gracious, merciful, and long-suffering.
I need You!
Please teach me how to possess Your characteristics.
You know how to do that. You know everything.
You Know it All!

I know You're going to transform me.
I know You will perfect that which concerneth me,
(from the least of my issues to the greatest),
because Your mercy endureth forever. It won't be long now.
Whatever You do, as always, I'm going to seek You,
and I will yet praise Your name in everything!
You're awesome! Through Salvation You've already done so much!
I'm going to praise You, no matter what happens,
on the road to my expected end of victory.
But You know that, because You know everything.
You Know it All!

Chapter Three
Love the Difference

Lisa had only been asleep four hours when she felt God's presence. Oftentimes, He awoke her when there was minimal distraction. For weeks, she had conditioned herself to ignore His nudge. Yet this early Monday morning, He met her by her bedside as soon as she knelt to pray. As she praised Him, He reminded her of things He had spoken into her spirit almost three years prior. He told her that He would use for His glory, everything that she had encountered. It was as if, while she was hopelessly wandering around the past few years, feeling stagnant, God had secretly pulled her aside.

God had given her a vision to start a community organization to teach values such as self-esteem, and self-respect. Lisa had a passion for working with young people. She dreamed of someday using a secular setting to teach them Biblical principles, as well as instill in them the importance of education.

She could hear God clearly saying, "I'm a God that cannot lie." He prompted her to once again read Isaiah 66:9, as He had done three years prior, "Shall I bring to the birth, and not cause to bring forth? saith the LORD: shall I cause to bring forth, and shut the womb? saith thy God."

God had called her to an awesome task. She wanted to walk boldly in it, but she often felt there were things blocking her way. Add to that her lackadaisical ways, and the fact that she had allowed her focus to be deterred by her temporary career in Corporate America, she now felt far behind. She decided right then to unmask herself before God. She listed the things she needed resolved. So that she could face God in peace, and live comfortably with herself.

The first thing that came to mind was her constant dependency on men, currently James, because of her fear of neglect. She also recognized the trickle of resentment that existed toward her parents for her lopsided upbringing. Thirdly, was the constant financial distress she experienced. She wanted a raise, but she also knew that she was overspending and overindulging—a habit she picked up in college when she was introduced to the credit-card-frenzy. The healing of her finances, within itself, was such a complicated request.

Her mind went back to her conversation with the credit union rep. She repented for being argumentative. She recalled Proverbs 15:1, which says it is "a soft answer [which] turneth away wrath: but grievous words stir up anger." She wanted to perfect the art of giving a soft answer. And she knew that she should pay her debts on time. Psalm 37:21, states that "the wicked borroweth, and payeth not again: but the righteous showeth mercy, and giveth." She did not want to be wicked by borrowing money that she did not have the means to repay. And she certainly did not want such things blocking her direct path to God. *These are the issues I know of,* she told the Lord. *Please search me and cleanse me of even my secret faults. Send Your grace and mercy speedily into my situation,* she prayed.

She was reminded of the prophecy that had gone forth in exhortation in worship service: "Offenses will come, but I'm ready to place the miracle of love in your heart, but you have to allow me to!" She lifted her hands and worshipped in the Holy Spirit. *Lord, please make my root clean, then inevitably we'll get the rest of me together! I love You so much!* she prayed. As she closed out her prayer session, Lisa was grateful for relief, not because anything had necessarily changed or improved, but because she was pregnant with God's promises.

Lisa also took notes for her Sunday morning leadership course. She had six weeks left. Elder Saunders assigned them the task of seeking God for their destined direction of ministry, their role in the local church, and the spiritual gifts He had imparted into them. During the second week of the course, Lisa told him that she had been called to teach. She asked for his counsel so that she would follow God's instructions to a tee. He advised her to use the time to allow her gift of teaching and administering God's Word to be developed, and to seek God for further instruction. Truly, God had given her guidance and direction that morning.

She also spoke with her pastor about teaching. It was as if he had been listening in on her conversation with Elder Saunders. He told her that God was going to use her mightily and that she should continue to fast, pray, study The Word, and get ready for God to impart into her even more. He did not tell her at that time, but he was planning to appoint her to teach the young adult courses.

Within the same time frame, Elder Peterson, had laid hands on her and prophesied to her that God was fixing her heart and that her divine purpose and destiny were waiting on her. Lisa had been taught that laying hands and imparting were used to establish and strengthen God's people. Imparting was God's way of transmitting quickly what it could take years to teach. Lisa was excited when Pastor Lindsay explained that impartation could be compared to infrared beam technology. "Technology is finally catching up with what God's been doing," he had joked. "They think the concept of being on-line is new, but for years the saints have been saying Jesus is on the main line."

Lisa's gift had been affirmed and confirmed several times, right after which, things began to progress quickly. She was elated, yet overwhelmed. During that time, she began to feel a need to separate herself from James and enjoy freedom from relationship drama. The stress associated with obtaining her master's degree would also end in less than a year, and she was counting down the days.

Lisa also had a wonderful prayer session on Tuesday morning. She had been taught to get with God, "while the spirit was moving." On Wednesday morning when her alarm sounded, she lay back down. Two hours later, she realized that she had missed the weekly Early-Morning Prayer Service.

Lisa had a lot to do that day and she was tired just thinking about it. She had set aside that day to consecrate and pray. She tried not to focus on the fact that she was hungry. She was determined to make it until 5:00 p.m.—the time that her consecration expired. She was already anticipating eating the leftover fried chicken, vegetables, and rice she had cooked the day before.

If she was not extremely busy, she often went to Afternoon Prayer Service during her lunch hour. As Cliff would say, there was, "a need to take a pause for the cause." But today she did not make it to either prayer service. She had a meeting after lunchtime, so she planned to sit in a conference room and read her Bible and pray. She needed to hear from God and did not want any distractions.

While tidying her cubicle, she heard her cell phone vibrating. The caller ID screen said, *The Parents.* Her brother had given that name to their mom and stepfather based on a hit flick. She had programmed it into her cell phone. She figured it was her mom's daily, morning call. Lisa enjoyed their conversations, even when her mom shared songs she taught the senior choir. Her mom was not a famed recording artist, nor was she Lisa's favorite singer, but her voice was tolerable. And Lisa had grown to love and appreciate her mom's cheerfulness in song, which always showed up in their conversations.

When she answered the phone, she was shocked to hear her brother's voice on the other end. "Hey, lil' sis," Mike said. "How's your day going?"

"Great. How about you?" Lisa hoped she was not about to get an update on the latest fiasco between Mike and his wife.

"Good! I can't complain," he replied, "uh, I'm here with 'The Parents.' Your mother just got off the freeway reenacting a scene from a demolition derby."

"What are you talking about?"

"Well, let me start by saying that she's fine now. She was released from the hospital about an hour ago and only has a few minor scrapes and scratches. She was going to do some early-morning shopping, when apparently a dude on his cell phone cut into her lane, and ran her off the road. So, she swerved, hit the median, went across three lanes to the other side of the freeway, skidded up the embankment and finally landed upside down."

"Oh, my goodness," Lisa practically screamed. "So, Dad wasn't in the car?"

"No, Mr. Townsend wasn't in the car," Mike corrected her. He never could bring himself to call his mother's husband his father.

Lisa was too concerned with her mom's well-being to notice. "I'm going to wrap things up here. I'll be there shortly." Lisa put away her laptop before she hung up. She prayed, and was expecting her mom's total recovery. She did not want her wonderful day to be scarred. A few years prior, Lisa probably would not have been in such a hurry to see her mom. Through her teenage years she had harbored a lot of anger toward her parents.

She peeked into her boss's office. He was not there. She sent him a voicemail message about her mother's mishap and told him that she was taking the afternoon off. When she got back to her cubicle, she remembered that it was Cliff's late day and he did not go into the law firm until after noon. She connected to the IM software using her cell phone, hoping he would be on-line.

Mona Lisa says: Mornin'.
The Righteous are Bold as a Lion says: Mornin' sweetie. How r u?
Mona Lisa says: I'm leaving work. Mom was in an accident. She's at home.
The Righteous are Bold as a Lion says: I'll meet you there before I go into the office. I'll be praying for her. And I'll pray that God consoles her little baby girl, as well. (SMILE)
Mona Lisa says: Thanks! Love ya and TTYL.

When using IM from her cell phone, Lisa used abbreviations because it was so tedious to type. "TTYL" was her quick way of saying, "Talk to ya later."

The Righteous are Bold as a Lion says: TTYL

Lisa's Aunt Josie, her mother's older sister, and her stepfather's two brothers were already at the house when she arrived. Their viewpoints always seemed to clash, so Lisa never knew what to expect. Yet they all usually had some wisdom to share. And although she was not happy that her mom had been bruised, she was grateful for an opportunity to bond with them.

Lisa finally left her parents' home at 8:00 p.m. She drove past the freeway entrance ramp. Although the traffic was light, she decided to take the scenic route so she could spend time expressing her gratitude to God for sparing her mom's life. She did not want the moment to end too soon. She actually drove the speed limit, which was a rare occurrence.

After she got home, Lisa read Lamentations 3:21-26, "This I recall to my mind, therefore have I hope. It is of the Lord's mercies that we are not consumed, because his compassions fail not. They are new every morning: great is thy faithfulness. The Lord is my portion, saith my soul; therefore will I hope in him. The Lord is good unto them that wait for him, to the soul that seeketh him. It is good that a man should both hope and quietly wait for the salvation of the Lord." Lisa meditated on the Word. She recognized that she did not have another hope, neither was she looking for another. God was her portion—her inheritance, her everything. If He could not fix her issues, then there was no hope for her.

Around 10:00 p.m., it seemed that all of her friends were settling in from Bible Study and calling to see where she had been. She did not answer several calls, but she did talk to Tina about their leadership class. "Sister Wilson, I want you to quote the theme scripture verbatim," Tina said, mocking their instructor.

"Second Samuel chapter 23, verse 3, '—The God of Israel said, the Rock of Israel spake to me, He that ruleth over men must be just, ruling in the fear of God.'" Lisa had studied that scripture for hours.

"Wow! I'm still working on that," Tina said.

"I went home and studied after that last pop quiz. I didn't do very well and…"

Tina cut her off. "Hey listen, I didn't see you at Bible study and there's something that I wanted to talk to you about." She did not allow Lisa to respond. "I think God is telling me that Cliff is my husband. What should I do?"

"Absolutely nothing," Lisa replied immediately. "And I'm only going to say this once—God doesn't force our mates on us. Brother Cunningham taught us that God presents, and we choose from the choices He gives." Lisa was trying to be sympathetic. She knew all too well that the devil had tricked people into the mentality that God would make them marry folks that they had never even dated. "Now, if, in fact, Cliff actually told you that he's interested in you, and if God says, 'Yes, Cliff is an excellent choice,' then and only then would you respond to Cliff's advances. It's the man's role to pursue and the woman's role to respond. Now that may sound old-fashioned, but it works. I always say, there are absolutely no shy men! No matter what a man does, you should pay closer attention to what he says. Just because he takes you out doesn't mean he wants to marry you. It could just mean that he was hungry." Lisa laughed. "Trust me, if a man wants more out of a relationship, he'll tell you clearly. There won't be any question."

"You sound like my grandma. But I need to be sure. Is it okay for me to ask him how he feels? I mean, I'm not trying to pressure him, but I don't want to waste time."

"Well, it depends… But if and when you ask, be prepared for his response."

"I'm prepared. And I'm glad you said that God allows us to choose, because I was confused. Sometimes Cliff seems interested, and then sometimes he seems preoccupied. And if he's not serious, then I can move on to this other guy who asked for my number. Actually, I think the other guy's a better choice."

"Did God tell you that, too?" Lisa laughed.

"Are you making fun of me?" Tina was laughing, too.

"I'm a little tickled at how quickly you were able to move on," Lisa said.

"Hey, ain't no use in crying over spilled milk, right?"

"Amen!" Lisa replied.

Tina promised to e-mail Lisa the notes from the leadership class, then they hung up. Lisa prayed that God would give Tina wisdom. Lisa had been blessed by their brief conversation. She remembered being Tina's age—being "young and dumb," as Aunt Ellen would say. Her self-esteem was very low, and she was very needy for the attention of men, no matter how detrimental. Back then she majored in crying over spilled milk.

Lisa also prayed for Cliff. Since Ahnna, he had seemingly lost his mind and was on a wild rampage after every skirt moving. Lisa knew that most of his issues were his fault because of his flirtatious ways, but she still asked God to show mercy and to also give him wisdom.

The rest of the week, Lisa spent the bulk of her days working overtime. She was helping her boss with an annual presentation, and did not have much time for her family and friends. She kept her regularly scheduled Saturday morning hair appointment and went into the office afterwards. By the time Saturday evening rolled around, she immediately plopped into bed. When she awoke, it was 6:13 a.m. She had missed Early-Morning Prayer yet another week. She promised herself that she would not miss prayer again, and went back to sleep.

After prayer service, Cliff and Melvin looked for Lisa so that they could go to their usual breakfast spot. Lisa was nowhere to be found. Ahnna had also decided to grab some breakfast. As she sat at the counter placing her carry-out order, there was a lot of commotion. She heard a familiar voice and spotted a group of guys entering the restaurant. Out of the corner of her eye, she saw Cliff approaching. Melvin had stopped to speak to the other Sunday morning regulars.

Cliff walked over and sat down. He placed his elbow on the back of her stool, leaned over the counter, and stared straight into her eyes. "Good morning! How are you today, Ms. Chambers?"

Ahnna was irritated that he thought they were still buddy-buddy and that he could be so close in her personal space. She gave him a half-smile and looked at him without saying a word. Then she turned her head slightly toward the TV on the wall.

Cliff reached into his pocket, pulled out his set of keys to her car, and slid them across the counter. "You asked me for those several weeks ago," he said.

Ahnna felt like fainting. Several thoughts raced through her mind. *Why is he doing this? Does he think that I still want him? Is he telling me that he still has feelings for me? Is he trying to work his flirting mojo on me?* Well, he could forget it. She was not going to let him win this one.

Before Ahnna could catch herself, she turned towards Cliff, and kissed him loudly, right smack on the lips. "Thanks!" Then she pushed him away and said, "Mojo meets Mojo, huh?"

By this time, Melvin was watching with a huge smile on his face. Cliff walked to the table and sat dumbfounded. "Did I miss something?" Melvin asked, laughing uncontrollably. "Do the saints need a hotel? The saints just fornicated, or should I say forni-kissed right in public? Can you explain what just happened?"

Cliff pushed him. "You saw the whole thing."

Melvin was still laughing. He barely heard what Cliff was saying.

"Man, shut up before I give you 'The Big Leg' right here in public." Cliff was referring to a wrestling move that he and Melvin often used to tackle one another.

The waitress gave Ahnna her food and she walked politely past them without saying a word. Melvin rushed pass her to the door and opened it for her, then he took her bag and walked her to her car.

"What just happened in there? As if I don't already know, huh? You guys are sickening!" he said. "I wish you would stop playing these games."

"Thanks, Mel," she said as he opened her car door. "Love ya!"

Melvin shook his head and walked away. Ahnna simultaneously started her car and called Lisa. Driving away, she saw Katie pulling into the parking lot. Too bad she had missed the show. Then again, Cliff would not have been so freely in her personal space had Katie been there.

Ahnna had forgotten how early it was. Lisa answered the phone sleepily.

"Good Morning!" Ahnna said. "You won't believe what I just did."

"What time is it?"

"Lisa, get up. It's 7:41 a.m., and why weren't you at Morning Prayer, anyway?"

"I overslept. You should have called me."

Ahnna told Lisa that she would be sure to call her the next Sunday. Then she told her play-by-play about her moment of temporary insanity.

"No way!" Lisa said. "Now, I could see myself doing that, only if I were having one of my silly moments. But I can't believe you did that."

"I think you're rubbing off on me."

"I was no where around." Lisa could not stop laughing. "I can only imagine that as large as Cliff's ego is, he was more upset that he didn't think of it first."

Lisa thought it was so awkward to see Cliff with Katie. Every time Cliff brought her around, Lisa distanced herself. Cliff had noticed that she gave Katie "the cold-shoulder." Lisa had explained to him that she was just trying to distance herself from a "circle of foolishness." Besides, she was not interested in validating, what she called, his "friend-of-the-month club." It seemed that every month he was introducing her to someone new.

Cliff swore up and down that he initially met Katie because he inquired about her mother. She was in the hospital and Katie was taking it very hard. Lisa figured he had been his normally charming self, and Katie had taken it as an opportunity to cry on his shoulder. "That's how you stay in trouble," Lisa had told him, "You're too sensitive to women's needs, for your own good."

Lisa tried to console Ahnna: "You should've gone back in and slid him the keys in front of Katie and said something like, 'Oh, here's the keys back,' then winked and said, 'Mojo lesson number one!'" Lisa was on a roll. "That would be a great commercial for Mojo jeans, wouldn't it? The slogan could be—These jeans will help you to get your man back."

"You're banned from watching TV," Ahnna said. "And your cousin is a nut!"

"Yeah, but you love that nut, so…"

"Can you say emotional roller coaster? Why'd God make us this way? Why'd He give men the ability to shrug things off and stick us with this excess estrogen that makes us extra emotional? Why am I the unstable one, here?"

"You're silly. You sure you're using that term in the right context?"

"Of course not, but it makes me sound super-educated."

"Well, I think that in order for men to be providers and leaders they need to be less emotionally driven and have more sound judgment. So, God gave them more physical traits to compliment their more physical responsibility. He gave them testosterone and gave us estrogen. Ha! Since you want to get technical. Most of the time, I'm so annoyed with their seemingly nonchalant ways, but then again, I appreciate their innate ability to be carefree; I mean we can't all be estrogen monsters. Life would be a huge mess!" Lisa laughed.

"Yeah, but it's almost like they're invincible, as if they don't ever hurt."

"They hurt, they just don't show it as much," Lisa said.

"Yeah, but it just seems to come naturally for them!"

"Are you saying you wish women were more like dudes?"

"No. The guys at the office have labeled one of my coworkers as the man in her marriage. It's like she's programmed herself to not respond. Yet you can see past all of that, and see when she's hurting. She's the other extreme."

"No! Don't hold stuff in. Release it to God. He listens, helps, and at the same time, keeps your business a secret."

"That's okay though, I won this battle. I worked my mojo on him," Ahnna said, sniffling as if she had just won a rough fight with the neighborhood bully.

Lisa felt her poetic creativity stirring up. "I got the floor, and I'm about to flow with some revelation knowledge." She cleared her throat. "You say you worked your mojo on him, huh? Well, the mojo is just a superficial copy of love. It stings, but it won't stick. It has no substance. It doesn't require reciprocation, which is what every person in love seeks. The mojo only thrives when it connives, but true love is like a machine gun. And if you pull the trigger on the right one, they won't be able to recover." They both burst out with laughter. "Please, hold your applause," she continued, as if she were on stage performing. "I must conclude that when necessary, the barrel can be reloaded." Lisa paused as if awaiting the applause to cease. Then she continued, "Thank you. I love you all."

Ahnna loved Lisa's poetic moments. "You're in rare form today. Wow! I guess you wake up creative. That was good, though. It's hard to believe someone so silly can be so talented. I'm going to share that with my coworkers. They love talking about relationships."

"Don't disburse it too freely or I'll sue you for copyright infringement."

"Whatever! As you said, the mojo *is* superficial." Ahnna sighed. "I find myself struggling back and forth between loving Cliff, and, at the same time, hating him. Sometimes I just go with the flow. And every now and then I have to pull back if I feel I'm becoming too dependent upon him again, of course, then he calls even more. Either way, I'm miserable. I think I need to make a decision and stick with it—either be content with where we are now, or put him out of my life forever. There's no easy answer. The 'valley of indecision' is mentally draining. Perhaps things will get better with time, but for now I need to keep fasting and praying. I don't want to go into my old age as a bitter old woman. I mean, I can understand not wanting to settle down, but geez. I wish he'd just be by himself, instead of involving others in his foolishness. I guess at some point he'll eventually make his intentions clear, but until then, it's hard to assess how I really feel because I've tried to protect myself from investing any personal feelings in him."

"Yeah, I know." Lisa could not help herself. "Women should never allow their feelings to move faster than men's, right?"

"Easier said than done, huh?"

"Easier said than done, but perhaps most necessary!" Lisa could relate to Ahnna's sentiments. "And the bottom line is that the male version of 'not settling down' is slightly different from the female version." Lisa laughed. "But we'll talk later, Ms. Mojo."

Lisa went to class and morning worship service. Tonya had called because she could tell that Lisa was not herself that day. Lisa was planning to do some work, but ended up taking a power nap. However, when she awoke again it was midnight. A few hours later she awoke, somewhat angrily.

She considered herself a writer, but, more than that, a student of God's Word. Yet sometimes she thought that she got inspired at the most inopportune times, but even a pseudo-professional writer knows that inspiration must be sited as soon as it hits, or it may be lost forever. It never failed that Lisa would never remember her thoughts in their entirety if she tried to wait. Then she would get even more frustrated. "Good Morning, Lord," she whispered. Lisa knew that she needed to get her thoughts down on paper but, it was hard to break her sleep.

She opened her eyes slowly, preparing them for the seemingly blaring light coming through the blinds from the street lights. She turned her body, and lay outstretched for several minutes. Then finally, she sat up and grabbed her pen and paper, which she left neatly tucked under her pillow each night.

Her writings were more like devotionals. David called them, "Lisa's Psalms." Periodically, she reviewed them, and used them to take mental notes on her spiritual progress. This time, as she began to write, her thoughts were racing all over. She did not stop writing until she exhausted her brain and drained the current inklings of her spirit.

Love the Difference

She is typically driven by emotion.
Well, it's not extremely bad.
It's why she's freely able to express herself
(whether happy, in-between, or sad).
He is typically focused on the physical realm
and what he can see and touch.
And in all actuality,
he doesn't require very much.

However, she seems to want to talk
about everything to no end,
while he would rather relax and watch sports TV,
with his legs outstretched, in the den.
Of course, there are times when he thinks it's important
to spend quality time—without drama, without a brawl.
While she wishes that he would learn to enjoy
bonding as they spend quality time in the mall.
Yes, statistics prove that she will likely
speak more than he within a given day.
Yet to her, their relationship would flourish
if he expressed himself more in a verbal way.
In her opinion, it's her way of not overlooking issues,
and allowing them to be openly discussed.
But in his opinion, it's something that can be worked out
without taking another opportunity to fuss.
To her, he often seems nonchalant and uncaring,
perhaps even somewhat callous.
But she knows it's what makes him who he is,
and thus allows him to comfortably be what he must.
She is more likely to get hysterical,
when things turn into a mess.
But he doesn't like to exert his strength
on every situation of distress.

He focuses on her curves
more than she cares to admit,
And she focuses on his virile embrace
finding comfort and strength in it.
She loves the charisma and gait of this man,
which shows that he's confident and proud!
And he loves the way she has mastered her dainty sashay,
yet avoids being offensively loud!
He likes to flex his muscles,
and she enjoys his strong attitude, as well as his playful wrestle,
because she has come to grips with the fact,
that she is, indeed, the weaker vessel.
Now, this is not an instance
where she becomes a doormat or walks in low self-esteem or shame,
for she recognizes that they are both
heirs and partakers of God's grace, just the same.

Neither one is someone the other can live without.
Neither one is labeled as the one who is always wrong!
They're just very different,
and must find a way to add a tune to this great song!

He is ever so sure of himself
and knows exactly what he wants.
Even if it's considered out of his league,
he is up to the challenge of the hunt.
When he walks confidently in his manhood
it's an occurrence a wise woman will particularly enjoy,
because she would rather deal with a real man any day,
than find herself involved with a childish boy.

A woman who is unashamedly moderate,
yet draws attention with her presence.
It is femininity at its best!
Yes, it's a wonderful lesson!
An intelligent man appreciates the value of a woman,
who walks in her role proudly and gives her best,
rather than a simple or contentious woman,

which will not allow even the earth to rest.
Her husband's heart safely trusts in her.
With the law of kindness she speaks.
Focusing on what's best for the entire household,
Constantly, God's wisdom she seeks.

Men and women are very different, and admittedly
there are some things they may never understand.
After all, she *is* an incomprehensible woman,
trying to understand an incomprehensible man.
But they learn to make it work,
And they appreciate the chance.
Since there can only be one leader,
He leads, and she follows, and they enjoy doing this dance!

They both hurt, cause hurt and bleed!
They both show love, support, and mercy!
They both have the ability to bring happiness, joy, and peace,
and when done purely, it is a wonderful thing!

Yes, they must tell the truth,
that they are in very few instances the same.
And it is God who made them this way
and gave each their distinguishing names.
The man was created first
to represent mankind;
with the woman being made from him—
not as an afterthought, but a help at the appointed time!
He is the designated provider; under Christ,
He is the leader and head of the family.
And submitting herself is a joy,
as she helps urge them both into their joint destiny.

The Bible says that when first made,
they were both naked but not ashamed!
And that's the sincerity they should exemplify now.
And let them both proclaim:
That there is Man and then there is Woman

It is true, though it doesn't always make sense,
the most peaceful and effective way to get through life
is to grow to enjoy, appreciate, and love the difference!

Chapter Four
Tweaked

Lisa turned on her overhead light, unlocked her laptop and booted it up. She flipped through her *Daily Devotional Calendar* that her stepfather gave her, which reminded her that she needed him to repair her dishwasher. The scripture for the day was John 15:2, "—Any branch in me that does not bear fruit [that stops bearing], He cuts away (trims off, takes away); and He cleanses and repeatedly prunes every branch that continues to bear fruit, to make it bear more and richer and more excellent fruit." *That's good,* she thought. *God knows I'm in the "constantly purged" crew*. She chuckled. *But at least I'm in the crew.*

She stood on her tiptoes to look over her cubicle and see if her boss was in. She wanted to speak with him about their energy audit projects with the local utility company, before he got bogged down with meetings and conference calls.

She was somewhat happy that he was not in, so she could be free to check her e-mail. Lisa had eight e-mail accounts—four personal (so that she would have unlimited storage space), two work related, one for school, and one to solicit information for the non-profit community organization she planned to start someday. She opened one of her work-related e-mail accounts. She had thirteen engineering reports to review and recommend technical improvements for the electrical distribution systems that fed some of their most sensitive plant equipment and operations. *These reports are going to be the death of me,* she thought. She added the tasks to her "to do" list.

As Lisa logged into her online news group, she noticed that Cliff had just sent her an e-mail entitled "Are you there?" which meant he wanted to talk. In the evenings and on weekends, they spoke via IM. However, there was a firewall at work which would not allow him to download IM software. She replied and told Cliff to give her a few minutes. Her Marketing Management instructor had posed two discussion threads. They were to pick a commercial, and discuss the target audience, and discuss if the commercial was successful. He also wanted them to discuss the importance of companies having a mission statement. The responses were due the next day. The online classes were more demanding than she had originally imagined, but she was determined to finish.

She laughed within herself, as she discussed the bug spray commercial. In her opinion, the commercial had accomplished its goal. It aired during a prime time teen show rerun, and was quite humorous. It was not only targeting parents, but young adults. If she were a teen, and saw a bug in the house, after seeing the commercial, likely that brand of bug spray would have come to mind. She counted her response to make sure that she had 200 words. She drafted a response regarding mission statements and saved it until the next morning.

Before she could finish her assignment, her indicator told her that Tonya had signed onto IM. Lisa was always tickled at Tonya's screen names, which she changed daily. Her screen name for the day was "Cous Cous Asparagus," a combination one of their friends, Angie, had cooked, along with some ribs made from lamb. Lisa's screen name stayed the same, which was her stepfather's nickname for her, "Mona Lisa."

Cous Cous Asparagus says: Good Morning.
Mona Lisa says: Good Morning! How r u today?
Cous Cous Asparagus says: Well, I've been trying to talk to you for bout a half-hour, but now I'm going out into the field. I'll catch you after lunch. TTYL.
Mona Lisa says: TTYL

Cliff had sent another message. "I was on the phone with Ahnna until 3:30 a.m., having plain-old good conversation. She says she misses sharing her life with me, and of course, I admitted the same. Am I being selfish? Is simply telling her my intentions to remain friends sufficient? I don't want to hurt her! Help me! It's obvious I'm at a loss when it comes to those of the female persuasion."

Lisa could not believe it. Was Cliff actually thinking of getting back with Ahnna. Lisa hoped he wasn't just bored with his friend-of-the-month club. The previous summer, Lisa had gone out with one of Cliff's friends and Cliff had labeled her a cheater. He said she went out with him just to have something to do. "Adam really likes you. It's not fair for you to keep seeing him, knowing that you're not really interested. You're cheating the system," Cliff had told her.

Lisa felt that Cliff was a phenomenal lawyer and capable spiritual advisor, but when it came to women, he could not make sound judgments because he had not yet come to grips with the fact that as long as he insisted on keeping his options open, he could never find and focus on one woman. She would have never told him that to his face. She entitled her reply "Cheater." Inside she wrote, "Does the void you feel have Ahnna's name on it or could anyone fill it? I know that somehow it just feels right to have someone during this summery autumn (the birds are singing, and the leaves are showing off their romantic splendor), but is this a chapter in your life you want to revisit?"

Cliff knew that he was opening up a can of worms. Lisa and her clique seemed to get their livelihood from giving their opinions of the male species. He replied, "How dare you use my own words against me? (SMILE) And for the record, I love her, but I don't want to rush into anything."

Lisa knew that Cliff cared about Ahnna's well-being, but he seemed to be at such a selfish state in his life. She felt that he needed to be alone until he was sure that he wanted to proceed into a long-term, committed relationship. She could not understand, for the life of her, why he was so afraid to commit to someone he "loved more than anyone else."

She had spoken with her coworker, Saiheed who was juggling four women. And since he only had sex with two of them, the others were "just friends." Yet single saints did not have the luxury of that distinction. Lisa had told Saiheed that women may still view such relationships as committed, but he did not listen. He got very upset when one of his "friends" introduced him to her family as her boyfriend, though. Lisa was annoyed with Saiheed's philosophy. However, it seemed to be the going trend. It seemed that whenever men and women tried to be friends, one of the parties ended up liking the other, and then chaos began.

Growing up, her Youth Pastor taught them group dating was "the safest way to get to know someone without all the strings attached. They may not even know you're watching, and, therefore, they are more prone to be themselves and not try to be impressive," he had said. However, that did not work well, because most of them looked forward to having one-on-one contact at some point.

He also taught the young ladies to do things in a scriptural manner. Based on Proverbs 18:22, "Whoso findeth a wife findeth a good thing, and obtaineth favour of the LORD." He told them that they could not be found if they were not lost, and were always up in a guy's face. Lisa felt that this often put women in the awkward position of waiting around for a guy to initiate a commitment.

Lisa had fussed at Cliff *and* Saiheed for unnecessarily victimizing women and perhaps being unknowingly abusive by leading them on, and then moving on and seemingly detaching themselves without a hitch. Lisa could not believe that she and Cliff were back at square one, with her telling him to stop his madness.

She knew that it was not all his fault or responsibility. Ahnna needed to be careful when dealing with him. And she knew that there could be a boomerang affect, and that men could find themselves being "left high and dry," but in most cases, it was the woman who got hurt. Or maybe it was just that she was a woman and was more sensitive to women's issues. Nonetheless, Cliff knew better. And she was not going to pacify him with kind words.

As she was considering her response, Paul had sent her an e-mail message. The subject was blank. She did not want to take on the menial task of once again proving to him that they had nothing in common. Their relationship had ended on a very sour note. The last time they had gone out, he had forced her onto the couch. She had to practically fight him to get him off of her. That frightening evening, she told him that she did not want to see him anymore.

She also had a message from Mandy. Lisa knew that eventually she would have to speak with her, but right then she was not in the mood. The last time Lisa decided to "hear her out", she had basically lied again, and Lisa ended up making a list of several of the things that Mandy had done to her. "These are the reasons why you are invisible to me," she had written. Lisa had called her a liar and a female impersonator. She had sarcastically ended the letter with "Can't you feel the love?" which had been one of Mandy's favorite

Lisa replied, "Well it's your move, so make it carefully!"

Cliff replied, "I'm getting there, but I need time if this is going to last forever. Hey, the best thing to do is make sure you keep your sister-in-Christ in your prayers. And let's not get caught up in a whole bunch of vain jangling. It's not going to help the situation. Well, I got some work to catch up on, so TTYL."

Lisa would not have expected any other reply from Cliff. He was very good at avoiding conversations and subjects in which he did not wish to partake. And she was sure that he had reached his maximum level of tolerance on the subject of dating Ahnna. After all, she was dealing with "Master D", a nickname she gave him because he was the "master at deviating" from uncomfortable topics.

"Talk to you later, Master D!" she replied. Lisa was somewhat agitated that Cliff had cut their conversation short, yet relieved because she did not want it to appear as if she was trying to tell him what to do. She could not help but wonder if he was telling her to pray, as just a quick, catchy cliché he threw out, in order to close the conversation. Well, Lisa was going to pray for Ahnna, and Cliff. It was time he grew up, matured, and left his old ways in the past.

Lisa was somewhat distraught because she was dealing with her break-up with James. Cliff and Ahnna were having issues. David was having difficulties with Susan. And her best friend, Krystal, was occupied with running from what seemed to be the perfect relationship with the perfect guy. It seemed the season of relationship drama was blowing in their direction. *Or is it always the season of relationship drama?* she asked herself.

She sent another e-mail entitled, "One more question." Inside she wrote, "Why do you keep going back to Ahnna? Are you in love? (That's two questions, huh?)"

Cliff's reply came back immediately. "Define 'being in love.'"

Lisa thought out her reply carefully. "Let's say there are three levels of love— general love for mankind, familial or friendship love, and relational love between a man and a woman, or "being in love." This means you've reached the point where you want to forsake all others to be with her."

Cliff replied immediately, "I guess being 'in love' is what matters between a man and a woman. No one wants to hear that you love them on the same level as your cousin, or neighbor. That being said, I think I can live without her. So, I'm not in love. And that being the case, perhaps I should move on, huh?"

Lisa was amazed at how quickly he replied. She wondered if he was going off of what he felt at that moment. She replied, "I'll assume that was rhetorical."

Right then her boss peeked into her cubicle. "I was about to come get you," Mr. Sweeney said, "I've been looking over these numbers for this business case, and they just aren't adding up. I thought the simple payback was shorter. And I was assumed that the utility was charging us $0.047 per kilowatt in that region. Can we review this over lunch? Hopefully you don't have anything else on your plate? Well, even if you do, let's treat this as top priority."

Lisa really wanted to spend her lunch break delving into the Bible. She had been learning about having a pure conscience, having the right attitude about money, and learning not to engage in vain jangling and "foolish talk," as her mother would say. She had been so excited that she had called Cliff and shared her study notes with him over the phone. He now used the term, "vain jangling," every chance he got.

Mr. Sweeney thinks everything's top priority, she thought, *and, it is now that he waited until the day before the executive staff meeting. I gave him that information two weeks ago. I know he's busy, but geez. I wish he'd be more considerate. It would help if he got a competent secretary.* Lisa had been frustrated with her current job position for quite some time, and this little escapade did not help. However, she excused her boss (as if it mattered) because he was a man in authority, and very accustomed to his subordinates doing things when and how he suggested them.

Lisa loved math and had pursued a bachelor's degree because she had the potential to be a great engineer. Her career had started off with a bang. And the first three years, she received several promotions. There was a time when she could see herself happily working in that position forever. But after working feverishly for years, she no longer possessed the passion she needed. She could barely relate to her coworkers, 75% of which were men that had been working there almost longer than she had been alive. Although they were a good group of guys, they seemed obsessed with their careers.

Deep down, she wanted to impact the lives of at-risk youth—meeting their academic and civic needs, as well as planting Godly seeds into their lives. She had heard, all too often, "people don't care how much you know until they know how much you care." God had confirmed that He would eventually move her into a career which would coincide with her ministry and purpose.

God had not prompted her to move on just yet so she paced herself accordingly. For now, she was inconspicuously learning the ropes of business management. She felt that if she had sought God while in college, instead of choosing a major on her own, she would already be in her dream position. Yet she realized that sometimes the route taken was not as important as reaching the destination.

Mr. Sweeney really needed her assistance, so she told him to meet her by the elevator in fifteen minutes so that they could walk to the cafeteria together. She spent the afternoon making corrections and adjustments to the business case that they discussed over lunch. Her coworker, Jasmine, who was always in a playful mood, walked into her cubicle for afternoon small talk. "Hey Lisa. I didn't see you in the cafeteria for lunch? Were you on a date or something?"

Lisa ignored Jasmine's last question. "I met with Mr. Sweeney over lunch."

"Oh, how boring." Jasmine was disappointed. "I was hoping you'd gone out with the guy from the eighth floor. He's cute. Why do you keep avoiding him?"

"Here you go talking crazy," Lisa said laughingly. She did not want Jasmine to see that she was annoyed. " Look, I'm not interested in that dude at all. So let it go."

"My, aren't we in a cranky mood? You never did have a poker face. I came over to see if you could spread some sunshine into my dilapidated relationship, but I can wait. My boyfriend is acting crazy this week. Maybe *I* should go out with the guy from the eighth floor, huh?" she said laughingly.

Lisa took a deep breath and tried to calm down. "I'm sorry. I'm not trying to be in a cranky mood. I just have a lot of things on my mind. I have to finish up this business case, which Mr. Sweeney changed…"

"At the last minute," Jasmine laughingly completed her sentence.

Lisa laughed, too. "So, you know I'll be busy for the rest of the afternoon, and probably tomorrow morning." She was hinting that she needed to be left alone. "But I'll look for you in the cafeteria tomorrow, okay?"

"Alright, hon'!" Jasmine said. "I'll see you then."

Lisa closed the work day by checking her messages. Krystal had sent a text message about the wonderful time she and Shana were having in New York. Her mom had left a voicemail about a Bartlett Hartins, who was a friend of her Godmother's that needed help organizing and computerizing his files for his real-estate firm. His name sounded familiar. Her "moms" were always volunteering her for something and had likely assured him that their "baby can do anything with the computer." Also, James had called three times within the past hour and left a message, stating that he missed her.

Lisa made a mental list of the items that she needed to finish first thing the next morning. She was tired. All she wanted to do was go home, take a shower, and spend some time with God, resting her body, soul, and spirit.

After what seemed like the longest drive home ever, she took a quick shower, and put on her favorite pair of comfy pajamas that her aunt had bought her for Christmas. It was actually a "work outfit" in Aunt Ellen's mind, but Lisa had turned the slacks and long-sleeved T-shirt into relaxation garb. She was in such a lazy mood. She decided to eat a bowl of cereal, as she waited for her frozen cuisine to finish cooking in the microwave. She ate and watched cartoons, a habit that she had not broken since her college years, while snuggling up on her futon. She was mentally exhausted. She knew that at some point within the next 24 hours she needed to post her three-page paper and finish up her discussion questions. She also knew that she needed to speak with James, and that was adding to the stress she already felt.

She was sad that the wonderful friendship she had established with James was ending. She had grown to love and trust him, and confide in him regarding every area of her life, something she had not done with any other guy she had dated. What she would miss most about him was his child-like sincerity and simple faith in God's Word, and of course, his lovely smile. She would also miss their long conversations about their future goals. Yet she knew that something was missing, and that she could not proceed and give the relationship her all, since such strong feelings had surfaced. She had enjoyed the ride, but this was her stop and opportunity to get off. She prayed to God that this would not be the worst mistake of her life, and that eventually she would share love again.

The doorbell rang several times before Lisa realized that it was not the TV she was hearing. She was not expecting anyone, but she had a feeling that James would not allow the silence between them to continue much longer. They had not spoken in several days, which was very unusual. The moment she dreaded had arrived. She opened the door, forcing a smile onto her face.

James barely allowed Lisa to get a word in. "You been avoiding me?" he asked very calmly. "I know when I'm being ignored. I thought we agreed that when you were having issues we would go through them together."

James assumed that Lisa was having problems with her dad, or that something stressful had surfaced at work, which usually caused Lisa to withdraw herself. James always tried to reassure her that he would gladly share in her issues so that she would not feel that she had to solve them alone. He assumed that this time things were no different, and that he was there to console and counsel Lisa, as in times past. He did not have a clue that Lisa had been contemplating how she would go about breaking things off between them.

"We do need to talk," Lisa replied.

James looked down at the staircase landing, where he suggested Lisa leave her keys since she had locked herself out several times. "Uh, before I forget, I'm going to move the truck for you and put it under the carport. It's supposed to rain tomorrow morning, and I don't want my girl out there fumbling in the dark."

"Thanks!" Lisa said softly. As he went outside, Lisa sat at the dining room table, which was their usual spot to powwow. She had not quite contemplated how she would start off the conversation, but she knew that when it ended, she wanted she and James parting in peace. Part of her wanted their relationship to last, yet she had vowed to never hold a man hostage by holding on to the past. Yet it was rough to go through the motions of tweaking the future—adjusting life to purposely detach something that had been attached just long enough to become a routine habit. It was like constantly turning the dial to find the perfect clarity of an a.m. radio station.

She had seen too many times the bitterness and resentment that surfaced when folks found themselves in the "break-up zone." Unfortunately, Lisa had been there herself when John Davis left her. She was not interested in going there again. She had spent countless hours trying to convince him, and herself, that their relationship was worth saving, and of course, giving him a piece of her mind for wasting her time. For months after they parted, she had been mentally and emotionally distraught and did not think she would ever find the strength to move on. She had loved him dearly. The memory of moments they had shared seemed to remain vivid for a long time, which made it very hard for her to imagine her life without him. She did not want to experience such sorrow again. She had fought long and hard for her sanity, which made her even more determined to let James go, without looking back.

Tweaked

We have decided to move on!
We should not hold on or look back!
So in the best interest of both,
there is severance of all unnecessary contact!

"Never say never,"
is a realistic rule,
But for now, we push forward,
using wisdom as a tool!

We cannot share our lives and special moments,
as we looked forward to doing in the past.
Why waste such time, sincerity, and emotion
on a relationship void of longevity—one that will not last?

Strong emotions have surfaced
that should be released before the setting of the sun.
We forgive and move beyond
all the hurtful things said and done.

So good-bye to a perfect friendship.
We did not prepare for it, but its future was tweaked.
And farewell to what could have been,
as it was abruptly interrupted, with an unborn opportunity to peak!

Chapter Five
You Are that Spirit

It was 7:43 a.m. on Saturday. Tonya could not sleep. She had a long talk with God, and even tried to watch TV, but it was turned down low so that she would not wake her husband, and she had gotten frustrated trying to hear it. She glanced over at Mark. She wanted to talk to him, but the last time she had awakened him on a Saturday morning he had been very irritable. She knew he was tired since he was up late the night before working on his parents' plumbing, so she did not wake him. She decided to wake up her cousin, Lisa, instead.

She went downstairs and peeked into the den. Mark Jr. was half asleep. Maya was eating cereal and watching her favorite girl-power cartoons. Her three-year-old son was with his older sister for now, and she had at least another hour before they began their next sibling rivalry. She quietly went into the living room, plopped down on the couch, and dialed Lisa's number.

"Good morning, are you sleeping?" Tonya sang.

"I hope so. I hope this is a dream," Lisa whined back.

"Girl, please! Be glad I didn't call you earlier. What time did you get to bed?"

"I don't know. It was probably after 3:00 a.m." Lisa replied.

"What were you doing?" Tonya asked, as innocently as possible. They had spoken briefly the night before, and Lisa told her that James was visiting.

"Whatever!" Lisa said. "You know, you're calling about James."

"Right, so start talking." Tonya admitted.

"Whew!" Lisa started her confession. "First, James is highly upset. I explained to him that I just feel like we need time apart so that we can grow more. We certainly haven't accomplished much growth as a couple."

"Well, I'm sure he didn't take well to that."

"No, he did not!" Lisa said. "He was defensive and accused me of blaming him because I'm not growing spiritually, then he went into this big ordeal about me comparing him to others—basically, David and Mark, but he didn't admit that."

"So are you blaming him for feeling stagnant?"

"Well, I'll just say that our relationship was not as spiritual as it could've been. And anyways, He's only been professing Christ for two years, as opposed to seven for David, and what, 15 for Mark? I've never compared him to them, or said anything of the sort. So I don't know where any of this is stemming from."

"Honestly, I never did like that boy! And he's right. He's definitely not of the same caliber as my man, or David for that matter," Tonya said laughingly, "James is educated, has a great job, and thinks he's 'God's gift.' I, personally, don't see why you gave him the time of day in the first place."

"Yes, I know!" Lisa mumbled. She had heard it all before.

"James's issues are no worse than any other average twenty-something male. But he has a lot of worldly habits. He's too busy trying to keep up with the Joneses. The length of time he's been professing Christ isn't necessarily a factor. It's more a matter of his lack of sincerity and refusal to surrender to God's way of doing things. He still curses every now and then, and still listens to WRNB. I mean, how can you grow in the things of God, feeding your spirit with lyrics about fornication and God knows what else? How are unregenerated, unanointed singers ministering to you. He's taking on yokes, instead of destroying them. I guess he has the same mind-set as Uncle Joseph, huh?"

Lisa's mother and her siblings considered Uncle Joseph an outcast. They had grown up in strict holiness, but when he became a pastor, he lowered his standards. Amongst other things, he told his congregation that they could listen to secular music and love songs, if they did not condone explicit lyrics. He got mad at Lisa's mom when she told him that it was not good for single Christians to listen to love songs, which helped put them in the mood for sex.

"Don't start!" Lisa begged Tonya to leave Uncle Joseph out of it.

"Okay, but either he's too carnal, or I'm just too spiritual!"

Tonya has to be the most opinionated person in the world, Lisa thought. Out loud, she laughingly said, "Well, it's probably a little of both, but I hear you. James has a friend who constantly combats him on the music issue. I told him that I found that deep down people really want to see an uncompromising Christian that's effectively implemented God's principles. So, he shouldn't feel bad if he makes a stand. He should be proud."

Tonya laughed, too. "Yeah, but you have to be confident in who you are."

"Well, I told James to stop comparing himself to others and seek God to find out what He wants him to be. He blew up even more, after that. I guess I understand since it's kind of ironic that I'd be advising him on how to live right, when we've both been carnal. But the truth is, and not that I'm a spiritual giant, but it seems that even when I try to do good, evil is present, or should I say, James tries to convince me to do otherwise. I need someone who'll help me do better, not cater to my foolishness." Lisa was being silly. "I can't afford to lose my relationship with God for anything. I need God's spirit in order to survive. And that's why I can't be with him. He supports my foolishness." Lisa was still laughing. "But seriously how can I submit to him and I'm the one holding this thing together, constantly playing the "spiritually mature" role. He's too content with mediocrity. If I married him, I'd probably wake up mad every morning."

"Why do you say that?" Tonya asked.

"Well, as you said, he comes off as someone who's always trying to impress others, which causes him to make bad decisions. And if I were going to spend the rest of my life with him, then I'd like to be able to at least trust his judgment. I mean, just last year he started leasing that truck. Well, a few months ago he got a huge bonus, and called me from the car dealership after he purchased a convertible two-seater because he and his brother vowed to have matching sports cars. He got upset when I said that wasn't a good investment. He said he really wanted it and decided not to pay off his student loans, as we had discussed."

"But at least he's not struggling to pay any of his bills," Tonya said.

"True, but we've had many discussions about making rash decisions. I mean, how often do you get a chance to pay off your student loans? And instead, he goes and picks up another debt for a 'weekend ride.' Whatever! That ticked me off. I don't think I could handle that for the rest of my life. And I'm not about to try to change him, either. Some of the brethren I'm willing to work with, but somehow he doesn't fall into that category."

"Well, submission is very important. And it does help if you can put some element of trust in your mate's decision-making habits," Tonya interjected.

"Right. So, I think it's best that we move on now while there are minimal casualties. I mean, I really hate to walk in hindsight revelation, or use a bunch of cop-out excuses. I loved James, but…"

"Hold on one second." Tonya turned her attention to her eight-year-old daughter. "Maya, what did you say?"

"I said, 'Are you talking to Cousin Lisa about her boyfriend?'"

Tonya glared at Maya and spanked her hand. "First of all, I would advise you to stay in a child's place. You are not to eavesdrop on adult conversation. And if you happen to overhear, you are certainly not to comment. Do you understand?" Tonya had one eyebrow raised.

"Yes, ma'am," Maya said.

"Now you're dismissed to go back into the den and watch TV."

"Mommy, I'm sorry!" Maya started crying.

"It's okay, sweetie," Tonya hugged her. "Mommy doesn't want you to think it's okay to pry into other people's business." Maya went back into the den. "She's trying to make me go postal on her tail," Tonya said. "One of my biggest pet-peeves is for a child to comment on an adult's conversation. I am not your peer. Where was I?" she asked. "Oh yeah! We were talking about submission."

"Right," Lisa said.

"Submission *is* important," Tonya said, without allowing Lisa to respond. "I mean, at least you have a conscience and a repentant heart. James just seems to go with the flow. And anytime lust, instead of love, is the basis of a relationship, then it's bound to fail. Love stands the test of time, but lust is always out looking for its next victim. Based on what you said about his playful sexual advances, he plays with fire too much."

"Exactly!"

"Listen, people need to take some time to allow God to clean them up. We have to put off the old man with his deeds, and the things we picked up in the world. Sanctification is a process, and for some, that requires exclusivity. Otherwise, you'll bring bad habits into everything, including your relationships."

"That's so true," Lisa agreed.

"Put it like this, James can only love based on his capacity to love, which appears to be quite limited. If a person is generally rough and rigid, then more than likely the best love they'll ever be able to give will come across as rough and rigid. On the same token, if they're considerate and trustworthy, their love will be, too. Right now, it seems that James's love is just too carnal."

"Yeah, and we have to be realistic about the kind of love that we enjoy giving and receiving, or at least know what we don't want."

"Don't I know it? You have to be careful, especially with those rowdy, roughneck guys you seem to like," Tonya said laughingly.

"This is not the time for jokes." Lisa groaned as if she were on her deathbed. "My life has too much drama. Why does this keep happening to me?"

"Hmmm..." Tonya sighed. She was in counseling mode. " Honestly, you did the right thing if you really feel he doesn't have what you're looking for, but that's just my little opinion. It's not that James doesn't deserve a chance at happiness, or that God can't change people. He changed me. And it's not that James doesn't want to be changed, per se. It's more like he's enjoying taking the slow route, when he should be seeking God for the most expeditious path to his purpose."

Lisa agreed. "I'm not blaming James for anything. He really does have potential, but based on Grandmother's definition, we both know that means..."

"Right now, he ain't doing nothing," they said laughingly at the same time.

Tonya continued. "That's right. And it's a waste of time to put all that emotion and energy into a relationship with no future, or hope that the person will eventually change. You have to accept them for who they are, and conclude that if they never change, you're willing to work with them and love them anyway."

"I agree, but sometimes I'm confused. I thought I knew what I wanted—a man who loves God and will love me as Christ loves the church. I'm not picky. Add a great sense of humor, and voila! Basically, I just want simple companionship. What were you looking for?" Lisa asked.

"That's it in a nut shell. However, I was very specific. Spiritually, I wanted a man who would be a covering for me and our children. I wanted someone who was rooted and grounded in God's Word because he studied it himself, and not because he was repeating what he heard someone else say. In addition, he needed to have ambition, and goals, and the Holy Spirit who, as we were taught, is essential for living right. I mean, I need a man who has experience with God and will stand firm in adversity. And having the baptism of the Holy Ghost just makes it that much easier to stay connected to the things of God."

"Amen!"

Tonya paused for a moment before she continued. "Naturally, I wanted a man with a steady career and steady income. And he surely could not be intimidated by my sometimes slightly forceful personality." She laughed. "Also, he had to be able to laugh and have a good time. My worst nightmare was to be stuck with a dry man. And of course, physically, I needed to be attracted to him."

"Yeah, you sort of threw physical attraction in there," Lisa teased.

"No. Physical appearance is very important. I didn't list them in any certain order, Missy. I asked God to not only give me what I wanted, but what I needed."

Lisa knew that a man who was too serious would not be able to appreciate or understand her sense of humor, which could be extreme at times. She was reminded of a Christian couple her mom introduced her to. They were both saved and filled with God's Spirit, but they lead such boring lives. They had no interests or ambitions other than their jobs, their children, and what the Pastor had preached. They hardly ever cracked a smile. Lisa frowned in disgust. *Yuck. Together they make a dry toast sandwich.* Lisa she knew that she could not be pleased living that way. *Hey, if it rocks their boat, then who am I to complain? But that type of relationship doesn't even float my boat,* she thought.

She turned her attention back to Tonya, holding in her laugh from her slight "joking spasm." Tonya was still talking, "I personally don't think that relationships have to be as deep or hard as we try to make them. There doesn't have to be a white light shining down from heaven, and God saying, 'This is the one I've chosen for you, blah blah blah.' Basically, a guy approaches you, and you determine whether he's someone you can wake up to every morning and submit to, or should I say, submit to his ego." They both laughed.

Lisa hoped Tonya would not start on her spiel about the importance of catering to a man's ego without compromising your position as a woman. Much to Lisa's dismay, Tonya continued. "You know how I feel about a woman allowing a man to be a man. You have to be confident in who you are. See, women have to realize that it makes a man feel good to know that his wife trusts him, and is not afraid to praise his decisions, even if they're not exactly the way she would've done things. And every woman should want her man to be happy."

Although Lisa wished that Tonya had gotten to her point quicker, she agreed whole-heartedly. She did not like to see a woman boss a man around. It just did not look good. One of the reasons that her brother's marriage was on the rocks was because his wife combated every decision he made.

Tonya was still talking, "But I'll save that for the marriage class in the morning." Lisa listened attentively, without butting in. Tonya had a knack for picking up right where she left off. "...back to what I was saying. It's a given that these are two people who love the Lord and live according to His Word. They seek God to make sure that He approves. And next, spend time getting to know one another to determine if they possess qualities that will enhance one another. Then bang! Next thing you know, they're in love, get marriage counseling to make sure they're going into the relationship with their eyes wide open..."

"...And live happily ever after, right?" Lisa finished Tonya's statement.

Tonya continued. "It takes some of us a little more time, but that's about the gist of it. I was just telling Krystal, the other day, that if she's not ready to commit to Jarret, then they should slow down a bit—that way, the relationship won't be so lopsided. He's seemingly picturing himself standing at the altar and her walking down the aisle, and in her mind, she hasn't even made it to the church yet."

Lisa laughed. "You're funny."

"Lisa, I guess I said all that to say, just be prayerful, and don't commit to someone or proceed in a relationship unless you're sure that you're moving where and when God wants you to move. Don't even get me started on the importance of having the correct timing. If one person is ready and the other person isn't, that will also complicate things," Tonya concluded.

Lisa had learned that lesson the hard way. Her relationship with John, the illustrious love of her life, proved that timing was very important. In her mind, they had been perfect for one another. However, they were at two different phases. He was not ready to take on the role of provider—perhaps financially, but not mentally or spiritually. He was still trying to figure out if Lisa was "the one." John had a lot of women approach him, which definitely has a tendency to deter a man's focus. He had admitted that he still had "a roaming eye." Lisa trusted him, and he had never cheated on her, but he still could not narrow his selection down to one woman, forever. Lisa had told him that he needed to make a decision to marry her or move on, and he chose to move on. Lisa felt that he would have dated her for 10 or 15 years without ever asking, if she had allowed him to. They remained very close friends for almost a year after he had supposedly "moved on," until finally Lisa put him out of her life for good. Ever since then, she had run for her life whenever a man tried to befriend her.

Lisa finally said, "And here I was thinking that you just happened to find a preacher man with a successful career and a great personality."

"Well, I expressed to the Lord what I thought would make me happy, and he refined it and presented me with a handsome, virile, holy man of God that..."

"Tonya, that's easy for you to say now," Lisa interrupted.

"Girl, please. We both had some growing to do before we could even discuss marriage. We've grown a lot in the past 10 years, but we still have a ways to go. The key is to trust the person with your deepest thoughts and feelings, knowing that whatever issues arise, you'll work through them and grow together. I guess when you get to a certain point in a relationship, you realize that what you've found is worth preserving. No, Mark is not perfect, and I'm not either, but I like to think that our love is perfect simply because of the grace and mercy, better known as forgiveness, we extend to one another, through the love of God. The Lord is faithful, which encourages me to be faithful. Persistence is what brings perfection. Marriage, or any relationship, is about giving selflessly. As a matter of fact, I need to go make sure my husband and children don't need me right now."

Tonya was being chatty, but Lisa was sorry that she cut their conversation so abruptly. "Well, I must say, once again, that I appreciate you more than you'll ever know. You'll always be my phone preacher." Lisa was fighting back tears. As she hung up, Lisa had a lot on her mind. For some reason, her mind kept going back to the days when she was in the "break-up zone" with John Davis. Lisa had been devastated because she had always pictured them going through their life's struggles together. And after he left her, she realized that she loved him and would have done just about anything to make their relationship work.

She had been through a lot. She had experienced things that she had never told anyone. It was during that time that she contemplated suicide. She felt that the things that she had worked hard for had failed her, and that the very person she loved had turned his back on her. It was also during that time that she had physical heartache. For several weeks, she hyperventilated. She also experienced a slight discomfort in her chest and felt her heart rate increase. Her attention span had been very short during that time. Later that Fall when her god-sister was killed in a car accident, she had really noticed an increase in her heart rate more frequently. Doctor Seven had told her that it was normal to have such symptoms, called heart palpitations, upon suffering a deep loss.

Lisa knew that particular time in her life had the potential to either make her or break her. The devil had tried to attack her and get her to walk away from her purpose, but something inside of her would not allow her to quit. After months of depression, she decided to finally get closer to God. It was during that time that she became more dedicated to writing her Psalms collection. She also began having morning praise and worship services. She did everything she could to regain her sanity and rid herself of the spirits of depression and distraction.

She haphazardly came across an article in a Christian magazine, written by a young lady who had a similar experience. The young lady stated that she had come to grips with the fact that she was grieving the loss of true love. And although at the time her ex-boyfriend was the possessor of her love, and the object of her affection, she was not necessarily mourning over him. He could be replaced. Once she came to that conclusion, she could go on. She had prayed that God would fill her void so that eventually she could love again. Her story had ended wonderfully, and she married the man of her dreams.

The young lady had highlighted the pros and cons and admitted that the things she experienced were unhealthy spiritually, mentally, emotionally, and physically. Yet that disaster had taught her that true love is not easily shaken, nor does it look for ways to give up. She learned that true love is worth salvaging, even though it can also hurt like crazy. After months of meditation, she had finally reached a point where she could move on without focusing on her own issues.

Lisa had appreciated that young lady's story. It had strengthened her and shown her that she, too, could move on. Lisa gave her heart's desires to God. She gave up on worrying about the situation, because worrying about what she could not control only brought her grief. She finally got to the point where she thanked John Davis for releasing her and kicking her out of his life because he was wasting her time, and, *furthermore, he doesn't bring out the best in me,* she had thought.

Lisa was also glad to hear things from Tonya's perspective. She and Mark had been married for almost 10 years and it was refreshing to see them still happy and still in love. Tonya had concluded that she and Mark possessed a perfect love. She had boldly emphasized that they weren't perfect, but their love was. *How can Tonya be so confident in her seemingly unrealistic statement? Perfect love? Does such a thing exist?* Lisa thought.

Lisa was very emotional and confused. She knew that God was speaking to her, but for the life of her she could not grasp the full understanding of what

He was saying. She got on her knees and prayed for revelation knowledge. Rivers and rivers of tears seemed to stream down her face endlessly. She did not say much, but she knew that God had heard her ever-so-faint cry.

She did not want this thing to continue to overtake her. She cast her cares upon her God. And even though she did not know how or why, deep down, she felt that He would deliver her from herself, and the issues and sins of her past. She was convinced that as God promised in His Word, all the things she experienced (good and bad), would work together for her good, because she was called according to His purpose. She thanked God for the call, which was something that no one on earth, nor any devil in hell, could take away from her. She also thanked Him for having a mind to answer the call.

After praying, Lisa felt better. As she lie in bed, Tonya's comments about the Holy Ghost were fresh in her mind, before which, she had never thought of the importance of her mate having the Holy Ghost, at least not quite as Tonya had expressed it. But she had to admit that the Baptism of the Holy Ghost was the quickest way to determine whether someone had really taken the time to clean out themselves unto sanctification and honor. Perhaps it was the factor that James was missing. Not everyone would agree with her newly found knowledge, but she quickly added the Baptism of the Holy Ghost to her mental list of "must-haves" for her mate.

She wondered why the Holy Ghost had become such a controversial issue in the church. In college, she had a huge debate with some of her friends who told her that the Holy Ghost was basically optional. Yet she had been taught otherwise. "It's like offering someone a million bucks, and they refuse to take it because they just don't know how they'll use it, or don't think it's necessary, because they already have the basic necessities," her mom had told her.

She remembered a song from her childhood Sunday school class, "Breath of God!" As a child, she did not understand it, but now she saw that the song writer was saying that the Holy Ghost is as necessary as the air that's needed to breathe. She thought about the creation of mankind as described in Genesis, and God breathing the breath of life into man's nostrils that he could become a living soul. She envisioned God breathing His Holy Spirit into His people so that they could have God's wisdom and power. *How can we live without the air we breathe? And how indeed can we move in the things of God without His Spirit?* she thought.

You Are that Spirit

You are the Spirit of Truth
If you are involved, there will be Integrity!
You are the comforter,
If you are involved, there will be love, joy, and peace!
You are the teacher,
If you are involved, there will be wisdom!
You come from God, the Father.
You testify of Jesus, the Son.
You are the witness given to them that obey God.
You remind us of what Christ has said and done.

How can we prophesy
and speak in tongues unlearned and unknown,
except you come and quicken us,
as a rushing mighty wind blowing?
How can our infirmities be helped,
and our spirits be built up,
How can we have power,
except we allow you to come upon us?

When we do not know what to pray,
And we need an extra push,
(with groanings that cannot be expressed in words)
you intercede for us.
…stubborn, and uncircumcised;
reluctant to cut away, we resist you.
We're deceived into neglecting
our wisdom, our teacher, our peace, our truth!

We recognize that you are, undoubtedly,
the third person in the Trinity.
Yet we vex one another in debating

just how deeply immersed in us you should be.
Others try to purchase you with money,
when the inevitable change in us they see.
Once partakers and enlightened, how can we be restored,
when we fall away from you, and to us, you were free?

If we walk in your character,
we can deny and mortify our fleshly lusts,
and the foolishness and sin that was once in control,
will be of none effect in us.
You help us to walk not in the flesh,
But freely in your essence.
And through revelation knowledge,
we recognize that you exemplify God's presence.
As a consuming fire
that burns within our souls,
and as a wellspring of living water,
out of our bellies you shall flow.

If we do not walk righteously
and in God's Word live,
and if we do not possess you,
we are considered none of His.

Just as inhaling and exhaling
are requirements for having life,
and just as Jesus Christ in three days did
defeat death, hell, and the grave, and still arise,
and as the valley of dry bones
was by God's breath revived,
You are the designated breath of God,
And we must have you on the inside.

Chapter Six
A Grim Look Explained

Shana and Krystal were having the time of their lives in New York City. This was the first vacation Krystal had taken in 18 months, and she was enjoying every second. She had not thought about her job at all since they stepped off the plane. The ladies had made plans to go during the spring, but Krystal had canceled twice. Due to her work schedule, she barely had any time to invest in her personal life. However, this time Shana would not take no for an answer. They had finally arrived in the Big Apple and were planning to go see a Broadway show for the evening, have a mini shopping spree on Saturday, then take an early Sunday morning flight back to Detroit.

Shana and Krystal had gotten very close since Krystal was dating Shana's brother, Jarrett. Shana was hoping that Krystal would eventually be her sister-in-law. As they rode in the taxi, Shana started her usual badgering of Krystal about the status of her relationship with her brother.

"So," Shana said, "when's the last time you spoke with Jarrett?"

Krystal just looked at Shana and smiled. She was surprised that Shana had not started prying on the flight in.

Shana kept talking as if Krystal had responded. "I think you guys are the cutest couple ever. I remember the first time he brought you over."

"Uncle Allen's birthday party!" they both said.

"My parents were trying to get you to stay later and sing on that bootleg karaoke system they had hooked up, but you had to leave to go to your neighbor's open house," Shana said. "Remember?"

Krystal nodded her head indicating that she remembered the event vividly. Jarrett's parents had performed an oldies-but-goodies song from the sixties.

"After you left, Uncle Allen told Jarrett that if things didn't work out between you guys, he wanted your phone number. That was hilarious."

Krystal thought about Shana's last remark. "Well, he's almost my type," she continued. "How often does he pray and read his Bible? I've been strongly considering marrying a man twice my age, anyway. And Uncle Allen may actually be able to keep up." Krystal was laughing the whole time.

Shana was growing impatient. She put her hands on her hips and glared at Krystal. "Don't joke like that," she said. "My brother really likes you. And my mom, dad, Kenya, and I have decided that you're the one for him. I wish you'd stop playing the hard-to-get role. My brother, as most men, is too unenlightened to appreciate that anyway! I don't know what it is you're trying to prove, but…"

Krystal could not hold her laugh in. "I have nothing to prove. I think Jarrett Mansfield is a perfect gentleman."

"So what's the problem?" Shana asked. "Why aren't you guys officially a couple? I know it has nothing to do with my brother, and everything to do with you. He worships the ground you walk on. Trust me, I know!"

Krystal lifted her brow, and cut her eyes at Shana. "You're so nosey. I don't even know why I set myself up and came on this trip with you!"

"Just spill the beans," Shana said, not letting up.

"There are no beans to spill."

"Yes there are! For example, what's taking you so long to commit to him?"

"Okay. Okay. Listen, he knows exactly where I stand. No one's playing hard-to-get. No one's playing any games. I've been up-front and honest from day one."

"Forget all the colloquialisms," Shana said, half pouting. "I want to know the real deal—minus all of the flowery wording, okay."

"I'm sorry." Krystal was being purposely evasive.

"Yeah. Whatever! Let me give you some conversation starters. First, you can elaborate on what you've been up-front and honest about."

Krystal started off slowly. "Look, Shana, since you must know, I told your brother that I believe in taking things slow. I really don't have time to cater to Jarrett the way he wants me to. I mean, he expects us to talk or go out and do something every single day. And my life is just too hectic for all that right now."

"So, what's wrong with that?" Shana interrupted. "You should be glad someone wants to spend every waking moment of their time with you."

"As I was saying, before I was rudely interrupted, I didn't plan for my career to be so consuming, but that's how things have panned out, for now."

"Freedom is played out this season, trust me," Shana joked.

"Ha! Speak for yourself! As I stated earlier, I've expressed my concerns to your brother." Krystal hoped that was enough to hold Shana for a while.

"Continue!" Shana said. "There has to be more to it than that."

By this time, they had taken their luggage to their hotel room and arrived at the café for lunch, where the waitress was taking their orders. "That's it! There's nothing more to tell," Krystal said. "That's my story, and I'm sticking with it." She tried to divert Shana's attention by asking the waitress a series of questions about the menu.

Krystal's diversion did not last very long. Shana ordered her food then continued. "Alright, if you want me to pry, I will. You'd make time for a personal life if you really wanted one, wouldn't you?"

"Hmm…" Krystal refused to respond further.

"Okay, so when was the last time you were in a committed relationship?" Shana asked. "Can you at least answer that question for me?"

"Geez, we just cut right to the chase, don't we?"

"Yes, we do. And we're not ashamed," Shana laughed.

"Look, I'm about 90% complete with my goal of just enjoying being single and not looking back," Krystal said laughingly. "Perhaps soon your brother and I can really get this party started, although I don't expect him to put his life on hold."

Shana looked knowingly at her, "He ain't got nothing else to do. If he knows what's good for him, he'll wait and play his cards right. Anyways, his previous choices were just flat-out horrible. He's too nice, and he let them take advantage of him badly. This last nut even had him paying her mother's utility bills. With you, we don't have to worry about that."

"You sure? My mom is going through a slight financial hardship right now," Krystal joked.

"We trust you to do right by him," Shana said, mocking a character from a movie they had watched on her laptop on the flight in. "We're not worried at all."

"Oh, great! Just what I'm looking forward to—nosey in-laws," Krystal said laughingly. "He told me you guys weren't too fond of his ex-fiancée."

"Not at all! No one in the fam liked her. Kenya told her that her hair weave was big and scary. And you know how nice she usually is," Shana paused. "I didn't forget my question, though."

"Oops! I did," Krystal said jokingly, "Can you repeat the question?" She laughed. "Okay, Okay. First let me say that I have made a pact with myself, that I will not go into my next relationship just to be in a relationship. I want to have realistic expectations. Hey, don't get me wrong, I've learned a lot, and I'm not one for holding on to the past. I say, make the best of what you've got. And I don't preach that you have to be totally 100% over one dude (if that ever happens), in order to start a fresh, new, successful relationship. All that looks good on TV, but in reality proof of getting over a past relationship is relative. And I know that may sound bad, but it exemplifies reality for me."

The waitress had brought them the check some time ago, but Shana was not ready to let go of their conversation, so Krystal took the initiative. "Hey, we've wasted enough shopping time. Before you know it, it'll be time to get ready for the show tonight. You've got all day to be in my business. We can talk and shop at the same time, can't we?"

They paid the check, left the waitress a hefty tip for bearing with them, and headed toward their favorite department store.

Krystal continued without Shana begging her to expound. "I guess it's been about six years since I've been in a committed relationship, or felt the need to be in one. Of course, before your brother, I occasionally went out with different guys here and there. But none of the relationships were ever a threat of anything serious, that is, until your brother came along and tried to rearrange my life." She grinned. "Back then I was engaged to my college sweetheart. We both stayed in the local area of the University once we graduated. A couple years later, things didn't work out, and so since he stayed there, I moved back home. And that's basically the end of the story. We both lived happily ever after." Krystal smiled.

"Yeah right, the end of the story!" Shana rolled her eyes. She could tell that Krystal really did not want to talk about the subject, so this time she left it alone. "So you moved back home just to separate yourself from him?"

"I sure did," Krystal said. She could see the confusion in Shana's facial expression. "Hey, I know that some people may consider that a cowardice move, but I found that leaving town in an effort to rid yourself of a past relationship is not a bad idea. It actually worked very well for me."

"But didn't it make you feel like you gave up and uprooted your entire surroundings over a man, that nine times out of 10, wasn't worth it?"

"Nope! It made me feel like I was moving on, and that I could take some stress off my brain from constantly worrying and thinking about why he decided to turn his back on me and spend the rest of his life with someone else. I was living in the same environment where we fell in love and spent many years together. It was a constant reminder of things we shared and the quality time that we'd spent building our relationship. It was just too much for me."

"I guess so. But it just seems like you could've become an even stronger person had you stayed there and not allowed him to affect you."

"Hey, you're entitled to your opinion. But based on the experiences of other women I've spoken with, I know I did the right thing. This time, I opted to learn from other peoples' mistakes. But I'm not saying that's the best choice for everyone. Hey, be a 'shero' and prove me wrong, if that's your flavor. But I felt like the odds were against me. For a while, I was carrying the load of the relationship. I told him that my love was strong enough to carry us, when he wasn't sure what he wanted. Well, that turned out to be a huge mess. And once I decided to move on, I wasn't sure how much contact I should have with someone I was trying to separate myself from. I felt if I stayed there it would take me longer to move on. And trust me, trying to separate yourself from someone that you had sex with and have soul ties to is nothing to play with, not to mention the emotional ties. Let the truth be told, I would have to say that it almost takes more guts to leave than it does to stay and bear it."

"Wow, so I guess now I understand why you're so careful," Shana said.

"Exactement!" Krystal exclaimed in her pseudo French tone, "I'm making sure that I go into my next relationship without harboring bitterness. I don't want to constantly compare this relationship to my past faux pas. I'm not saying that sometimes I don't still feel the pain. But I can honestly say that I've moved on. I mean, I'm not a robot, but when I feel the pain of my past, I simply take a deep breath, swallow, and try not to allow it to affect my behavior. I literally prayed that I'd become numb to the pain. And I learned to grin and bear it in the meantime."

"Numb to the pain, huh?" Shana said doubtingly.

"Well, you know what I mean. I may not be numb, but I would at least like to be able to ignore the pain. I want to go into my next relationship with a clear head. I don't even care if I'm labeled as a giddy woman who'll do whatever it takes to keep her man happy. Of course, I don't want to be fake. I want to genuinely learn the art of forgiveness. I want to have fun and be blissfully happy. I'm talking holding-hands-skipping-through-the-park happy. I'm talking cavorting to the max!"

"Yeah, that sounds wonderful!" Shana was still doubtful.

"Realistically, there'll be ups and downs, but I won't mind if we go through them together. The man I marry won't be able to get enough of me. He'll be treated like a king. I'm tired of everybody giving up. I've vowed that once I settle down, that's it. I'm going to do it right. I'm ready to move forward in victory and make sure all the pain I experienced was worth it. I'm expecting pay back for every failed relationship." Krystal was pumped up at this point.

Krystal and Shana woke up bright and early on Saturday morning. After focusing solely on their shopping for several hours, the ladies decided to sit on a nearby park bench and take a break. "I've had my share of pain in relationships," Shana started back up their previous conversation.

"Yeah, let's talk about your life," Krystal said.

"Uh, that's what I was about to do, until I was rudely interrupted," Shana said, mocking Krystal.

"Well, start talking!" Krystal was mocking Shana.

"Well, my personal life is in a holding pattern right now. William and I had been seeing each other for about two years, before we broke up five months ago. You know how that is. We're still 'friends', so we still talk and go out a lot."

Krystal looked at her knowingly. "Girl, I don't ever recommend playing 'the friendship game' with a man. Seems like they win every time."

"I know…" As Shana was talking, Krystal looked across the small park area and thought she saw Lisa's cousin, Lauren, and her brother, Charles. "Hey Lauren! Charles!" she yelled. Lauren turned around. At first, Charles thought that she was hearing things until he saw Krystal waving both of her arms in the air.

"Oh, my goodness. Well, what a surprise!" Lauren said.

Charles gave Krystal a huge kiss on the cheek.

"What are you guys doing here?" Krystal stood up to hug Lauren.

"Actually, I had a job interview in Manhattan yesterday," Charles said, "of course, Lauren came to do some shopping."

Krystal introduced Shana to Lauren and Charles. Lauren was such a bubbly person. She hugged Shana before Shana could even stand up.

"We're shopping, too, of course," Krystal said.

"Well, you guys look tired. You've accomplished a lot today, huh?" Charles asked, as he looked at the many bags they had stacked between them.

"Yeah, we're taking a break," Shana said.

"...talking about life, love and the pursuit of happiness," Krystal said.

"The pursuit of happiness, huh? I just got off the phone with my significant other. She's going through changes because I'm considering taking this position," Charles said. "She doesn't know that I'm going to ask her to move here with me."

Krystal cut her eyes at him.

"No one said anything about shacking up, so just calm down," he said.

Krystal had grown up with Lauren and Charles, as if they were her cousins. They were both younger than she and Lisa, so they had always taken it upon themselves to boss the two around. "Amen!" Krystal exclaimed. "But wait a minute. Are you talking about Dawn? I thought you guys broke up."

"No, I'm not talking about her. That's what you get for being so busy. You'd have known that I've been dating Shelly for almost a year."

"Well, what happened to Dawn?" Krystal asked.

"Oh, brother. Please don't get him started on that!" Lauren shrieked.

"No, I need to keep up with you guys' lives," Krystal said. Then she looked over at Shana. "We will finish our discussion about your life later." Shana smiled. She was glad to be off the hook. Krystal turned back toward Charles. "What happened? You guys were such great friends."

"Where should I begin?" Charles said. "Well, that relationship ended up very wickedly, to say the least. I actually cursed at her. And before that, I hadn't cursed in about three years."

Krystal shook her head. "We're going to pray that cursing spirit off of you."

Charles continued. "Well as you said, we started off as great friends. It was actually a group of us that hung out. We basically did everything together."

"Yeah, it was such a ridiculous little clique," Lauren interjected.

"Quit interrupting your brother!" Krystal said, in her parenting voice.

"Common sense would have told me to just leave that knucklehead alone. But we both know that common sense is not so common." He laughed. "I knew first hand that she was a canine in the making."

"Oh my goodness. Keep your language pure, please," Krystal begged.

"Alright. Sorry! Well, I knew she was into playing games, but she convinced me that she'd changed. And I thought I'd 'covered all the bases' and asked all the right questions. I figured she was a mess, but it didn't matter because she belonged to me, and I could deal with it. She told me that she was honored that I would give her the time of day. Well, everything went well for about three months. Then all of a sudden she turned on me. When I called, she would say she was busy. Then, finally, she admitted that she wasn't happy, but didn't want to tell me because she knew I'd be hurt. Naturally, I was devastated. I thought that people married their friends and that friendship was the perfect ingredient for a perfect relationship. Nonetheless, she said she thought of me as just 'one of the guys.' She loved me as a friend and was concerned about my well being, but wasn't interested in more. So just like that, our relationship was over. Needless to say, the next month I found out that she was pregnant by this other dude."

"Oh, no!" Krystal exclaimed.

"Right! And our friendship was ruined. Sadly, I still loved her. I used to think about her a lot. I considered begging her to take me back because she was the first woman I ever truly fell in love with. But you know how that goes. We're always hoping that we're the exception, and the one who causes the other person to change for the better, but we live and learn."

"Everybody has a story!" Shana said shaking her head.

"Makes you wonder why we fools even fool around with love," Lauren said.

"Yeah, it seems like the hurt and pain suffered is more intense than any love received. The truth is that love hurts, but it's worth it in the end," Krystal said.

"Yeah, and it's quite interesting that they were good friends, yet she was able to walk away so easily. I just hate the fact that Charles loved her so much, and she seemed to be so carefree with his feelings." Lauren put her two cents in.

Krystal remembered feeling as if someone had ripped the very breath of life out of her when her fiancé cheated on her. Jarrett, on the other hand was so genuine. She trusted him with her life. He kept telling her that he wanted to marry her, but she was hesitant. His sincerity and adoration were almost unreal. Yet she knew that if she did not want to lose him, she would have to respond soon. She finally spoke up, "Well, the Bible says that husbands should love their wives, even as Christ also loved the church, and gave Himself for it. That means that a man must be willing to die for his wife. Go figure! And I think men should love women more. Women need adoration. We need to feel needed." Krystal hoped that they would not think her philosophy was too old-fashioned.

"That's so true! Break out the violins and the tissue," Lauren said, jokingly.

"You're such a clown," Krystal said to Lauren. She wholeheartedly understood Charles's pain. "Well, don't feel bad about believing that she had changed. Or even wanting her back after all the ill things she'd done. That's just the way love is," she said. "Love is seemingly always willing to give it one more try. I'm just glad to hear that you didn't get rid of her because she couldn't cook or something." Krystal was poking fun at the teenage Charles, who said that he was going to keep his woman in the kitchen, barefoot and pregnant.

"Hey, I was a kid then. But now, I don't require much. I'm just a simple dude looking for love. On any given day, a smile and a soft word will beat out a greatly cooked meal accompanied with a frown," Charles said. "I found someone to love me back and she smiles all the time. And this relationship is working out great. She can even cook a little, too. Actually, you might remember her. She's a teacher at the middle school where Lauren worked last year."

"That's right. I'll take the credit for fixing my brother up with a good woman who won't take advantage of his niceness," Lauren said.

"Shana, right?" Charles asked. "You have to excuse my sister, she didn't take her medication today."

Lauren pushed him. "Oh! Whatever."

Krystal interjected. "Lauren is just being her super-exuberant self. And believe me, Shana can relate!"

"Super hyper is more like it," Charles mumbled.

Shana was cracking up. "Don't worry, Lauren. I have an older brother. And I'm in the process of making sure that he ends up with a good woman, too."

Krystal ignored Shana's comments, but Lauren caught on. "That's right you're Jarrett's sister." Lauren hugged Shana again. "Welcome to the family!"

"Thank you so much!" Shana said.

Krystal ignored them both.

"Hey! Have you guys eaten anything? I'm starving. And we walked past this café with a very cute waiter standing outside. That's where Charles and I were headed," Lauren said.

"Actually, it's been several hours and I could use a snack," Shana said.

Charles began to cough. He was just getting over a slight cold. "Yeah, and I think I should stop and get something for this cold before it flares back up."

"Oh, suck it up!" Lauren said. "Take it like a woman! It's just a cold."

Charles refused to get into that battle in the presence of three women. He grinned at Lauren, but he dared not open his mouth.

As they walked to the café, Lauren gazed over at a handsome young man walking towards them.

"You got caught looking again," Charles said. "But this time it's not a bad looking dude."

"Yeah, he's cute," Krystal said.

"No, he is stunningly beautiful," Lauren corrected them. "He has to be a model or something."

"Yes, indeed," Krystal said, taking a second glance. "He just looks so sad."

"He probably just had a bad day or something," Lauren said. As they passed by, she smiled at him and nodded her head.

He forced a smile at her, and kept walking.

Lauren quickly reminded Charles that he had been flirting with the young lady who had tried to pick him up earlier by introducing herself and giving him her business card. "Well, you know how that goes. Once you're in a committed relationship, you somehow become more attractive. No one wants someone who ain't nobody else interested in, anyway." Charles was defending himself.

"That's your story, and you're sticking with it, huh?" Krystal laughed.

"Anyway, I wonder what was that guy's story?" Lauren asked. "Someone so gorgeous should not have such a sour look on their face."

"Yep, we all have a story." Shana repeated her sentiment from their previous conversation.

"Yeah," Charles said, "but God can change the ending of our story, if we submit our wills to His will."

"Amen, let's go eat!" Lauren said. "All this talk about beautiful people and the looks on their faces can wait!"

A Grim Look Explained

The blow was straight to the heart.
I stood stunned for quite some time.
I decided not to give up without a fight.
I prepared myself for the battle within myself.
I punched the air!
In integrity, there was not much else I could do physically
to defend myself against my enemy.
This was going to be tough.
I swallowed hard!
I stood there bleeding inside
with a grim look on my face.

As she smiled at me,
the person standing next to me
told me I should get rid of the grim look I carried.
She convinced me to smile.

But if she had experienced my pain,
she would have known firsthand
that the look was justified.
I was trying not to let pain and anguish overtake me,
so I fought it inside
with this grim look displayed outside!

Yet she was very cordial, so I decided to smile back!
After conversing, I found that she
had experienced a blow of her own.
Her story, was my story. And my story, was her story.
Yet her smile was so bright, so genuine.
I remembered the blow I had experienced,
and now it seemed so major, yet so minor.
I swallowed hard again,

and girded up the loins of my mind.
I felt the pain of my past,
but at the same time I was numb.
I realized the feeling might stay awhile,
But I still had a desire to smile again!
I wanted to live outside the four walls in this box I had created!
I wanted to live outside of my wounds!

Later, as I walked through the street,
I watched the faces of others.
Many were sad and grim.
I wondered how I could help erase that look—
eliminate the cause of their pain.
And I remembered how that gal gently helped me
And I smiled at them.
Some smiled back.
Others kept the grim look.
But I didn't take it personally
because I assumed that they were feeling "the pain."
And instead of lashing out at their enemy
they were doing their best not to let it overcome them.

And I prayed that they, too, would win the battle—
that they could feel the pain,
and simultaneously realize
that they could still smile again.

Chapter Seven
Drama

Lisa tried to pull herself together, but tears fell continuously without her permission. "God have Your way," she whispered, as she slipped into her S.U.V. She found a napkin in her glove compartment and blotted her eyes.

Pulling into the church parking lot, she saw her niece, Ashley, along with Maya and Mark Jr., running towards her. Strolling at a modest distance behind was Tonya and Mark. Lisa assumed that Ashley was being tossed between family members, because her brother and his wife were having marital problems again. She was also reminded to call him to finalize plans for her mom's fiftieth birthday dinner. Lisa could see that Tonya had a big grin on her face. She got out of her vehicle and hugged the kids.

"You look like you need a hug!" Mark said.

Lisa welcomed his embrace. "It's your wife's fault that I'm in this state."

"Well, I do what I can to bring the sisterhood closer to the Lord," Tonya joked, "and closer to reality."

Lisa was smiling, but she had forced herself to attend church that morning. She really wished she could just stay home and spend time with God, minus the bother of interacting with others. She had considered visiting another local church, or even staying home to watch a televised church service. However, she knew that she would not be happy. God had placed her in that assembly to be ministered to and to minister to His people. Her flesh could always come up with an excuse to miss church, but in her spirit she knew that church was the place she needed to be to help strengthen her with a word of encouragement. She had found that missing church was more detrimental than helpful. It never failed that when she chose to stay home, she felt far removed from the things of God. Some days, the circumstances of her life made her feel as if she was not worthy of going to the House of God. "Ain't that just like the devil to try to convince you that you could ever actually be worthy of God's grace," her grandmother would always say.

As they all walked into the church, Lisa scanned the lobby for Krystal. It was still early, so she had probably not arrived. Lisa was not in the mood for small talk, but she knew it was inevitable. She could hear Pastor Lindsay's voice as clearly as if he were preaching right then, "Ministry is people. You need to grow up and learn to deal with all types of people. How else can God use you to effectively help others?"

She still wished she could stay home sometimes. There were always those saints who vexed her every chance they got—always causing strife and division—but she wanted to learn to show God's love towards them as well. The fact that they had issues getting along with others was not an excuse for her. *Lord, please help me to get rid of all of my hang-ups,* she prayed silently.

Unknowingly, she was setting herself up. Before she could finish, she saw Kim and Nicole approaching her. She called them the "Church Critics." They were always ready to critique whatever drama was going on in the lives of their prey. Well, she was not in the mood, which obviously did not matter to either of them because they immediately started questioning her.

"How is Jamesey Pooh?" Nicole asked. "We heard about his grandfather."

"Oh, his grandfather's doing much better." Lisa did not want to give them the slightest hint that things had changed between she and James.

"Is he here yet?" Kim asked.

"Uh, yeah, I'm sure he is." Lisa hoped that was their last comment, but of course they went on and on about how nice James was and how good-looking he and his brother were. *Lord, haven't I suffered enough torture?* Lisa thought. She politely smiled, and gave them both a hug. "See you guys later," she said.

Perhaps Lisa was overreacting, but it appeared that her worst nightmare was unfolding. She was officially involved in church break-up drama. She was about to be introduced to cowering in order to avoid answering questions about her not-so-happy personal life from people who already had preconceived notions, and who would likely spread her business erroneously, like a wild fire.

On top of the rumors, James was one of the most eligible bachelors at the church, so she also had to prepare herself for seeing him with other women. She did not really care whether James was dating again or not, but she did not want to see him and his new woman prancing around.

One of her good friends had left their church because she was tired of seeing her ex-boyfriend and felt like she could not grow with him constantly around her. She said that it had been too much to interact with him on several committee events. At that very moment, Lisa totally understood her pain. No one wanted a constant reminder of a failed or severed relationship. Lisa also had a fear of being marked as someone who could not be taken seriously, which was the stigma attached to those who constantly "played the field." She knew she was only on break-up number one, but she also knew that those numbers could grow quickly. After all, her cousin, Cliff was on try number six and counting, and her friend, Dina was on try number eight. Those statistics scared the life out of her.

Her love for church was being tainted by mixed emotions. Whenever she came, she was reminded of the power and authority she possessed to overcome. Yet some days it was still very hard to show up. She prayed that soon she would be able to walk through the church doors freely, not allowing anything to weigh her down. She longed for the day when she would not care who was there, what they were doing or why, who liked her, and who did not particularly care for her.

Today her dealings with James, or lack thereof, were such a distraction. She dreaded facing him in such a public arena. She almost convinced herself that if she stayed away, it would benefit both of them, and would help to alleviate the awkwardness and stress associated with seeing one another.

However, Lisa was a hard-working, active member. Whenever she missed even the smallest of events, everyone seemed to notice, and that usually caused her more drama than if she had attended. Besides, she wanted to be found in place, and not putting the burden of her share of the load on someone else. She had a feeling deep down on the inside that if she just stayed in place, God would reward her for her diligence. And so she painfully walked around the corridor before service started, doing her usual hobnobbing and greeting God's people.

She cringed when she saw James coming her way. It was like he was wearing a banner which read, "Hey, Lisa I'm the one! That guy that you couldn't have a successful relationship with, that's me! I'm that guy who you said you would love until the end, and yet turned your back on!"

Lisa braced herself. *I must kill this flesh!* she thought. She knew that the drama would likely never end. There would always be an issue to deal with. So, it was best if she ended the fight then, laying her personal issues aside so that she could give and receive what she needed from God and His people.

Out of the corner of her eye, she saw James laughing and joking with Elaine Peterson. Her feelings of discomfort were overwhelming. She wished she had gone straight into the sanctuary and prepared her mind for service. Just then, Krystal walked up and rescued her.

"What's up, Diva?" Krystal walked up from behind. Lisa was so glad to see her that she hugged her and kissed her on the cheek. "Whoa! What's wrong with you? What happened to your rule about unnecessarily kissing women?"

Lisa barely heard her. "I like that suit. Did you buy that in New York?"

"Yeah! I bought you something, too, and it is gorgeous, if I must say so myself. And you're looking mighty spiffy. Are those boots new?"

Lisa might have looked good outwardly, but inwardly, she was a wreck. She pulled Krystal into a nearby corner. "Look, enough small talk." She laughed. "I'm having drama. I asked you to call me no matter what time you got in last night."

"I know, but I didn't get back until this morning. I figured you'd prefer I got some rest so I'd be sober and could think clearly. What's so important anyway?"

"I finally told James that we need time apart. I prayed about it, and I just feel like the Lord is doing some things in me that require me to separate myself."

"Time apart? You might as well say you two broke up! And why do you people always blame God when you dump somebody?" Krystal was annoyed. "Just say you want to be alone. Well, actually, that's not true, is it? You and I both know that if the right guy came along, you'd make an exception."

"Whose side are you on anyway?" Lisa glared at her. Perhaps there was some truth to what Krystal said, but Lisa was not about to admit it.

Krystal started talking really fast, as she was known to do once she got excited. "Look, just admit that you initiated this breakup, because if God did tell you to break up with him, and you didn't want to, you'd likely shrug it off as the devil playing tricks with your mind. Don't blame God unless He really told you that. And if He did, He likely told you before you got into the relationship. Although I need you to explain to me why God wants you to be by yourself. It's possible to have a man by your side and grow spiritually, too, Pooh Pooh!" Krystal rubbed Lisa's back. "It just has to be the right man."

"The right man? Oh, you mean like Jarrett?" Lisa teased.

Krystal ignored Lisa. "It's more like you guys' relationship was a bit too carnal for you. And you already know it's a pet peeve of mine for people to act deep and spiritual—as if God is anti-relationship. But I know that if you do your part, He's willing to work with you." Krystal was giving Lisa a brief synopsis of a discussion they had had several times, and would likely have again.

I can always count on Krystal to give me a reality check, Lisa thought.

"What I really want to know is how you're feeling?" Krystal asked.

"Uh, I was feeling horrible until just now! Thanks!" Lisa said.

"Well, I'm glad you feel better, and we'll definitely talk later. In no time, you'll be able to look back and say you've survived yet another attack of the enemy in his quest to discourage you, and it will be a sweet victory." They hugged again and then went their separate ways to find their favorite seats in the sanctuary.

Lisa braced herself and went into the sanctuary, "as a mature saint ought." She continued to rebuke the spirit of distraction so she could totally focus on the service. Pastor Lindsay preached, "The Making of a Leader!" He talked about God's divine purpose that is entangled in our trials. "They won't destroy you, but make you into the person God's called you to be," he said. He blew Lisa's mind when he said, "God choosing you has nothing to do with you, but everything to do with His mercy and foreknowledge of your purpose. God doesn't call us because our pasts are so great that He doesn't want to miss out on our futures. He calls us knowing we'll fail, but uses it all for His glory."

Lisa's situation had not changed, but she felt such assurance in knowing that God would not give up on her or abandon her, like so many others in her past had done. She prayed she would be able to hold on until God gave her the desires of her heart, and fulfilled the promises He had given her. All she really wanted was to walk effectively in His will and purpose for her life.

As she pondered what Pastor Lindsay said, a guy two rows in front of her jumped up and yelled, "Yes, God!" Lisa looked over at her friend, Barb and smiled. Of course, his wife jumped up five seconds later and yelled, "Hallelujah!" Then they gave each other a high five. Lisa was really tickled.

She and Barb made eye contact again. "They're overdoing it!" Barb whispered. Lisa could hear some of the young people snickering. Alisha looked back at both of them, as if to say, "it's not right to judge someone else's praise." Lisa was still laughing.

I agree that praise is "comely for the upright," because of the awesome goodness and mercy of God, Lisa thought. Sometimes she wished she could hold up cue cards saying, "Sit down, now!" or "Hush up and pass the candy!" They would be for the extra special people who always had a loud comment, or stood up before Pastor Lindsay could even finish his thought. She shook herself and started back focusing on the message.

Lisa left church immediately after the benediction. As she pulled into the carport, she was glad she had come home. Krystal and the crew had invited her to go to her favorite restaurant, but she decided to go home, sort out her feelings and allow the Lord to continue to minister to her.

The next day was very peaceful. Lisa went to work, and then went home, studied the Bible for a few hours and then went to bed. Her Tuesday went much the same way. She started her Wednesday morning off with Early Morning Prayer at church. After prayer, as she was driving along Route One, on her way into the office, she heard her cell phone vibrating. As the traffic light was turning yellow, she slowed down so she could grab it. The person behind her was obviously heated as they blew their horn, swerved around her into the next lane, and zoomed through the light. Thinking it was Tonya she answered the phone fussing, "Why are you calling me this early in the morning? You know my phone is in the bottom of my bag and I'm in rush hour traffic," she said laughingly.

"Excuse me?" A male voice came through the receiver. "I didn't know I needed to make an appointment to call my E.A."

She was so embarrassed. It was Bartlett. He had teased her about being an overeducated, know-it-all. He called her his executive assistant (E.A. for short) to remind her that he was the boss. "Oh, I'm so sorry!" Lisa exclaimed. "I thought it was my cousin, Tonya ... Well it doesn't matter. How are you?"

"Great, considering the fact that I've been bawled out and haven't done anything wrong yet," Bartlett joked. Lisa apologized again. Bartlett quickly got to the reason of his phone call. He needed her help reviewing some correspondence, and wanted to e-mail it to her that afternoon. He also wanted her to attend his staff meeting so she could meet his employees. Lisa assured him that she would make herself available so she could earn the title he had given her.

By the time eleven o'clock rolled around, Lisa had been in three meetings.

She felt they were all a big waste of her time. She loathed non-value added exercises, and the last meeting was definitely one for the record book. She had met with some of their customers which, in her opinion, loved to hear themselves talk. It seemed like they all spent the whole time trying to prove how smart they were. Lisa sat and counted how many times one of them started off a conversation by saying, "Well, I have nothing else except [blah blah blah], but that subject should probably be handled offline in a more relative meeting!" It happened a total of four times. Lisa could not believe how obnoxious they were, especially Mrs. Kapowski. It was as if she had to mark her female territory and prove that she knew everything, all in one meeting. The meeting lasted an hour, only about fifteen minutes of which was relevant.

Finally, Lisa cut them short and said she needed to make her 11:30 a.m. conference call. She could tell they were upset about her cutting them off from talking about nothing, but she did not care. She could only take so much of their babbling. She agreed that energy conservation and electrical safe work practices were important, but she was anxious for God to release her, so she could spend 40 hours a week doing work that would touch people's souls.

It was about noon before Lisa finally got to go through her daily ritual of reading her inspirational calendar and checking her e-mail messages. She was elated when she saw Bartlett V. Hartin's name on her list of unopened e-mail messages. She was tickled because he had finally told her his middle name was Vernon. So now she knew his whole name—Bartlett Vernon Hartins. His mom had named him Bartlett because she met his dad while bartending in college. He said he had been teased and called "Brat" throughout grade school, and that his friends and family called him "Big Bart" or "Big Hart" because of his height and because he was the eldest son. But Lisa had told him she was going to call him, "Brave Heart." "I'll only respond to that because it's coming from you," he had said.

Lisa spent the remainder of the day reading her work-related e-mail. Then she shot Krystal a message to remind her that they were having dinner with David and his parents for the weekend. She checked her e-mail one last time before she turned off her computer, and noticed that she had not even opened the message from an engineer who worked in one of their manufacturing facilities. They had spoken the previous week about an energy conservation proposal he was planning to submit for changing out the Metal Halide lighting fixtures in several of their facilities. She opened his message and skimmed through it. She replied, letting him know she had received the message and that she would get back with him, the following week. This was yet another reminder of the humdrum career of which she wanted to rid herself.

Lisa's day had gone by fairly quickly after lunch, and she was glad. While eating dinner, James called, but she did not bother answering, and since he did not leave a message, she figured it was not important. She could not wait until he stopped calling completely. She cared about him a lot, but she knew that it was not good for them to be together. She was also hoping that she would not run into him at mid-week service that evening.

As usual, Lisa was glad she had attended church. Pastor Lindsay said, "We must kill this flesh, and not allow our current emotions to stop our future purpose in Christ." It was exactly what Lisa needed to hear. After church, she made a point to greet her family and friends, particularly Tonya. Tonya had left a message saying that Lisa was still being antisocial, and she was beginning to take it personal. So Lisa made sure that she showed her face before she left. As soon as she turned out of the church parking lot, her cell phone rang.

"Hi Angie," Lisa said, as she answered the phone.

"Caller I.D. is such a wonderful thing, isn't it?" Angie responded. "How are you? I haven't been able to find you at church the past few weeks, but I wanted to invite you to Brandi's birthday party this coming Saturday at 4:00 p.m. She'll be three. Let's pray that the terrible two's are behind us."

"Our little baby is growing up. Well, I'm sure that I'll at least be able to stop over," Lisa said. "David's finally coming home, and his mom is cooking dinner. My mom's party is the next day, so this is going to be a very hectic weekend."

"His mom is cooking dinner for us," Angie repeated mockingly.

"Don't even start," Lisa warned. "David is like a brother to me."

"Anyone can tell he's interested in being more than your brother. That's why I don't have a man. You have two, and can't make up your mind." For some reason, Angie thought Lisa and James would eventually get back together, if David did not snatch her up first. Angie continued. "And I almost forgot that my cousin tried to fix you up with one of her coworkers. Why didn't you like him?"

"I thought you called about Brandi's party? And how many men are you going to fix me up with in one conversation? Do I seem that desperate, Missy?"

"Well, you are always frauhnjilating," Angie teased.

"Trust me, I wouldn't waste any frauhnjilating on him," Lisa laughed. She had not heard that term since college. They had made it up to define flirtatious women, and used it especially for a girl on the third floor of their dorm who was always prancing through campus with high heels and tight jeans.

"Why not? He's cute," Angie insisted.

"He's not that cute," Lisa said.

"Well, he's a very accomplished young man. You could at least go out with him, even if it's just to have something to do other than watching cartoons."

"Been there, done that, got the T-shirt! I can't find fulfillment in that. Dudes like yourself, however, seem to have no problem. But at this stage in my life, I'm not looking for something to pass the time. I'm waiting for that man who wants to be known as my Provision! Forget the rest! Can I get an Amen?"

"Yeah, I got ya, but I'm going to go ahead and have some fun. I mean, Brandi's father had me tied down for years and then when she came along, somehow, we fell out of love so quickly. But I guess there's an unwritten rule that if you have a child with someone that's not 'ready' for commitment, then things go bad immediately. But there's nothing wrong with going out with no strings attached. How else will you find someone?" Angie was trying to plead her case.

"Yeah, if you go out with folks who you might actually consider marrying," Lisa was picking on Angie who was known to give any guy a trial period.

"Are you trying to be funny?" Angie asked.

"Who, me? Of course, not!" Lisa said sarcastically. "I'm just saying, I need more. But hey, do your thing, Missy."

"And you know I will."

Lisa quickly finished up her conversation with Angie, then she clicked over to speak with Lauren, who had called on the other end.

"I could have called back if you guys were talking about something important," Lauren said.

"We weren't," Lisa laughingly assured her. "She was torturing me and giving me bad advice about going out so I won't be bored."

"Well, I agree. It's very healthy for you."

"Perhaps, but you two aren't the ones to plead that case," Lisa teased.

"Oh, no. Here you go! You know that clown, Chad, called me the other day." Lauren was annoyed just thinking about that situation.

"Perhaps because you sort of led him on and kinda-sorta stretched the truth a tad bit, so now he's still kinda-sorta searching for the truth and still kinda thinks there's maybe some hope for you guys. Perhaps he sat back and watched you say one thing and do another. Could that be why?" Lisa was not letting up.

"Okay, I messed up," Lauren admitted. "I told him Andre and I were just friends, and that we weren't talking, but hey, things happen."

"Lauren, that would only be a valid point if you hadn't already admitted that you only dated Andre to have something to do and/or if your relationship with him had actually lasted more than a week." Lisa was really letting her have it. "And then after him, there was Minister Taylor, who you practically threw yourself at."

"Okay. I know! I know!" Lauren was tired of her issue with Chad.

"Hey, you know I'm being honest, and hopefully you'd do the same for me."

"Is he going to find a new issue every day, though?" Lauren asked.

"He would never do such a thing. Unless of course, the untruths and issues just continue to unfold," Lisa said, hoping that she was not being too harsh.

"Okay, so I told him two or three untruths, but he stretched it into 200 or 300. I apologized several times. How long will I have to pay for this?"

"Hey, only you and your healthy-relationship-having-self can answer that. Just be sure you've genuinely changed and that you're intentions are pure. Is that too much to ask?" Lisa asked in her parenting voice.

"Hey, I've learned to be open and honest about my intentions."

"No, don't misunderstood me. I didn't say be honest about your intentions. I said make sure you have pure intentions. There is a difference."

"Ha! Charles said my opening line should be 'Look dude, I know I'm cute, and I want things my way or no way! You need enough money to support my shopping habit, and we'll get along just fine."

"Exactly," Lisa said.

"Whatever! And if I use that line, they'll likely agree that I'm no different than any other woman," Lauren said laughingly. "I think I'm recovering from my foolishness now, though. Hanging around you, there was no way I could continue in my folly anyways. Thanks Cous.'" Lauren was sentimental. "I don't know if I've ever expressed that to you! I appreciate having you around as my role model."

"Who me?" Lisa was shocked. "Thanks, but I'm just a small fry who Christ is working on. To know Him, is to know that we can't comfortably stay how we are. Trust me, I have a lot to work through, too. I've been through so much foolishness, though, I ought to know a little something by now." She laughed.

"No, seriously, I just think about how whenever you're in a relationship that's going sour, you handle your business quickly. When you realized that John wasn't ready to commit, you sent him on his merry way. And you did the same with James. That's why you don't have any relationship drama."

"Are you kidding me?" Lisa asked. "Trust me, both times I went through a lot emotionally. I missed both of those jokers like crazy."

"Yeah right! You're so intelligent," Lauren cut her off. "You're just sailing along through life. You got rid of your excess baggage. You're getting your Masters. Your career's booming. You have a great family life. You're active at church. And you stay focused on your goals. I bet you never feel complacent."

"Wow! So that's how it looks from the outside?" Lisa asked. "Sometimes I think others have higher expectations of me than I have of myself. I'm so insignificant. The Holy Ghost taught me everything I know. Trust me, nothing comes easy for me. I have to work extra hard for the basics. Anyways, I wish I were as confident as others view me. I guess I'm just good at faking it." She laughed.

"Yeah right! Some days I wonder if there's anything you don't know."

"Girl, that's because I am the queen of copycat. Mostly everything I do, I've researched on the Internet. Might as well, since it's free, and so easily accessible. Trust me, I just know how to fake it."

Lauren laughed. "Lisa, please. I know nobody's perfect, but at least you constantly look for ways to improve. That will always overshadow your mistakes."

"Well, I always say, 'Why do anything if it's not going to be done right?' Remember that time you asked for help with your finance homework? I got online and found the equation. Then I found my old homework, and about an hour later, I had jogged my memory enough to help you out." Lisa was pulling up in front of her house at this point. "Well, I'm not trying to rush you, but my mom is on the other line. Love ya!"

"Love ya, too," Lauren sang.

By the time Lisa clicked over, her mom had hung up. She decided to eat and prepare her lunch and clothing for the next day before she called her back. After she spoke with her mom, although tired, she decided to catch up on some reading for her class. She could barely find her book before the doorbell rang.

Drama

Drama is defined as a prose or verse composition telling a serious story
intended for representation by actors; impersonating a character
and performing dialogue; a serious narrative work
for television, radio, or the cinema; a theatrical play of a particular period.
It is a succession of events having the dramatic progression
or emotional effect or characteristic of a play.
It exemplifies something arresting, powerful, or forceful in appearance or effect—

Or, at least that's what they say!
But I say, it is usually a performance of grand proportion
from a very colorful character, and is an indication of something or someone
that you would rather not deal with at the time.
It symbolizes that situation or person
that causes vexation of your spirit and irking in your mind.
Oh, don't get me wrong! It has been known to bring about laughter,
but, of the sarcastic and disparaging sort.

There's ministry drama—folk think you have to be perfect if God has called you.
There's church folk drama. Lord, show us that we can't all be in charge.
There's financial drama. We need to give, not borrow our way out of debt.
There's familial drama. Kin folks major in cutting one another down.
There's career drama. We spend too much time on menial tasks.
Then there's male/female relationship drama. Mending that can take forever.

Drama is as drama does!
It's usually caused by picturesque individuals that enjoy stealing the show.
Actually, we all possess the ability to portray an aura of drama.
In our own way, we write sitcoms daily.
And we have coined the phrase "Save the Drama for your Mama"
because she's the only one who cares enough to waste time consoling you
in your pretentiousness, which will only be repeated if it is appeased.

Oh, did I mention that drama lasts forever? That's Right!
It monopolizes the stage! Drama will never exeunt!
It simply changes partners, replacing those who star in the leading role.

Chapter Eight
The Attitude of a Friend

"Just a moment!" Lisa yelled, as she rushed to get dressed. She ran down the stairs and flung open the door.

"How are you, Ms. Wilson?" James said, flashing the smile that always charmed her.

"Great!" Lisa said, barely cracking a smile. "What are you doing here?"

"I've been thinking about you, and since I'm in the neighborhood…"

"Really?" Lisa could not believe that he had the audacity to stop by, but she was determined to remain Christ-like. "Well, I'm preparing for bed," she began.

James had already invited himself in. "I'm thirsty. You got some pineapple-orange juice in the fridge?" he asked. The whiff of his cologne, was like a nebulizer—awakening her to the emotional dependency she had established on him. When they first separated, she had had to force herself to stop calling him, especially when his grandfather got out of the rehab center. Also, the last time she spoke with her dad she had been flustered, and wanted James to console her. She could not believe the feelings that were resurfacing, yet she followed him into the kitchen with the intention of putting him out within the next few minutes.

Tonya, the relationship guru, had assured her that she was normal for still having feelings for him. "Just because you moved on doesn't mean that your feelings toward him will go away immediately. All the things you liked about him are still there. And, you still possess the qualities that he loved and adored." The last time she saw James her heart had skipped a beat, as he kissed her on the hand. "I loathe that part of me that wants to take him back," Lisa had told Tonya.

She sat down and watched him make himself at home. "So how's life been treating you?" he asked without turning around.

"Great!" Lisa replied. "How about you?"

James poured himself another glass full of juice, and then walked over into the dining room. Lisa was still watching silently as he took off his jacket and sat down. That evening, James did most of the talking. Lisa remained quiet as he apologized for being irresponsible and told her that he missed her and wished that they could pick up where they had left off. Finally, he looked over at her and said, "Lisa, I love you. How do you feel about you and I being together?"

Lisa was caught off guard and speechless for several seconds. "James, I care about your well being, but I don't think we should be together. I'm enjoying being free to sort through my life without dragging someone else along for the ride. I know I've made the best choice for this stage of my life."

"I appreciate your honesty." He was seemingly staring into the abyss. He stood up, put on his jacket, kissed her on the cheek, and let himself out.

Part of Lisa really wanted to accept James's apologies. She was tired of being alone. She wanted companionship with someone that she loved and someone that loved her, and James qualified. Yet she knew that she would not be happy settling for anything less than her soul's yearning.

Lisa had an extended lunch with Cliff to tell him about her drama the evening before. "You worked your mojo on him," he teased. Then he said the magic words she needed to hear to move past her loneliness. "You made the right decision since you don't have the heart to continue that relationship."

Lisa sneezed. "When I woke up this morning, I felt sort of under the weather. I'm still nauseous," she whined. Lisa did not feel very well, but she was glad that she had not stayed in bed all day sulking as she had originally planned.

"You're such a big baby!" Cliff said. "You want a little cheese to go with that whine?" Cliff asked. "We're going to have to work on that, so by the time Mr. Right comes you won't scare him off."

"Hey, there's a technique to whining." She had a sneaky smile on her face.

"Oh, so you only whine to me because I keep babying you. Well, I'll fix that," Cliff joked. "I don't know why I keep falling for it. Everybody knows that whining is a woman's way of manipulating the circumstances in her favor."

"Oh, please! Statistics prove that men are much more whiney than women."

"You just made up those statistics."

"You can't prove that. And let the record show that I'm not getting married. I'm tired of this drama."

"You've gone from whining to talking crazy!" Cliff was getting serious.

"No, I'm serious. Men and women are always at two different phases. My goodness! Women are always ready for marriage, which scares men half to death. And then the woman has to end up moving on to another man, which she's really settling for because she's still stuck on her first love."

Cliff smiled. "Interesting!"

"Okay, maybe I should just speak for myself, huh?" she asked, after realizing how general, yet specific, her statement sounded.

"Lisa, there isn't just one person on earth you can be happy with. My dad says you make the best choice, and it all works out if you stick with it!"

"You can always count on good old Uncle Larry." She laughed. "But it hurts to hear you say that. It sounds like a ticket to settling for second best. I hope I never get so tired of waiting that I settle for whatever's out there."

"That's not it at all. Life won't play out the same for everybody. Some may marry their first love, some won't. But whatever you finally choose, stick with it."

"Yeah, if I ever run into a man who wants to settle down. Is it just me, or do men play games for a billion years first? Why is it that the one you want to be with isn't ready, and the one who wants to be with you is a mess?" Lisa was frustrated.

"Be patient. I think most men have an adjustment period, trying to find the balance between responsibly committing to one woman and loving her till the end, or playing the field, which is easiest. That generally takes no thought or effort. We all tend to get more offers than we can physically handle," he joked.

Lisa glared at him. "Yeah, okay!"

"Seriously! A committed relationship is just one act of compromising after another. Commitment ties you down, and both men *and* women have been known to enjoy the luxury of running from it," Cliff concluded, "I don't know why I always have to remind you that this is not a one-sided issue."

"It's the man with the God-given power to pop the question, and y'all can't seem to get that right until you hit 50 and are finally tired of being alone."

Cliff ignored her. "Plus, women scare men. How in the world is somebody who knows everything going to be submissive?"

"What? Why are men so intimidated? It's as if being accomplished or mature is a curse!"

"Well, I considered marrying a younger woman because I want someone who I can grow with."

"Yeah, I've had guys tell me that, but I think there's a huge misconception regarding independent women. If a woman has a decent career, owns a home, and appears to be established, most people think she can only be approached by a certain type of guy, which isn't true. Please, living from check to check doesn't constitute being established." She laughed. "I'm high-maintenance only because I require respect, emotional and spiritual guidance, and intellectual stimulation."

"Okay, I can agree with that. Everyone wants someone who they can relate to. But are you saying you're not looking for a man who can financially improve your current lifestyle?" Cliff could not believe what he was hearing.

"That's a stigma. Why look for what I already have? *I* maintain my lifestyle. Mature women can admit that independence wears off quick. I'm looking forward to the day when I can kick my feet up, become the copilot, and let my husband be the decision maker. But that's not an attitude a man can fathom." Lisa was disappointed. "When I was 20, it was about money, but I've struggled enough to know those superficial things are replaceable. Now, love's what it's all about."

"Yeah, but younger women expect less. They think it's an accomplishment for a man to own a home or business. An older woman thinks that he should have something to show for his years on the face of God's great earth. Katie is seven years younger than I am. When we dated, I played the role of her father. Whereas, Ahnna always had input, which wasn't a problem. It was just different."

"So, is the alternative someone who doesn't have an opinion and thinks that everything you say and do is right? Cliff, *you* don't even believe that!"

"I'm not saying that. I'm saying it felt good that my opinion carried so much weight. She willingly submitted. She wasn't so used to doing things on her own."

"Perhaps, you should go ahead and marry a fifth-grader. Not even a teenager would accept what you're dishing out! And do I have to wait for a man who's 56, and has three ex-wives and 16 kids in order to find someone that finally wants to settle down?"

"Drama Queen!" Cliff ignored her "fifth grader" statement. "Isn't it ironic that you gals tend to be ready for this stuff much sooner than we are, but God put us as the head of this train?"

"You're not funny! Guess I'll sit back and wait patiently for my God-sent 80-year-old."

"You could also marry the total opposite."

"Yeah, what world are you living in?"

"A world where God is in control, not statistics! You'll be alright. Ask God to prepare you and to teach you, and the rest of those independent women out there, how to be submissive, virtuous wives."

Lisa was stuck on Cliff's statement about Ahnna. "I've found that submission is a choice. Women don't submit because they think their husbands make the best choices, but because they trust him. And just because Ahnna gave more input doesn't mean she wasn't submissive or allowing you to be the head. She's just older and wiser, and grown more into her role as a helpmate. And I've seen things from both perspectives. It all boils down to making the best choice."

"Exactly!" Cliff said.

"My grandma was 14 years younger than my granddad. I wouldn't exactly use the term submissive to describe her. He didn't always hold up his end of the bargain, so she did her own thing and dared him to say something. She gave him the flux, but they raised eight children, and were married 46 years. It reminds me of that sitcom where the parents bicker, but at the end of every episode they'd say, 'But we're still in love.' That show depicts how familial life should be and the importance of balance and staying power. You know?"

"Yeah, I hear ya."

"So, if things were so wonderful with Katie, why aren't you still with her?"

"Well, the flip side is that she couldn't really keep my interest. Her conversation was limited, especially when it came to God. Hey, she's a nice young lady. And in all honesty, she got rid of me. She said that I was too bossy, and was always trying to change her."

"Yeah, change her into Ahnna," Lisa mumbled under her breath.

"What was that?"

"Uh, I was just thinking that I've always had ambitions and possessed a zeal to be mature in the things of God. I didn't just start at 28. I went to the top college-prep high school and had my own car. I pursued a degree in engineering, and the mere words 'I'm in school for my master's' scares folks. At church, I won Bible quizzes, assisted with Sunday school, and won the oratorical contests. So, I've always been labeled smart, accomplished, and, I guess, intimidating to men."

"Aren't you just God's gift?" Cliff could not help but poke fun.

"Whatever! I'm not trying to be arrogant or facetious! Add to all that the fact that I'm trying to hold up a standard of sexual morality, and that right there cuts out half the men who want to be bothered."

"Oh, come on! I don't think that's a fair statement."

"It's the truth. Not one man I've ever dated has appreciated my stance. Believe it or not. Plenty of men got mad at me because I did stuff like set a curfew, or had a three-month waiting period before we kissed, but why would I stress over them? Where are they now? I figured, one week they'd be asking for a kiss, and sex the next. Kissing gets old quick. There was this one superficial jerk who dumped me and flat out said he had plenty of female friends he could 'do that other stuff with.' It makes you wonder if folks can decipher between love and infatuation if sex isn't involved."

Cliff could not stop laughing. "At least he was honest, huh?"

"I was so glad that I had never even kissed him. Back then, I actually had a system. I paced myself and tried not to give up too much at once."

"You're so theatrical!" Cliff said.

"Whatever! My mom was a single parent from the time I was in kindergarten until I started ninth grade. And I was determined to defeat the odds."

"That's understandable, but I still think you were a bit extreme."

"I know!" Lisa paused. "Remember when John and I *almost* slipped up? We didn't even go all the way, and I was so paranoid that I took 10 pregnancy tests."

"I remember," Cliff joked. "You're too deep. You think too much. You're too analytical. You're like an Einstein or something. Who can keep up?"

"See!" Lisa whined. "That's why I'm not getting married. It's almost like I'll have to play the 'dits role' in order to be considered approachable."

"That's not true."

"Are you sure? Because it seems all men are looking for a physically gorgeous, opinion less, helpless, air head."

"Well, the spirit is willing, but the flesh is weak," Cliff joked. "Look, that's a myth. Men want smart women, but just not all the lip that goes along with it." He could not help but push her buttons. "No, seriously. We want someone who'll enhance us physically, spiritually, and intellectually—just as most women do."

"Right! Right!" She mocked him. "Seriously, don't you think a man would settle for a less cultured, less intelligent woman that's better looking?"

"I'll say, hopefully there's balance between the physical, intellectual, and spiritual attributes."

"Yeah, okay," Lisa was doubtful. "As visual as men are?"

"Are you feeling ugly today or something?" he joked. "Seriously, think about it, any person in their right mind would choose the road of least resistance."

"I guess, that's true, but seems like men want a woman's mind for business purposes only, otherwise, she's too analytical or fussy. And the missing factor is..." Lisa was thinking out loud.

"What's the missing factor?"

"I honestly have no clue." She laughed. "I'm still trying to figure it out."

Cliff gently massaged the back of her neck. "God's going to send you someone who loves you as you are. I, personally, don't think you intimidate one soul. The right man will walk boldly as your leader and help you advance further, and vice versa. You just got to trust in Jesus to send him your way. Now, He's the most faithful Brother I know. See, being head of the household, or head of the woman, as the Bible puts it, is no joke." He smirked. "Just as women think it's hard to get a good man, men think it's that much harder to find a good woman."

"Hmm. That may be true. I'm just hoping the next man I love has already 'adjusted.' If not, life can get pretty messy."

"So, do women go through an adjustment period?" Cliff asked.

"Ha, of course not. We're born perfect," she said.

"Right! Right!" Cliff said sarcastically. "Well, we imperfect men have the simple request that you perfect women be patient. Y'all should be just that much more willing to work with us, right?"

The next day Lisa fasted to refresh herself. She did not want to be vexed or think that she could not have ambitions in order to get a suitable mate. It had weighed heavy on her heart. The week prior, she suddenly broke into tears while working. She had kept her vow of celibacy for years, yet the devil was playing with her mind. She knew it was not God asking, "And what if you don't get married for 10 more years or even worse, what if you still end up a single mom?" She prayed God would sustain her. Anything else would only bring reproach and guilt. While fasting, her stomach felt hollow. However, she knew she was receiving something from God that could not be seen with the natural eye. Fasting taught her the much-needed lesson of self denial, and simultaneously made her sensitive to God's voice.

Lisa was constantly fighting stress. Her boss kept trying her patience. She had a two-day headache. She was tired of her issues with the opposite sex. And she was playing catch-up on her bills since she upgraded her PC. But she put her mind on Bible Study. That week God's presence had visited them like never before, and she knew that He had purged and restored her. She also anointed herself with oil and meditated on her favorite scripture, Psalm 34:19. In the past, she had evaluated her days based on her emotional state, but now she did not allow emotion to be more prevalent than purpose. She challenged herself to evaluate her days based on her consistent prayer life through her psalm booklet. Besides, David was coming home, and she was excited. It had been a while since she actually had a heart-to-heart talk with him or Krystal, and the threesome forum was long overdue. She spent Friday evening and Saturday morning doing course work so she would be free the rest of the weekend.

She was about to dial her mom when David called her from the airport. Afterwards, she called Tonya, but Tonya rushed her off the phone because she and Mark were going out on their monthly date which they vowed to have in spite of their busy schedules. At dinner, Mark could not stop talking about the science fiction thriller they had seen. Tonya was just overjoyed to spend time alone with him. When they got home, there was a message from Mike reminding her to call her aunt for her birthday. She decided everything had to wait until the next day, when her in-laws returned the kids and their date was officially over.

While Tonya and Mark were courting, Mike was at home evaluating his life. He was a workaholic, but it was all in the best interest of his family. He wished his wife were home, but it was probably best for her to be out, rather than drinking, smoking and cursing in front of their six-year-old daughter. It was Dee's bold demeanor that initially drew him to her, but lately her attitude had been unbearable. "Lord, save my wife! I don't want to push her away," he said aloud. He called Lisa to make sure that she had confirmed the entertainment for their mother's birthday dinner the next evening, but Lisa did not answer.

While Mike was at home praying, Dee was shopping. "Lord, get me out of this, and I promise to get it together!" She wanted to be a better wife and mother. As she walked to the checkout counter, she saw Paul, Lisa's ex-boyfriend.

"Hey Dee! Remember me?" Paul sang. "And How's Lisa?"

He's so cheery! Dee thought. "Of course! How are you? Lisa's great!"

"I always said I'd get myself together and marry her," he said, reminiscing.

Dee smiled, thinking that he was still as arrogant and annoying as ever. "I'll tell her you said hi." *And that's the only part of this discussion I'll relay to her,* she thought.

Seeing Paul made Dee think about Lisa and how smart and ambitious she was. She envied her, wishing she possessed such stability. She loved her husband and daughter, but often wished she had waited until she matured more and gotten established in her career. *The grass is always greener...* " she thought. *Married folks trying to be single, and single folks trying to get married.* Perhaps running into Paul was not an accident. It reminded her of the trust that once existed between she and Lisa. She decided to give her sister-in-law a visit. She did not want to put Lisa in the middle, but she did not know where else to turn. As she drove towards Lisa's place, she dialed her mother-in-law's number.

Mrs. Townsend answered the phone hoping it was Lisa calling her back, but it was her daughter-in-law. Dee told Mrs. Townsend that she was only calling to wish her a happy birthday. Mrs. Townsend asked how Dee was doing, but Dee cut her off, so she politely thanked her for calling and hung up. After she got off the phone, she continued her previous conversation with her husband.

"Baby, you know your child wouldn't dare miss her mommy's birthday."

"I spoke with her once, thank you," Mrs. Townsend said sarcastically.

"Paula, you know how Mona Lisa is. Is she even in town?" Mr. Townsend could not help but make fun of his stepdaughter. She was always busy with work, school, and church, yet found time for "those knucklehead boyfriends." He told her that she switched boyfriends more than he switched his socks.

Mrs. Townsend gave her husband a look that said she was not in the mood for his joking, so he stopped. He knew that his wife would not tolerate anyone talking about her 28-year-old baby. She went into the den. They had been married twelve years, and she knew him like a book. He would come in soon, and kiss her on the cheek. He would not verbally apologize for making fun of their close-knit relationship, but that would suffice. She would also make him pay by not letting him watch the sports channel for a few hours. She would require his undivided attention, and he knew it. She sat patiently and waited for him.

At dinner, Lisa was in paradise. She loved Mr. & Mrs. Lewis as if they were her own parents. Mr. Lewis spent the whole time telling what Lisa referred to as "old man" jokes, which embarrassed David. Lisa wished he would lighten up, but it was hard to fight with him since he came home bearing gifts.

After they had eaten, David and Lisa went into the den. Krystal called saying she would be on her way soon, which let them know she was running later than usual. David wasted no time asking about James. "I know you've been holding back because you didn't want me to hurt that clown, but it's time you told the truth about that situation. So start talking, young one!"

"Stop calling me that. You forget I'm approximately two years, 11 months, two weeks, and three days older than you," she said sarcastically.

"Whatever, young one. That's been your name since forever," he said. David considered himself Lisa's overseer. And she was actually flattered that he called her "young one" because his grandfather had given his grandmother that pet name 63 years prior, even though she was his elder by six years. Lisa knew David's comments were all in love, so she did not waste much time defending her age.

"Anyways! Why are saints always looking for a fight?" Lisa joked.

"I don't want to fight him, just give him that extra push he seems to need."

"Thanks, but I've got it under control. We had a long talk the other night."

"Again? What more does he want you to say?" David asked, angrily. "Why is it so hard for you to get rid of him? Did you sleep with him? I want the truth."

"No!" Lisa shouted. "You sound like Cliff. Would you just calm down, please."

"I can't promise you that, but I'll try to let you explain without interrupting."

"Well, I only let him in is so that we could settle the issue once and for all. But he was trying to rekindle what I was trying to let die, so it took longer than I anticipated."

David cleared his throat. "Yeah, right!"

Lisa continued, ignoring his glares. "He said he missed me and that he reevaluated things and decided he didn't like not having me in his life; that he had changed and was looking forward to us starting over."

"What did you say?" David asked.

"I wanted to say, 'You know what? It's not about you. I've changed and so have my desires and goals, and they don't include you.' But I didn't go there."

"Maybe you should've!"

Just then, Krystal made her cameo appearance, greeted them, and went into the kitchen to fix her dinner. "Don't continue without me!" she yelled. "And be prepared to repeat everything I missed!" David and Lisa looked knowingly at one another and laughed.

"She's still crazy," David said.

"I know, but that's why we love her so much," Lisa said.

"Oh, and Lisa, I just got off the phone with your mom to wish her happy birthday. She's waiting for you to call her back," Krystal said.

"Oh, that's right," David said. "Today's her birthday. Tomorrow's her party."

David and Lisa called Mrs. Townsend while Krystal fixed her plate. When Krystal joined them, she handed Lisa a small note. "I keep forgetting I saw Mandy at the mall. She looked good. She was with some dude. And she looked pregnant, but I couldn't tell. Anyway, here's her phone number."

"She can kiss the hem of my garment!" Lisa mumbled.

"What?" David asked.

"Oh, thanks!" Lisa said not wanting to cause a scene. She stuck the paper in her pocket, wishing she could throw it away. She immediately switched subjects, "Hey, I think I'm going to have another round of that macaroni and cheese."

David took the liberty of catching Krystal up on the conversation. Lisa could not wait to finish the story. She knew they would be proud.

"I told him that I didn't want us to be together out of convenience. I said yes, we are attracted to one another, but attraction should never be mistaken as the foundation for a relationship."

"That was good!" David said.

"I don't know what it is. I just think James is used to women doing whatever he wants, and doing the bare minimum in return. I don't think he values the things God has placed in me."

"Why'd you go out with him, then?" Krystal asked. "Oh yeah, Aunt Ellen's friendly, advice giving, matchmaking self. That reminds me... She tried to hook me up with her neighbor's son. And then said I didn't need 'oomph or sparkle.' To some extent, I understand there's a thin line between that and superficiality, but I need something to make me stick around when he gets on my last nerve. But I won't get started. Or should I say, finish what I started?" Krystal laughed. "Anyways, honey, you don't owe that boy a thing. What is this, the ongoing saga of John Davis Part II?"

Oh, no! Krystal is fast-talking again, David thought.

"Right, but don't worry! I've seen this episode and I know how it ends. There's no way I'm going back to that. As he was talking, I thought about how I let John in and out of my life, and how much that cost me. That was my incentive."

"John was only able to hurt you because you truly loved him, and you can't feel bad for that." David was always sympathetic toward Lisa.

"Yeah, I heard someone say that we should thank those that hurt us. They're our true friends because it's through them that we learn about love and friendship. So, I guess John is my best friend ever." She laughed.

"Everybody has a story," Krystal said. "It's just good to be able to look back and have learned from your mistakes."

"Yeah, I actually got rough because he tried to get super spiritual, telling me to seek God before I gave up on us. I told him 'there is no us.' And if it was that deep, then he should seek God before he dialed my number again." Lisa's tone was raised. "I mean, I suggested we remain friends way before he had woven such a thick web of foolishness, but at this point, I'm not even interested in discussing the weather with him. I didn't even tell him that Elaine's friend had the nerve to ask me if he and I were still together. Oh, his bon voyage party was overdue." Lisa did not mention that she had almost fallen for James's charming smile. Since she turned him down, she had technically still won the battle.

David and Krystal both were proud of Lisa. However, they still teased her. "We crown you queen of relationship drama," Krystal said, as she stood over Lisa pretending to put a crown on her head. David joined in saying that he could sit back and take notes, and that she was the appointed guinea pig. "We're learning and growing together. I appreciate you, sweetie," he said sarcastically.

Lisa felt bad about being the center of drama, although she knew their teasing was their way of patting her on the back in support. Yet that evening she cried herself to sleep. She was thankful that God had put her friends in her path. She knew they loved her, but sometimes she felt like they ganged up on her and made fun of her mistakes. Although on the same token, it was refreshing to see herself through their eyes. She knew that an intricate part of friendship was being able to accept criticism, as well as praise. However, she could not help feeling like they had themselves "together", and she was a wreck. David had experienced minimal drama, and Krystal's drama had been over for years. She also felt that she had gone through a lot of unnecessary drama, and that somehow God had poured burdens on her, or at least allowed them to come her way. She had not done everything right, but she often felt that chastisement came immediately and lasted forever, yet her rewards were always on hold.

God had promised to deliver her, but she could not help but wonder when. She allowed her feelings to pour out through her tears: *God, thanks for being my best friend, and allowing me to cry on Your shoulder.* She quickly put her doubts in the back of her mind. She knew that it was pointless to whine and appease her flesh. How long should she allow the devil to trick her into doubting and giving up, which only prolonged her progress? As her grandmother would say, "What prayer and the gospel can't do, can't be done!"

She started singing a song that she had learned in Sunday school when she was only six: Trust and obey, for there's no other way to be happy in Jesus, but to trust and obey. She thanked her Heavenly Father for constant affirmation that she was His child, and for not only making her a joint heir with Christ, but for elevating her from servant to friend. She was thankful to Christ for being a friend who sticks closer than even a brother could!

The Attitude of a Friend

Friends are the necessary gifts
used to push you into destiny.
Friends know the inner you,
that others do not look hard enough to find.
Friends encourage you to do what is right.
And friends tell you when you are wrong.
Friends inevitably go through your growing pains with you.
Friends help you to become a friend—
congenial, supportive, merciful, and forgiving.
Friends bring out your smile.
Friends are not moved by your intermediate
displays of anger and frustration.
Friends don't let you sulk in misery for very long.
Friends are those persons that you
just cannot imagine ever turning your back on.
Their love is closer than even family ties.

Friendship prepares you for all relationships,
by putting you in a constant state of compromising
your feelings for the feelings of another.
You learn to be yourself,
and not focus on what other insignificant folk think of you,
because you have your friends by your side.
You learn to give your friends the benefit of the doubt.
You learn that love truly requires allowing hurt from others,
and not wanting to hurt them in retaliation,
and it's really still worth the hassle.

And as you mature
you learn the art of loving beyond the pain,
allowing removal of all bitterness,
especially when hurting
because of something done by an eternal friend.
Friends love at all times.

Chapter Nine
What is This?

Dee stopped in the park and slept in her car, after crying her eyes out. She drove to Lisa's home and hopelessly tried to smooth her hair and makeup.

Lisa was listening to a message from Paul when the bell rang. "Hi, Love. When you get a chance, I'm at three-six…" She deleted his message. "What a joker!" The doorbell rang again. Lisa was paranoid from her last unannounced guest. This time she looked through the peephole. It was her sister-in-law.

"Hi, Lisa. I hope you're not busy," Dee said, as Lisa opened the door.

"No! Come in." Lisa hugged her. She could tell that Dee had been crying.

"I want to apologize for the things I've brought on the family recently…" Dee began.

"It's okay. We all have our moments," Lisa assured her. "Are you okay?"

"No." Dee burst into tears all over again.

Lisa was glad Dee had come. She had been wanting to talk to her. "I was about to have a snack. You hungry? What do you want to talk about?"

"Life, particularly mine!" Dee said. She cut right to the point. "I feel terrible about Mike and Ashley."

"Have you and Mike seen a counselor?" Lisa asked, as she fixed their snack.

At this point Dee was really bawling. "Not recently," she answered through her tears. "We usually end up arguing, or me cursing while he just sits there. I have a lot of anger and resentment toward him because all he does is work. We do things for Ashley's sake, but we're in two different worlds. He keeps saying we need to trust God. And I want to, but how can I, after all of these years of doing things on my own?"

"Believe me, Mike understands. I understand too. If we could change on our own, we wouldn't need God. And the good thing is that He waits with open arms. And it's pretty rare to find a sure thing that's given freely and willingly. So, it's a big step, but it's necessary."

"I feel like I'd be starting at square one for the millionth time. I'm 37. I'm not a spring chicken, anymore. We've been through a lot. I don't know if I can just forgive him, and move on."

"I know that sounds hard, but it's very possible," Lisa said.

"Well, the way I grew up, everybody fended for themselves. If somebody hurt you, you cut them, family included. I didn't grow up trusting anybody to look out for my best interest, nor was I concerned about theirs. I was told that it's a dog-eat-dog world, and I had to make sure I was on the side not getting eaten."

Lisa knew Dee was all bark and no bite and all it would take to soften her was the genuine love of God. A broken spirit was the right attitude for God to speak to her heart. Lisa knew God had touched her and changed her outlook, and was certain that He could do the same for Dee.

Pastor Lindsay had preached "I'm Going Through to be a Blessing to You!" Lisa could see oh-so-clearly that God allowed people to go through things so that they could learn the lesson and teach it to others. Lisa wanted to blurt out, "I see why my relationship drama was so intense. You mean I'm learning to be the victor not the victim, and learning endurance so that I can have compassion and help folks like your crazy self?" It was on the tip of her tongue, but she resisted. This was not the time for one of her urges to be silly. Besides, despite all of her drama, she had never been in a covenant relationship, which is how she knew it was God giving her the words to heal Dee's situation. She thanked Him for His compassion toward her and was elated to pass it on. She even felt better about David calling her the group's guinea pig.

"Dee, take it from someone who knows, once you accept Christ, the Holy Ghost's love and never-ending mercy will allow you to trust not only Him, but Mike and others. And don't worry about your age, God knows how to turn back the hands of time," Lisa said.

"Okay, Lisa, what do you mean by all of this Christ and Holy Ghost stuff?"

"Well, it's like this. God, the Father, created the heaven and earth. Jesus, His son, or the Word in Flesh, was sent to earth to die for our sins. And the Holy Ghost, or the Holy Spirit, dwells inside of believers. These three are one, and Their names are even often used interchangeably."

"That sounds like three separate Gods," Dee said.

"No. It's kind of like going over someone's house that has a sign that says to use the side door in order to get in. It's the same house with three entrances. Christ is that designated door and the only way we can get to God."

"I guess that makes sense, but what's the significance of the Holy Spirit?"

"Well, we attain salvation through Christ, and maintain it through the Holy Spirit. I compare Him to our good conscience." Lisa was getting all choked up. "God giving His son to die for me, and His Spirit to dwell in me taught me a lot about love. I remember barely being able to love my parents. And I tried to drown out my inability to truly love someone, with my physical actions, thinking I'd be fulfilled. I was motivated by fear of neglect and pain and could only experience God's love on the surface. And since I couldn't sincerely love everybody, I felt really distant from God. I felt guilty trying to talk to Him, while consciously neglecting the people He'd placed in my path. I had a void only God could fill! Yet He healed me, and He'll heal you too."

"How?" Dee asked sincerely.

"Just believe that Christ died on the cross, and was resurrected. Confess your sins. Repent! And then ask God to fill you with His precious Holy Spirit and become Lord of your life." Lisa finally lost the battle with her tears.

"That's a lot." Dee was hesitant.

Lisa continued her mini-sermon: "God is pleased when we're able to forgive. Then we're ready to receive His forgiveness. Listen, no other religion, except Christianity, is based on relational love. Just recognize that you've broken God's commandments, and repent. You don't want to die and not be ready to meet Christ in heaven."

Lisa and Dee talked for several more hours, during which time Lisa convinced her to attend Mrs. Townsend's birthday celebration. When they arrived, it was as if she and Mike picked up right where they left off. There was no tension in the air, only a strong spirit of love, forgiveness and peace, which only the God above could have pulled off.

Lisa was happy for Mike. She knew how it felt to pray for something for a long time, and finally receive it. As she stood in the mirror wrapping her hair, she felt her poetic creativity rising. She stood calmly for her brief moment of stardom, and let her impromptu soliloquy roll off of her tongue. "There's an appointed time of waiting and preparation, but, there's an appointed time of manifestation of the promise. And once it's manifested, I'll know it was worth the wait. For they that wait upon the Lord shall renew their strength." She made up her own rigid beat and danced to her new song. "Preparation! Strength! Waiting! Strength! The Promise! Strength! Appointment! Excitement! Culmination! Manifestation! Elation! Manifestation! Relief!" Her voice cracked, as she yelled to the top of her lungs. Tiredly she moved slower, but could not stop, as if she were drugged with her new revelation. Finally she stopped and gave a sneaky smile. She would have never danced so aggressively in public. She gave a curtsey, left the mirror, and went to her desk to continue her thoughts in writing, "Lord, I am persuaded that I'm a stronger person as a result of waiting on your perfect timing," she began.

The next week, Lisa did not watch TV, and she cut out all of her extracurricular activities. Instead, she prayed for the marriages of her friends and family, so that the devil could not tear their families apart. That Sunday morning, Lisa called Tonya and Mark to tell them to expect Mike and Dee in the marriage class, but they could not talk long because they were running late, as usual. When they arrived, 20 minutes late, Mark started the session off with prayer, then went right into the lesson. Each week, they gave the couples a question. This week's question was "If you were the author of a book entitled, *My Marriage*, what would be your prescribed ending?" This was an opportunity for each individual to reflect on their role, and give profound insight on what caused their marriage to flourish.

Brother Tony gave the opening statements, "This book of marriage has all the questions, but not all the answers. Its backbone is commitment. I've come to realize that it's not a hopeless story, if allowed to be etched into the hearts and minds of the readers, and not merely penciled in or easily erased, nor omitted with the divisive sins that result from an unforgiving mate. I vow to make it last, just as Jesus Christ, the Author and Finisher of our faith endured the beautiful cross and now finds pleasure in His eternal reward."

Tonya took over. "As the author of the fate of my marriage, I would have an ending where Mark and I would have lived a happy, fulfilling 75 years together."

"Why only 75?" Mark asked. "Commit to at least 100, geez."

The class snickered as Tonya continued. "Our marriage would be filled with love, mutual respect, adoration, communication, and physical attraction from start to finish. We would never allow the sun to go down on our wrath, and we would wake up every single morning anticipating sharing our lives together, as one."

"That's just beautiful!" Sister Lane said. This was the general consensus of the women. They were all excited while most of the men sat with slight grins on their faces.

Tonya continued. "Marriage should start good and end better. Now, do we have any volunteers to go next in sharing their thoughts?"

Several hands shot up immediately, mostly women. Tonya always got a kick out of the newlyweds, so she let Brother and Sister Brooks answer first. They eagerly obliged. "Well, we've only been married seven months, 13 days, 17 hours and 43 minutes," Brother Brooks said, looking at his watch, "We've learned to work things out sooner rather than later. We will be together forever, and although the fire may die down, we'll never allow it to go out." Sister Brooks concluded, "As much we love one another, if we can't make this work, then I don't expect to make anything else in life work."

"Spoken like true newlyweds," came a comment from across the room.

"Let's all, from this day forward, consider ourselves newlyweds, if that's the case," Tonya said. "Sometimes we start off marriage with figurative prenuptial agreements. So, if it doesn't work we pick up our stuff and pretend like it never happened. Folk, we should start off by agreeing that this is a person who I've grown to love and appreciate, and will do my best to make it last forever."

Mark cut in, "Forever's a long time. Not many things last forever. So, automatically if something's going to last forever, it must require premium, quality maintenance."

The Mackenzires stood up to go next, but, as usual, Sister Mackenzire did the talking. "We've been married 36 years. That's longer than many of you have been alive. You young people said some great things, but I'm here to tell you that your faith in Jesus Christ is what will make your marriage last. You can trust Him when you can't trust your mate. The ending of our marriage is better than the beginning because we've found that there's a blessing in having someone to count on for the rest of life. You have to pray, not complain. Women, ask God to give you peace that passes human understanding. I can't even remember the last time Jay and I argued. We've learned to pray and come to an understanding without any excessively harsh words. Of course, I wasn't always this way. I was feisty in my younger days." She chuckled. "But it don't take no years of practice. You can start that in your seventh month," she said, pointing at Sister Brooks.

Sister Mackenzire was known for being long-winded so Tonya cut in, as soon as she paused. "Amen! Wonderful advice! As she said, particularly women, tend to want to talk and talk (which usually comes across as fussing), but we need to pray instead. We need to 'study to be quiet', as directed in I Thessalonians 4:11, and watch God work it out!" She pointed at Mark. "Okay, honey, it's your turn."

Mark grinned. "I'm not only author, but subscriber of the book of marriage. I've read it several times. It's my favorite book. I think of the main character, my wife, all day and night. She is the epitome of virtue, which encourages me to strive to be a better man of God. I love her. I never want to live without her. I need her. And I speak those words into her heart daily. Of course, some parts of the story I wish I could rewrite, or change the book's contents, but it doesn't matter, because all I really need to change is the ending. And when others read our book, and see the storms we've weathered, our story becomes more relevant and helpful. They'll learn from our mistakes and victories and their marriages will last forever too."

Tonya stood in front blushing as the class cheered. Mike and Dee had come in late, but they consented that they were looking for longevity. They advised the couples to take things one day at a time.

Tonya gave the students their assignment for the coming week. "We have time for a few quick questions," Mark said. "And I do mean quick."

Dean and Deborah Peterson, both Elders, seemingly never wanted class to end. Deborah raised her hand. She wanted advice for her 23-year-old son. She did not think he and his girlfriend should marry just because she was pregnant. She did not want the young lady to deter her son even "further from the faith."

Tonya thought the question was irrelevant. She looked at Mark, as if to say, "Handle this!" Mark picked up on her vibe. If the students had the gift of gab, then he had the rare gift of receiving gab, which his wife did not always possess. He began, "That'll lead us into a topic we'll address in the coming weeks—responsibility. Let me read the definition of the word responsible."

Mark found his notes. "Liable; to be required to give account; as of one's actions or of the discharge of a duty or trust; involving personal accountability or ability to act without guidance or superior authority." He continued, "A good example of the latter definition is someone such as a CEO, that has the ability to make major decisions without necessarily having to run them pass others. It refers to a maturity level where we're held accountable for our actions. Along with leadership, comes responsibility. A CEO makes major decisions on behalf of a company, but he or she had better be able to back up the basis of those decisions."

"I'd like to comment... When you're done, of course," Brother Brooks said.

"It'd probably be best if you guys write down your comments, and bring them in next week," Mark said. "As I was saying, CEO's usually have accountability to a Board of Directors, and surely we as Christians have accountability to God and our leaders. However, once counsel is given, we still have to make a choice."

"Uh hum." Tonya cleared her throat, which was she and Mark's cue that they were being too long-winded.

Mark continued. "Life's about choices. The choices we make prove how responsible we are. As we get older, our choices should get better, less self-motivated, and even help bail us out of past mistakes. And truthfully, everybody won't agree with our choices." Mark was trying to explain in an elementary manner. "Uh, is there anyone here whose in-laws weren't particularly fond of them before they married?" Three hands went up, including Elder Deborah. "Before we continue, you may excuse yourself if you need to, since we're already 15 minutes over."

"We don't have anywhere to go," Brother Charles said.

Mark raised his hand. "My in-laws didn't like me initially. Imagine that. See, sometimes our choices are based on an inner passion or motivation. And I'm not talking about infatuation or playing childish games. We're still talking about responsibility. I'm talking the kind of responsibility that makes us gladly get up for work on time."

"Our young folks need to hear that more often!" Dean interjected.

Mark continued. "Major decisions should be made by mature, responsible adults, not based on how we feel at the moment, or even how others feel. Again, don't ignore counsel and wisdom, but don't look for the easy way out either. Take the route that'll make life peaceful, enjoyable, healthy, and successful."

"Amen!" Brother Mackenzire said.

"Several people in Tonya's family, initially thought that I was too immature to handle the responsibility of a family. I was a skinny kid who had barely made a name for himself. But now they love me, right Tonya?" He loved to tease her.

She smiled. "You're the son they never had."

After the snickering died down, Mark asked for more details. "How long has your son been seeing this young lady?"

Dean answered. "Uh, I believe we first met her at Easter dinner. Although taking someone home to meet the parents doesn't mean a thing these days, cause he brought someone else home with him on the 4th of July."

Brother Hawthorne jumped in, "Shucks, My daughter's been seeing the same guy for three years. They have one child together, and one on the way. Yet she's not sure if she loves him enough to marry him. I told her she was shallow. I don't see how you spend so much time with someone and don't love them. That shows how easily we confuse sex with love."

"Please ladies and gentlemen, quiet down." Mark was trying not to laugh and lose focus. "We don't know the whole story, but if they've been dating for a year, and love each other, then there's nothing wrong with going to the next level. Many times we're teaching escapism; showing men how to indulge themselves in Fantasy Island by going into relationships looking for a way out."

"That shows lack of trust," Sister Brooks said.

"Exactly!" Mark continued. "That's the world's easy way out." He finally chuckled. "Now, men listen closely to my next statement. I want you to take it the right way. In a relationship the onus is automatically placed on the man. The growth of a relationship can't go any further than the desire of the leader, which God appointed to be the man. And then the question becomes whether onus is responsibility or duty. Responsibility is wonderfully enlightening if handled correctly, but 'duty' is sometimes a burden that we can't wait to get rid of."

"Is there a difference between duty and responsibility?" Sister Brooks asked.

"Let's say duty refers to requirement, but responsibility to a suggestion."

"Don't they coincide? Isn't duty a result of a required responsibility?"

Tonya cleared her throat again.

Mark was trying to rush. "Well, just because something is the responsible thing to do, doesn't mean it will definitely get done. Elder Peterson, I'll conclude that your son chose to date her because he saw something he liked, and hopefully it was something of substance. Then every day, for a year he chose to be with her and make the relationship work. Hopefully, somewhere along the line he chose to love her, and then unfortunately chose to sleep with her, and now he's choosing to marry her. Now, why can't we just take this last step, as a step of responsibility? Perhaps he wishes that he had done things in the correct order: marriage then sex, and perhaps this is his attempt to rectify it."

"Make it plain!" Brother Mackenzire said.

Brother Williams could not hold his peace. "Brother Mark, I agree. All this sleeping with people who you won't marry is foolishness. Folks are hiding behind that mentality and it's keeping everybody single. They're acting married, but without the responsibility that goes along with it. And there's seemingly no repercussion. People just do whatever they want and it's the kids who are suffering."

"Exactly!" Brother Mackenzire said.

Brother Williams continued, "What's worse—forcing shotgun weddings or forcing kids to grow up in single parent homes. Reality is, they need to get married, otherwise, they'll end up with a whole bunch of regrets. I don't see why people are so afraid of marriage. Marriage is a wonderful thing. I wouldn't want to be single for nothing in this world!"

Everyone was listening attentively, but Mark knew it was time to conclude. "I'm going to say this, and then I'll be done. We really do people a disservice by giving one-sided counsel or a lopsided viewpoint. Sometimes we mistake our personal convictions and teach them as doctrine, and we get people confused. I tell my brother constantly, just because he was hurt by a much younger woman, doesn't mean that he should preach to everyone that men shouldn't marry much younger women. I tell my cousin that just because she was hurt by a male friend, she can't preach to everyone that men and women being friends is detrimental. And on the same token, my wife always reminds me that just because I went through a series of failed relationships before finding her, I shouldn't preach to everyone I encounter, that you need to make sure you rid yourself of your past and get 100% free before you can have a healthy, successful, marriage."

"Uh hum." Tonya cleared her throat again. "What my husband is trying to say is that your son ultimately has to make the final decision and he needs to be a responsible young man and determine if he loves her enough to expedite the wedding vows or if he was just being irresponsible by being with her. Either way, he needs to make sure the child is being cared for."

Mark briefly added, "Uh, this last statement is for the men. We must be responsible for our actions, and learn to take responsibility seriously, allowing it to be a joyous duty realizing that the rewards are far greater than the toil we've expended. We must make predeterminations. And we're really out of time, so I'll pick this up next week." Mark nodded at Tonya to let her know that he was done, and she could make the final remarks. She quickly prayed and dismissed.

Afterwards, Elder Dean came over to Mark and shook his hand. He was glad that Mark had shed some light on the situation for his wife. He admitted that her constant nagging was taking its toll. His wife was also grateful.

"I know I added some excess, but I want you to consider both sides. That child deserves a home with both parents, and they deserve a chance to succeed, in spite of this initial blow. Back in the day, the two would've been forced to marry or the young lady would've been sent away to cover up the sin, with no question. But that's not the reasoning behind my statements, and hopefully I made that clear. I just can't give one-sided counsel that supports irresponsibility."

Elder Dean decided to give his viewpoint: "Yeah, I know exactly what you mean. Sometimes counsel is easy because folks do things that are blatant sins against the Word of God. But sometimes people's issues are not always black and white. And we can't always say don't do this and don't do that! Or, do this and do that! We have to be more open-minded in our approach."

"There is safety in the multitude of counselors," she interjected.

Mark loved that scripture. "That's what the King James Version of Proverbs 11:14 says. The New International Version says, 'For lack of guidance a nation falls, but many advisers make victory sure.' And I love the Amplified Version. It says, 'where no wise guidance is, the people fall, but in the multitude of counselors there is safety.' Now that word safety means deliverance and salvation. We can be delivered from most of the stuff we go through, if we seek God's wisdom beforehand. And again, our actions should not be used as an opportunity to run from responsibility, or a cop-out, but a means to help us out."

Elder Deborah agreed: "I think you're basically saying that my son will have to use wisdom. And we can't assume that because the relationship isn't traditional, or because they didn't follow a certain formula, it won't succeed. As a responsible adult, he has to make a realistic decision based on his love for her and his ability to handle the situation."

Tonya had joined into the conversation as well. "Wisdom shows us all sides of the issue so that we can go into the situation with our eyes wide open. We should not go in looking for excuses, perhaps not even a definite solution, but looking for resolution."

Mark was glad that everyone was grasping his teaching. He finished up where Tonya left off. "He must look at both sides, even though having a baby out of wedlock is not a reason to bind two people together, and even though starting off the marriage with a child means that they will have to go against those odds, along with regular newlywed hardships. All that needs to accompany the decisions already made, no matter how good or bad they are, is another decision to be responsible and ensure that things work out in the best interest of all involved. It's okay to make a wrong turn here or there, but he'll be fine as long as he doesn't continue down that road of irresponsibility."

"He hasn't been too sure what he wants to do," Elder Deborah added.

"Well, that's a sign of irresponsibility, which is probably mixed with a whole lot of fear. And signs of pressure from others always seems to rear its ugly head. But as he grows older, hopefully he'll learn to stick with his decisions. All it takes is a decision to be responsible and responsibly pursue the choice made. And if he's not sure what he wants to do, that's fine as long as he doesn't lead this young lady on." Tonya always enjoyed giving her input.

By this time, Dee and Mike had joined in. "If he loves her, then he should be trying to make it work, not finding reasons it probably won't. Obviously, it's been working out fine thus far," Dee said.

As the Petersons were leaving, Deborah whispered to Tonya, "I guess I wanted to see my son with your cousin, Lisa. And that reminds me, I've been meaning to ask you about this guy, James, who my daughter, Elaine's seeing."

Tonya laughed. She knew that Elder Deborah was only playing the role of a concerned mother. Tonya had no clue of James's intentions. And she did not want to taint Elder Deborah's image of him. "For the most part, he's harmless. But I'm sure that during prayer the Holy Ghost will reveal all you need to know." Tonya always teased her because she never missed a prayer service. Growing up they had given her the nickname, "The Holy Ghost's twin sister."

After the Petersons left, Tonya and Dee separated themselves. And Mike asked more questions about the class. "When you were talking earlier, I had wanted to ask you to give me some examples of the difference between sound doctrine and personal convictions."

"Well, sound principles don't change under any circumstances. If someone doesn't profess Christ, then the Bible clearly states that they're not born again, and are doomed to eternal damnation. And You'll know whether a person is spiritual or carnal by their fruit, or should I say, their lifestyle. If a person shows love, long-suffering, gentleness and faith, they're spiritual. But hatred, lasciviousness, drunkenness, and witchcraft, those are works of the flesh. Sound doctrine will hold up in any culture, any language, and in any situation."

"Amen!" Tonya was eavesdropping from across the room.

Mike picked up where Mark left off. "I see. And then personal convictions are things like we should not eat pork, women should not speak in the church, or women should wear their skirts a certain length."

"Well, you can find scripture to back those things up, but for the most part, yes, those are more personal convictions rather than sound doctrine because they are not really universal concepts. They're more so cultural."

"I'm looking forward to the coming weeks and I'm eager to finish this conversation about responsibility," Mike said.

"Yeah, we walk away from responsibility because we allow things to deter our focus, and we start thinking the grass is greener on the other side. And the grass may be greener, but it could be based on the perception of the position you're occupying. The devil knows how to shine the light on sin and wrong-doing and make it seem so appealing."

Mike agreed. "But once you get over there, you'll likely see that things are 100% better where you were. And hopefully, we don't get too far over to the other side that we can't make it back." Mike wanted Mark to elaborate on his advice to men. "Give me a hint of what you'd have said to the men, if you'd had more time."

"Well, I said the men particularly because God ordained us as the head of this thing. We need wisdom with that authority. I've had several husbands ask me if I think it's okay to go out to lunch with their secretaries, or do things with women other than their wives. And I said no! Emphatically, no! We can't love our wives one week, and then the next love the attention of our secretaries. It may start off innocent, but it's dangerous. We need to learn to abstain from all appearance of evil, in whatever form it presents itself. I had this conversation with my wife and your sister, and you know how silly they can be. Your sister said that she wishes she could invent a shot—like an immunization or..."

"Or a truth serum," Mike finished Mark's statement.

"Right, for men 21 and up, which would instill in them the need to be responsible and get married as soon as possible."

"That sounds just like something Lisa would say."

"The funniest part is that once the man married, he'd get a special pair of sunglasses to wear in public, which allowed him to see his wife only."

"She's so dramatic! And I'd probably never admit this in front of her, but, she's basically right. I've never read in The Bible about a man and a woman being 'friends'. The two most quoted scriptures of the Bible talk about a man finding a wife, and then leaving and cleaving."

"Yeah, cleaving, as in clinging," Mark said. "So, I guess that as men, we should be glad our wives are clingy."

They both laughed.

"True!" Mike said. "And you *do* have to be careful. It's seems so easy for men to flirt, often unknowingly, but women pick up on it and run with it. They're more keen to that kind of stuff and can be very convincing, controlling and conniving. Things can start off innocent and end up only God knows where."

"Exactly. So, as men, we must take responsibility and do what it takes to make marriage work. We have to detach ourselves from flirtatious ways so that nothing can be taken out of context. The Bible warns about strange women, which entice with their words, but their goal is destruction. They could care less about you or your family. They're just trying to fulfill their own agendas. You know, during one of the sessions, I started to ask the men, 'Who can give me an example of a time that good came out of you overextending yourself to a woman other than your wife?' Tonya threatened me, though."

"That's hilarious! That may be a can of worms you don't want to open."

"But you know, my point was simply that too many people find out the hard way that they've already made the best choice and that there's really nothing else out there for them," Mark said.

"...or as you said, that what's out there is strange," Mike said. He thought about all the women who had tried to trap him since he married. "I've run across many women in my day who have learned the art of manipulating and controlling men with sex, business relationships, guilt, and the list goes on and on. But since you're focusing on the men taking responsibility for their actions, I'm sure the wives will appreciate that."

"And if men stay in line, their wives will fall in line right behind them," Mark concluded.

Before they left, Mark and Tonya prayed with Dee and Mike, that God would continue to give them wisdom, love, knowledge and understanding for their marriage, and that he would continue to bind them together as one.

What is This?

This is a man and a woman becoming one person.
This is having two persons, but one desire.
This is having two persons, but one need.
This is two selfless persons, which equates to one self.
This is two persons addressed as plural, yet living together as singular.

This is one person hurting, so automatically two persons hurt.
This is one person breaking the chain,
and the other possessing the obligation to repair the link.
This is loving someone unselfishly,
knowing that the same love will be reciprocated.

For better or worse—
For richer or poorer—
In sickness and in health—
Until death separates.

This is not only about one man loving one woman.
This is not only about one woman loving one man.
This is about both persons together, loving unconditionally.

This is each person ministering and serving another someone.
That other someone is an extension of them—
That other someone is actually themselves.

This is falling in love with the choice to love the other person.
This is two whole, complete individuals, completing one another.
This is a life filled with compromise and servitude.
This is a life filled with happiness and growth, in love and friendship.

This is supreme unity between a man and woman.
This is an esteemed honor of covenant.
This is the ministry called marriage.

Chapter Ten
Consistency in this New Phase

By the time Cliff arrived at Lisa's home, she and Krystal were engrossed in conversation about his brother, Bryan, and his ex-wife, Sharon remarrying. "He told me yesterday that they're shopping for a new ring," Lisa was saying.

"Really? It's been, what, three years since they divorced?" Krystal asked.

"What are you guys talking about," Cliff asked.

"Bryan and Sharon renewing their vows," Lisa answered.

"I just talked to him," Cliff said, opening the car doors for the ladies.

"So, what made them change their minds?" Krystal asked.

Cliff plopped down into the driver's seat and started the engine. "I think it had a lot to do with her mom dying a few months back. It was a traumatic time and my brother was there for her." Cliff was struggling to put his seat belt on. "Somehow or another, her insurance policy had lapsed and he paid for the funeral. I'm sure going through that together brought them closer. And apparently they weren't divorced, that's just what they told us. So, we're all very happy to see them finally work things out."

"Wow," Krystal said. "I'm always a sucker for a love story. More couples should reconcile instead of running from one another, which is really only an effort to get away from themselves. Both parties are always pointing the finger, never accepting any blame. And it's good to see people get back together without having messed around with other folks in the process."

Lisa had gotten Bryan's side of the story. "He said he went to pick up their five-year-old one weekend, and she broke into tears saying she missed him and what they'd shared. It made him admit that she still held a special place in his heart, and that he still loved her. Right then and there, he got down on one knee and asked her if they could start over."

"Wow! Now that's romance. That's what I'm talking about!" Krystal said.

"I asked him what he would've done if she'd never said those words," Lisa continued, "and he said, he would've just went on without her because the thought of them getting back together hadn't crossed his mind."

"That cat is funny. It ain't no way he wasn't thinking about her, at least in the back of his mind," Cliff said. "How else could he propose that same day?"

"I don't think he was lying, but that he had put his feelings for her on the back burner," Lisa said. "And they resurfaced when she confided in him."

Krystal cut in, talking fast as usual. "Well, the way I see it, men always think their exes will take them back. But somehow they won't admit that, at some point, they were missing her too. How the heck can two people be reunited solely based on the woman's desires? But who cares? All that matters is that they're back together!"

Lisa agreed. "That's the role men play publicly, but privately they lick their wounds and hope for reconciliation too."

Cliff was outnumbered, but that did not stop him. "Hold on! I've met quite a few women with huge egos that think that every man on the planet wants them."

"Well, then that settles it," Krystal said. "I'm sure Cliff has dated enough women to collect accurate data."

Cliff shook his head. "Look who's talking, Ms. Love-'em-and-Leave-'em, Sr."

"Well, I had this conversation with one of my coworker's, and he's a bigger player of the field than Cliffy," Lisa laughed. "He thinks women can be talked into anything and that all it takes is to say all the right things to get a woman back. I don't know if that's accurate, but he has quite a few women at his disposal."

"First of all, I'm not a field player. If that's the case, we're all field players. Second of all, women play those games too. And for the record, it's not the woman who gets burned, it's the one who loved the most; male or female."

"Yeah, but most of the time it's women who can't let go as easily," Lisa said.

"Or is too insecure to think she'll find someone else," Cliff mumbled.

Lisa did not acknowledge his comment. "Women have been known to hold on to the pain of past relationships for years, even decades. Trust me. I grew up in the same house with one such woman for most of my elementary years."

Cliff did not like the way they worded their opinion. "Well, the Bible does say in Proverbs that it's better to dwell in the corner of a housetop alone, than share a whole house with a brawling woman, that a contentious woman and a steady rain drop have a lot in common, and that there are three things for which the earth is disquieted or agitated, one of which is an odious woman when she marries."

"It's true. I don't think it's coincidental that women were emphasized. Women are usually stifled because we generally become so much more emotionally attached to a man, than he is to us," Krystal agreed.

Lisa knew it to be true too. "Yeah, women are so much more susceptible to becoming bitter, old and lonely. That's why you have to ask God to take that odiousness up out of you." She laughed. "You can't let that stuff fester."

"Sounds like you gals are too emotional for your own good," Cliff said.

"Right, I can't think of the last time I saw a man crying over some lost love," Lisa said. "As a matter of fact, most of them act like we did them a favor."

"No," Krystal said. "What they do is force the 'double-dump.' They'll date you forever until you mention marriage. Then say they're not ready, but want to remain 'intimate friends.' Because they never really want you out of their lives completely. They treat you like a science fair experiment—see how long you can stick around before you burst, but by this time, the woman is fed up and tells him to beat it. Then he can say she got rid of him and it wasn't his fault that the relationship didn't work."

Cliff had had enough. "Oh stop the madness! As you said, a man expresses himself differently. It doesn't mean he wasn't hurt or attached because he didn't cry in public, call all his friends and tell them every detail of what his ex did to him for 13 months straight, or cut his eyes at the woman when he saw her. Don't be mad because we don't see the value in constantly crying over spilled milk."

Krystal and Lisa burst into laughter. "Calm down, Cliffy!" Krystal said.

Cliff continued, "And if you saw a man crying and being all super-sensitive, you'd label him a soft, little, wimpy punk, and look the other way." Cliff, once again, felt the need to tear down their out-of-whack philosophies about the male species.

"That's so true!" Krystal exclaimed, "Well, I guess just because men don't show emotion too well, doesn't meant they don't have emotions. Now, my brother and his wife, are very happily married. But I remember when he was thinking of marrying her. He called me saying he wanted to talk. And he didn't say he was in love and couldn't live without her, it was more so like, 'I've invested a lot of time in her and I don't want to start over with someone else.' I interpreted that to mean that they had shared enough to hold on to, and that he wanted to share the rest of his life with her." Krystal laughed. "So, I guess I can appreciate a guy who knows what he wants, but may not be as expressive. Emotional men, are more of a turn-off. I'd probably..."

"I'd *definitely* tell him to beat it," Lisa finished her statement.

"Okay, I'll say that somehow men are able to move on quicker," Krystal said. "But I guess it wasn't fair to imply that they don't get attached."

"So, why verbalize such foolishness?" Cliff asked, pulling Krystal's nose.

Lisa put her two cents in. "Women get more emotionally attached, whereas men get more physically attached. Now, I'm not co-signing a woman allowing her emotions to control her to the point where she can't be rational. But for women the emotional factor is definitely there. We deal with it constantly. So, if it's a matter of emotional versus physical, you have to admit that it's much easier to find a physical replacement than an emotional replacement."

Cliff looked as if a light bulb went on in his head. "That's probably the most sensible thing you've said all afternoon. I'll approve that one statement."

"Oh no!" Lisa exclaimed.

"What's wrong?" Krystal asked.

"I think I'm turning into Tonya!" Lisa said, wiping her imaginary tears.

"No, you're pretty opinionated. It has nothing to do with her," Cliff said.

"Oh, who asked you anyway?" Lisa cut her eyes at him. "Well, we can't help it. God's placed a spirit of teacher and helper inside of us women."

"Right! Right!" Cliff said sarcastically.

"That's right. We're here to help you find the truth," Krystal said.

"Help me to know the truth! Set me free, baby!" Cliff exclaimed.

"Whatever!" Krystal continued, talking fast again. "What Lisa was saying nicely is that y'all jokers tend to go ahead and get someone else, whereas women may continue to reminisce on what they had with one particular guy."

"Right! Right! I see what you're saying," Cliff said in his usual sarcastic tone. "Krystal, where do you get this stuff?" He could not take any more.

"Man, let's just go to the mall, please. And kill all this vain jangling about men do this, and women do that. Now, I'm not making excuses, but both men and women have issues. Let's just stay focused and seek God to help us all deal with one another. Now that we know certain things about the opposite sex, let's dwell according to knowledge. My dad says all the time, that was the best advice given in the Bible regarding women. You have to know what you're working with."

"That's hilarious!" Lisa said.

"But true!" Krystal interjected.

"We're just trying to give you things from a new and different perspective—the female perspective," Lisa said.

"Well, let me give you a few tips from the male perspective. Tip number one is save the drama for the soap operas, okay."

"We're just telling it like it is," Krystal said.

"Man, I wish you guys could hear how you really sound," Cliff said.

"We sound like women learning to deal with the male species," Lisa said.

"You really are in the wrong profession." Cliff had told Lisa that many times before. "You should be a counselor or a shrink or something."

"Yeah! Yeah! Yeah! So I've been told."

Lisa decided to give Cliff a break, but Krystal did not stop. She was talking so fast, Cliff was half-way tuning her out. "Answer this question, please. Why do men act like they're only looking for friendship, unless a woman has big breasts and a firm derriere to jump-start them into the phrase 'Baby, I wanna get to know you better?'" Krystal had just spoken with Shana, who was still wondering what to do about a male "friend" who had not made his intentions clear. "And y'all scare women, who really want to be with you, into settling for friendship, so they'll have some type of involvement in your lives, because you're too slow to tell them your intentions up-front." Krystal was frustrated. "You guys are looking for the wrong thing in relationships."

"Here you go again. Men are always doing this. Men never do that," Cliff said mockingly. "No, trust me! We're looking for all the right things."

"No! You want to have your cake and eat it too. You guys give friendship a bad name," Krystal exclaimed.

"Why would you want a piece of cake just to look at? Is that not what cake is for?" Cliff laughed. "The last time I checked, cake was still edible."

"Oh brother!" Krystal rolled her eyes.

Lisa had had that discussion with Cliff before and did not want to double-team him. He probably felt bad enough about several relationships where he had done misleading things which caused women to think he wanted more than friendship.

"And I thought that's what women were looking for, anyway—a friend to marry and spend the rest of their lives with?"

"Exactly. Not a friendship that leads to the inevitable statement, 'Uh, I thought I made it clear six years ago, that we were just friends."

"Six years, huh? That's funny!" Cliff was trying not to get upset. "Okay so the next time I meet a woman I'm going to either run for my life and politely find my exit, or I'm going to say look, Baby, you're too fine and virtuous for me to let you slip away into the abyss we call friendship. Let's get this party started."

"Sadly enough, that line will probably work," Lisa said, shaking her head.

"Well, if you want my advice…" Krystal began.

Cliff cut her off. "No thank you. Y'all the two most advice-giving females I've ever met, geez. Like I said, this ain't one-sided. As Pastor Lindsay preached we have to believe that God is making us into something lasting. Listen, I'm in this thing to win it. We've all been through a lot of changes, but just because we enter into a new phase, whether good or bad, doesn't mean we have to act brand new, or act like God's run out of grace. His grace was sufficient when you messed up, and when I messed up, and it'll be sufficient when we mess up again. Let's just pray. And let's not forget that saints have to walk in the spirit, and according to God's Word. As the Bible says in Galatians 3:28, 'There is neither Jew nor Greek, there is neither bond nor free, there is neither male nor female: we're all one in Christ Jesus.'"

"Amen!" Lisa agreed, hoping they were done ruffling one another's feathers.

Cliff continued. "I received Lisa's insight about the hardships that go along with men and women trying to be friends. And I also received the men-are-physical-women-are-emotional-bit, but the rest of you all's sermonette ain't gone bless nobody. It will probably vex them, as a matter of fact."

Lisa pushed the back of his head. "We made some valid points."

"Yeah, but they were mingled with a whole bunch of nothing," Cliff answered. "Stop all this male bashing. It just ain't right."

"We're sorry Pooh Pooh. That was not our intent," Lisa said.

"Ain't no Pooh Pooh's around here," Cliff said, "Oh, I like this song." He turned up the car radio and sang. "Lord, do it again. Fill my cup until it overflows!" This was a hint to the ladies that he was done with that conversation.

"Men can only take so much drama!" Krystal whispered.

"You can not continue to generalize men with such statements," Lisa whispered mockingly, in a masculine tone.

"So now we'll have to decide whether we're generalizing or dwelling according to knowledge," Krystal replied, as they laughed amongst themselves.

Cliff turned up the radio a couple more notches and sang louder. He knew they were whispering about him, but he did not care. In the mall, they ran into two of his ex "friends", including one who his brother had labeled a fatal attraction. Cliff knew that only gave them more ammunition in their plight to prove him wrong. He did not let it get him down, though. He was ashamed of the things he had done, but he knew that it helped him learn and grow. In the end, somehow it would all work out for his good.

On the way home, Lisa noticed that she had missed several calls. Her Aunt Ellen had called twice and left a long drawn out message about how Lisa had been neglecting her. After she got home, unpacked her new items, and took some time to wind down, she returned her call.

"Hi Auntie! How are you today?"

"I'm good, Sweetheart, except I can't figure out why it takes my niece so long to return my call." Aunt Ellen sounded unusually irritated.

"Is everything okay?" Lisa asked.

"Well, that's what I'm calling to find out. I spoke with your mother and she told me about that guy you're seeing. Now, I'm going to cut right to the chase. I recall meeting him once, and I don't like this fellow for you. I've always hoped you'd marry someone with a preaching background. James's uncle and his grandfather were both preachers. We know their family history very well."

Lisa was startled by her forwardness. "Aunt Ellen, you know how my parents are. They pair me up with everybody. We're just business partners."

"So, there's nothing else going on?"

"Right." Lisa was not about to have that discussion with "impulsive Aunt Ellen." After she hung up, Lisa lay on her futon to watch TV. She had thought about all the things Aunt Ellen brought up. She did not believe in picking up strays. She too wondered about Bartlett's background. She wished she had confirmation that he had not come from a line of alcoholics, or axe murderers. However, she knew it was not fair to hold someone to their unregenerated past. She had found some consolation when they ran into Todd Peterson at the movies and found that he and Bartlett had attended the same church, growing up.

"What kind of name is Bartlett anyway?" Aunt Ellen had said.

Aunt Ellen was the matriarch of the family since Lisa's grandmother died. Lisa appreciated her advice, but realized that she was not interested in an "arranged marriage", which others staged for her, or a relationship which supposedly had all of the perfect ingredients, but was not based on genuine love and trust. The very reason that she had given James a chance was because of Aunt Ellen. Yet that relationship had left her feeling very empty. Having a lineage of preaching was a nice addition, but it was secondary in Lisa's mind.

The more she thought about Aunt Ellen's words, the more frustrated Lisa became. She often wished she could move to Timbuktu, which would keep the well-meaning church folk and family members out of her business. She could care less whether her final choice was acceptable to the masses. Aunt Ellen had been the main one bickering and complaining about Tonya and Mark. Now she loved Mark to death. *Besides, the Bible says, he that findeth a wife findeth a good thing. Whomever I decide to be with is the finder, and I'm the good thing, and I can't worry about anyone else's hang-ups,* Lisa thought. *We haven't even been out on an official date, and already folks are giving reasons why the relationship won't work, geez. My intent is to enter my next relationship and make it last forever. All I want to hear are testimonies of folks who were seemingly incompatible but learned to love each other for many years.* Lisa was convinced there was no perfect formula for having a perfect relationship—only a perfect God helping two determined people perfect their love for one another.

Lisa had already experienced having outside input ruining a relationship. Her relationship with John had been tainted by outsiders who were judging her without even knowing her. Right when their relationship was starting to grow, his cousin had accused Lisa of trying to take advantage of him and his money. One of his friends also told him that Lisa was too educated for him. John had gotten a GED and had never actually finished his college studies.

Lisa was hurt when John relayed those concerns to her. *I loved you when you lived in your parents' basement and was driving a 10-year-old two-seater,* she had thought. Yet John had walked away and left her heartbroken. After that, she became very leery of allowing others to give her situational advice, based on their failed relationships. She felt like she had missed out on the best opportunity for love, and she would not even want her worse enemy to experience that.

Lisa had been hurt and became very close-minded towards the advice of others, but she had prayed, *Lord, Help me. I just want to keep Your word. I pray as David in Psalm 119:17, "Deal bountifully with thy servant, that I may live, and keep thy word."* God had answered her prayer and shown her to receive counsel with open arms. She studied Proverbs 19:20—Hear counsel, and receive instruction, that thou mayest be wise in thy latter end.

Lisa wanted to make choices that would bless her present and her future. She had gone from one extreme to the other—from welcoming counsel to despising it—from wanting to feel the validation of others, to not wanting their input at all. But God taught her how to be honest about her personal desires, and make choices based on the unction of The Holy Ghost. *Lord, I'm not sure why Aunt Ellen was so adamant, but as long as I have the approval of Your Holy Spirit, that's all I need. You speak to my spirit, as well as my intellect,* she thought.

Lisa did not want to settle for someone else's choice for her. Nor did she want to be in a relationship with the attitude of, "Oh well, I'm single and you're single, so we might as well be together." She wanted someone who would be her inspiration for waking up, which would make submission easy. She wanted her knight in shining armor to notice her in a crowd, and hand pick her. *It seems that no matter how many women a man sifts through, he knows when he's found what he's looking for. And I'm looking forward to the day when I'm that someone,* she thought. *I won't be able to rest settling for anything less.*

Lisa had eventually consoled herself regarding John, because she wanted to be with someone who got sick to their stomach at the very thought of her absence. However, John had been on a mission to rid himself of his love for her, because of the accusations of others, and so she had finally released him.

Lisa was looking for love and if Bartlett stepped to the plate then she would give him a chance. Lisa considered him even more now that Aunt Ellen had brought it up. *He would be a great catch,* she thought. She did not know exactly where their relationship was headed, but she was very comfortable with having him as a potential mate. They were establishing a wonderful friendship through their interactions for his business. She admired his charm, whit, and his sincerity. His very presence was such a refreshing relief. He had the utmost respect and concern for her and it showed in the way he treated her. *That man always has a word of encouragement or a compliment, and is always putting me "up on a pedestal,"* she thought.

Bartlett seemed genuine in his approach. He had shown interest in her dreams and goals, and in helping her accomplish the purpose that God had set for her life, which was what most of their conversations were centered around. And, unlike James, he had never made sexual advances or tried to play mind games with her.

She recalled running into Elder Deborah Peterson in the church corridor. "We're just friends, but you never know, based on some of the hints he's been dropping, things could eventually head toward commitment," Lisa had told her.

Elder Deborah had encouraged Lisa to not wait too long to find out Bartlett's intentions. She had also assured her that Bartlett was a nice young man from a great family. "Even though he does keep company with a lot of women," she had said. "That's not a big deal though, most men do that and know how and when to separate themselves once they find the woman of their dreams. Be honest with yourself about your feelings towards him, and be prayerful." She had also told her to make sure that the "Holy Ghost down on the inside was telling her to go ahead." And to be obedient if He said, "Let that man go!" These were phrases from a popular contemporary gospel song. Lisa had been so tickled at her attempt to be cool. Lisa took her advice seriously, though. She prayed that God would slow their relationship up if necessary, and that he would help them to proceed only in His timing. Regarding Bartlett's previous history with women, she prayed and asked God to deal with him. He was not her "man" and she did not want to confront him. She knew *that* discussion could cause more harm than good. God was the only one who could change his heart, anyway.

I just need to make sure I'm not being a desperate church woman trying to snag a man who doesn't meet my standards, or even worse, God's expectations, she thought. *Although, I enjoy spending time with Bartlett, I want us to seek one another's companionship for the right reasons.*

Lisa vowed to constantly pray regarding Bartlett, particularly during this early stage. They had flirted here and there, but he had never out-right told her that he was interested. God had spoken to her heart and told her not to be afraid to allow Bartlett to become her friend, but He had not authorized anything else. Lisa was too smart to stop seeking God and start doing things on her own, as she had done in the past. She knew that would only result in another failed relationship—which could again jeopardize her relationship with God. She had been in the situation before, but this time she was determined to pass the test. If she and Bartlett started a relationship and it failed, it would not be because she had not sought God every step of the way. Lisa hoped that however the relationship ended it fell in line with their individual, divine purposes.

Being a woman, and being extremely emotional, Lisa had mixed feelings about the whole ordeal. Sometimes she experienced an adrenaline rush, then sometimes she felt this was likely one of the most peaceful times in her life. She often nervously felt like she was between a rock and a hard place. Yet she did not allow herself to take things between she and Bartlett out of context. She wanted to remain clam and allow God to lead and guide her through every phase. She did not want to jump the gun. She wanted things to play out naturally.

Months later, Lisa lie in bed and finally admitted that she really wanted to be with Bartlett. And right then, her mind began playing tricks on her. She kept trying to calm down before she drove herself crazy, but her mind kept telling her that she was hypocritically going against her own belief that men and women should not be friends if attraction was a factor. Her heart began to beat extremely fast. It was as if with every heart beat she could hear the words, "You're settling for friendship again. You're settling. You're settling again. You're settling." She was so afraid that she would have another John Davis experience, (where she would have to force him to make a decision.) She did not know if it would be the right thing to do, or if he would react differently than John had acted, but she knew that soon, something would have to give, in order to ease her own spirit.

I was so mentally strong a few weeks ago, she reminded herself. She did not know what to do except just take things slow, and continue to pray and ask God for direction and count on Him to see her through, as He had always done when she found herself in emotional la-la land. God's mercy and grace had always sustained her in the past, and she was counting on it to be sufficient enough to bring her to her purpose and expected end for the future—in every aspect of her life, including her potentially blooming relationship with Bartlett. That night Lisa prayed, *Lord, I'm not trying to perform witchcraft or asking you to change his heart toward me. My plea is simply that if he loves me, he will tell me soon.*

Consistency in this New Phase

Death, lack of finances, broken relationships:
this year, all downfalls I've faced.
The enemy wants me to think
that I've reached my limit in grace.
I barely know if I'm coming or going,
unaware of my position in reaping or sowing.
This has been a time of strange,
unfamiliar, unwanted change.
Suddenly I hear a blast from the past.
The shaping of my character is going to Last!
Is this the never ending cycle
I'm destined to embrace?
No!
His name is a strong tower, wherein I can retreat and be safe.
I will remember to humble myself and pray,
I will seek God's face, and turn from my wicked ways.
I'm still His child,
And I'll continue the seek in this new phase.
It's a new day and a new millennium,
but I still have the same daily renewal of mercy and grace.

Chapter Eleven
I Wanna Holler

Bartlett had just pulled his S.U.V. into a spot about 50 feet from the door of the conference center where he and Lisa were meeting a potential business partner. "I hope you don't mind that I didn't use the valet," he said.

"No," she said softly. "But it would have been nice if you had let me out at the entrance. My feet are aching from wearing these shoes all day."

"Do you want me to take you now?"

"No, I'm fine. We'll just have to walk slow."

"No, you'll have to walk slow. I'll meet you inside," he joked.

After the meeting, Bartlett took Lisa home and again apologized for not dropping her off at the entrance of the hotel. "Sometimes I forget and think I'm with one of the guys," he said.

Lisa was always up for a challenge. "So, basically you're so comfortable with me, and have learned to love and appreciate me so much, that you can be yourself around me, just as with your male friends?"

He knew that if he pursued that conversation he would not come out on top. He got out of the car, opened her door, and walked her onto the porch. He took her key, opened the door, and placed her briefcase near the coffee table. "You're coming tomorrow, right?" he asked. Lisa nodded. She had a huge smile on her face. Bartlett nodded and smiled, then closed the door behind him.

Lisa could hardly wait for the work day to end. Finally 4:00 p.m. arrived, and she drove to Bartlett's office. He had the conference room set up with snacks so that they could relax as they reviewed. Bartlett could hardly focus on the work in front of him. He kept thinking about Lisa's irresistible wit and charm. He loved how she expressed herself so freely, yet daintily. Her overall character was spellbinding. Her laugh was so sneaky, yet inviting. Sometimes, she got on his nerves, because she was such a know-it-all, yet somehow he liked that, too. She was gorgeous outwardly and inwardly. He loved her business casual way of dressing, the way her thick eyebrows were always perfectly arched, and her signature scent, which he enjoyed inhaling.

He did not like her driving, and had become the designated chauffeur. It allowed him to study her small frame as she sat on the passenger side in his oversized leather seats. He had caught a glimpse of her high cheek bones so many times that he fell in love with her left side-view profile, which included a small mole in her left brow. Because of such small detail he knew he was sprung. He could not deny that he was beginning to fall in love with everything about her.

What he liked most was Lisa's pseudo-shyness. She was self-conscious of her every move, yet liked to play the role of being overconfident. He thought her personality was so cute and lovable—so real. He looked up at her quickly, trying not to stare. He was enjoying watching her out of the corner of his eye, as she twirled her brown, shoulder-length hair around her finger and concentrated. After a couple of hours, he was done, but he waited patiently for an indication that she was finished. He was enjoying her and did not want the moment to end.

When they first met, he thought she was just another rigid, critical, bitter, and whiny woman, wearing a mask of pretentiousness to cover her true self. He knew the type well. *I can break her,* was his original thought, *the only question is what I'll do with her once I've accomplished it.*

Lisa stood up. Bartlett was startled at her abrupt departure. "You're leaving?" he asked.

"Yeah, I've been finished for about 15 minutes. I was trying to go through some of it a second time, but I just remembered that I have somewhere to be in a half-hour. I didn't want to disturb you. I put my comments in red. Besides, creativity leaves me after a certain amount of time and I have to regroup. I'll be free in a couple of hours if you have any questions or anything."

"Oh! Yeah, well since you're in such a rush, I'll just give you a call if I have any questions." He was clearly disappointed. "You got a date or something?"

"Of course!" Lisa said emphatically. Bartlett did not react outside, but on the inside he was torn. Finally she said, "Well, it's a date with my stepfather."

Bartlett was relieved. "Oh, because I was about to say, I know you're not stepping out on me already, with some other cat. Well, let's plan to meet at my mom's house over the weekend, okay."

She could not believe how openly he was flirting. She raised her eyebrow. "Sure! Oh, one more thing, babe! I can assure you that you ain't never looked at Lisa Wilson and thought of no dude." Then she picked up the rest of her things and walked away, swishing her hips, knowing that his eyes were closely following.

Lisa felt like such a high school girl. A few days later, she called Cliff to get his opinion on the scenario. "Ask him!" Cliff said. "You're always encouraging folks to keep their relationships open and honest. Now let's see if your rules will work for you." Cliff told her that he was in a rush and had a conference call in a few minutes. He did not tell Lisa that it was with David, whose elderly aunt needed legal advice.

"Now that we're done, and since I have you on the line, I might as well ask you something."

"I wonder what that could be?" David was being sarcastic.

"I'm glad you asked!" Cliff was not backing down. "Why haven't you and Lisa ever gotten together? I have her version, but I'm interested in yours."

"What's her version?"

"Man, lawyers invented the art of answering questions with a question."

"Here I go explaining this for the one millionth time," David chuckled. "Why is it so hard for people to believe that Lisa and I are just friends?"

"She's a woman and you're a man, *and* you spend a lot of time together."

"We started getting close because we'd both gone through a series of failed relationships. We're like sister and brother—providing advice, input, and love."

"So, you two never even talked about being together?"

"Of course! When everyone else made a big issue out of it. But I didn't want to mess things up by trying to make a move on her during her vulnerable stages."

"Man, my cousin is never vulnerable." As they laughed Cliff defended Lisa. "Well, that's the role she plays. She's such a critical thinker and a perfectionist—always beating herself up, and trying to change, but somehow, it works against her, and makes her so vulnerable. I don't even think she realizes it."

"Yes, she does. All women do. And hopefully that's not a sexist statement."

"No. It's not."

David continued. "I love her too much to play with her emotions. And one day she's going to be that strong woman that she always tries to portray."

"I have no doubt in my mind that she will," Cliff said.

"We care deeply for one another, but decisions were made to remain friends and so that's the end of that. And we're both satisfied," David concluded.

"But you could have spent the rest of your lives *together* instead of helping each other mature, for someone else to enjoy," Cliff said.

"No one's giving anyone away. We're always going to be friends."

"Dude once one of you ties the knot, you won't have time for each other."

"Well, that's a sacrifice I'm willing to make, I guess. I know this could have made a wonderful love story, and large box office hit for the movie theater. I'm told that all of the time. But we have no regrets. This type of relationship is for mature audiences only. We never crossed the line of friendship. We never kissed or anything, not even that time she tried to force herself on me." He laughed.

Cliff's heart jumped. "No way! Are you serious?"

"Just kidding! Thought I'd give some of the drama you people are always looking for."

"Whew! Man, you almost gave me a heart attack."

"Sorry! Now, does that answer all of your questions?"

"Nope, one more question. Are you attracted to her?"

"Okay, let me break this down for you. I would have to say, yes."

"I knew it! I…" Cliff said.

"But," David cut him off. "It's not necessarily physical. We're attracted to the fact that for this appointed season we have someone we can count on to pray, encourage, and even rebuke us—which is no different from any other friendship."

"Or any other marriage," Cliff mumbled.

"I heard you," David said, "but I'm going to ignore that."

"Well, I guess it's possible for men and women to be friends, as long as they don't cross the line, which I personally never had any success at," Cliff admitted.

David used that as an opening to pry into Cliff's business. "So what about you? What happened with Katie?"

"I don't know. I just don't think I love her as much as she loves me."

"When was the last time you allowed yourself to love a woman, anyway?"

Cliff paused. "This is payback, huh? Well, I honestly can't say."

The last woman Cliff had loved had crushed his heart into pieces.

As he sat thinking, John called from the lobby and invited him to lunch. Cliff had already planned to meet Bartlett. He thought it was such a coincidence that David and Bartlett had wanted to meet with him and both around noon. Now, John Davis had popped up. He could not wait to tell Lisa about his busy day with all of her men. When he got downstairs, both men were in the lobby. Cliff was hoping that his lunch hour would not turn into a disaster while meeting with Lisa's ex-lover and her current potential. Although, he thought it might be good for John to be around some young men that could be a good influence on him.

Cliff walked over to Bartlett, shook his hand, and told him that an old college buddy had called unexpectedly and would be joining them. Bartlett, being his usual carefree self, said that it was no problem. Cliff was looking forward to seeing John, yet he hoped and prayed that John would not bring up Lisa. He sent up a quick prayer for a peaceful lunch, and then walked over to John.

"Hey man, it's good to see you," Cliff said, as he gave John a handshake with one hand, and hugged him with the other.

"John Davis, meet Bartlett Hartins," Cliff said as they shook hands.

"Good to meet you," Bartlett said, but John had turned back to Cliff.

"So, what's been going on?" Cliff asked.

"Nothing much. The same-old, same-old thing," John said.

"I see you're wearing a wedding band, so something must've changed."

"Yeah my girl and I eloped last month. We were living together anyway, so you know how that goes."

"Dude, yeah I know how that goes," Cliff said, sarcastically. "And I'm glad you rectified that."

"Man, that's why I didn't tell you. I didn't want you to waste one of your good Sunday morning sermons on little old me."

"No, it wouldn't have been a waste. I can't let you act crazy while I'm the appointed 'watchman on the wall.'" Cliff punched him in the arm.

"How am I under your watch when I left that church stuff a long time ago?"

"Because I'm not giving up on you. You have too much imparted and planted in you to just walk away from the things of God. You'll be back."

"Yeah, maybe one day when I get myself together."

"That's backwards. Give your life to Christ and let *Him* get you together. Tomorrow's not promised." Cliff was trying not to sound preachy, but at the same time he wanted John to see the urgency of his need for salvation.

Bartlett felt comfortable enough to add his two cents. "It's better to be saved when Christ comes, than to be out there still in the process of getting yourself together, and still be lost. Repent now and spend time with Christ getting yourself together."

"Exactly," Cliff said. "That would be a mess, and unnecessary since you know the way. It's all about a determination of the will. Your love for Him must go beyond your general love for mankind, or your love for your family and friends. You must love Him enough to spend the rest of your life in relationship with Him."

"So, both of y'all preachers or what? Look, I said, I'm thinking about it."

"Okay, I'm not offended. You're rejecting Christ, not me," Cliff said.

"No, I'm not. And can't you give your opinion without giving a scripture?"

"I don't have an opinion other than the Word that saved my soul," Cliff said. "I don't see how people live without God's Word or His voice in their lives; no church, no prayer, no nothing. That has to be an empty lifestyle."

Bartlett tried to break the ice. "Time can be your enemy or your friend."

"Alright. Let's just eat." John did not like being ganged up on.

"You knew I'd be telling you about the Lord today, right?" Cliff asked.

"Yeah, I knew that."

"Well, then. But I'm done for now. How's married life been?" Cliff decided to save the rest of his concerns for a one-on-one conversation with John.

"Great. Although, I think I'll always have feelings for your cousin."

"What are you saying?" Cliff asked, as they walked into the restaurant next to his office building. "Don't admit that! That's terrible, dude!" He was trying to divert the attention off of Lisa. "You're a married man now. That's all you need to focus on."

After they selected their table and sat down, John continued. "You know what I'm talking about. I really messed things up with her. By the time I realized my mistake, it was too late. But I vowed that I'd never mess up that bad again."

"Oh, yeah," Cliff finally told Bartlett. "John dated Lisa a few years back."

"Oh!" is all Bartlett managed to get out. He began to size up John, trying to get a glimpse of the guy who Lisa had fallen for. And even though John was married, he could not help but wonder if they were trying to set him up for an altercation.

John continued. "I met my wife at the casino, but before you say anything, she's a church-going woman. I can't wait for you to meet her. You'll like her. She's good for me. She's willing to work with a dude, and I appreciate her sincerity. Of course, she's the typical woman who fusses a lot, but I'm the typical man who knows how to ignore her, yet pretend I'm listening," he laughed. "Anyway, I did promise her that I'd get back in church, soon."

Cliff mistakenly started preaching again, "Listen, you don't want to wear her out and make her wish she'd never given you a chance. If you made promises to improve, then keep them. You're the head of the household, and the more responsible you are, the smoother things will run. I remember when you were once a great soldier in God's army," Cliff said reminiscing. "I don't know what happened, but this is a great time for you to get back in place."

"All this talk about responsibility makes me nervous," John said, laughingly. "This is too much for my brain. What I don't know can't hurt me, right?"

Bartlett was trying not to butt in, but it was inevitable. "Sometimes gaining knowledge does make us uneasy. Solomon says in Ecclesiastes that he that increaseth knowledge increaseth sorrow. The more you know, the more you become accountable to act upon what you know. But of course, this doesn't mean that we stop seeking wisdom, which helps us to make informed decisions."

John had been very attentive while Bartlett was speaking, and Cliff could tell that they were getting through to his heart.

"You know, it's actually funny that you guys are saying this. Just last night, I asked God to help me to be a better husband. I just had no idea that he'd answer so quickly. I need a little more time." John was such a jokester.

"Yeah but once we know better, we should do better. Now as it relates to foolishness and gossip, the less you know the better. But this is good stuff, and the more you know the better," Bartlett said.

"Yeah! Yeah! Yeah! I got you." John wanted to change the subject.

"Trust me, we're just trying to help you keep your woman happy, which will keep you happy," Bartlett said laughingly.

"Ha! Are women ever happy?" John asked.

"If you treat them right, they'll stay happy. Whether they're whining, fussing, or whatever. You just show them a little loving and they'll be okay. They just want to know that you care," Bartlett said.

"I guess so. But all that whining and fussing can get on your nerves. Are you married?" John asked Bartlett.

"Not quite," Bartlett said.

"Oh, you're engaged? Congratulations!" John did not wait for a reply.

Bartlett and Cliff looked at one another knowingly. Bartlett continued without responding. "If you act nonchalantly about the whining and fussing, their reaction to that will get on your nerves even more, trust me."

"Don't I know it!" Cliff said. "That's the quickest way to a fight."

"That's probably true. And when did you become such an expert on women?" John looked over at Cliff.

"Expertise comes from experience, and experience usually comes from lots of mistakes," Cliff said. He had gained understanding, wisdom, and compassion. He knew how it felt to be in relationship with an all-knowing, perfect God, yet make mistakes and have unresolved issues because of his imperfections.

"I hear you, loud and clear," Bartlett said.

By this time, they were done eating. They paid for their food and walked outside. "Just promise me that you'll think about what we've said. We need you, my brother!" Cliff said.

"Alright, I promise, but I didn't grow up in church like you," John said.

"What does growing up in church have to do with anything?" Cliff asked.

"It's not about how long, it's about how quickly you surrender. Just keep telling Him 'yes.' Surrender your will to His will, and watch him make a change in you," Bartlett said.

"You're an all right dude," John said to Bartlett. "It was nice meeting you. And Cliff it was good seeing you again. I may even come to church on Sunday."

"I'll be looking for you and your wife," Cliff replied.

"Well, we never did get the chance to talk about my uncle's business, huh?" Bartlett asked after John left.

"You guys just had some quick questions, right?"

"Right, it shouldn't take more than a half-hour or so."

"Are you guys free for a quick conference call this evening? It would probably be better if he were included in the conversation," Cliff said.

Bartlett's uncle was a retired educator. He had been a high school principal and owned a property management business. He wanted Cliff's advice on the legal ramifications associated with donating property. Cliff's expertise was usually litigation, but he did not mind offering friendly advice. Bartlett's uncle appeared to be quite the comedian. They had talked business for five minutes, and for 20 minutes he told Cliff of stories of properties he had purchased and people who kept promising to pay their rent. He also kept referring to Lisa as his niece, which Cliff thought was hilarious.

Cliff called Lisa to give her a heads up about his encounter with John. He told her that he and Bartlett had made a lunch date, and that John had unexpectedly shown up at the office and joined them. Lisa was glad John was finally improving, although she was not sure how she felt about he and Bartlett breaking bread together, therefore, Cliff did not discuss his conversation with David or tease her. Lisa had asked Cliff why he met with Bartlett, but he told her that he was not at liberty to discuss his client's business with her.

Lisa sat at her desk daydreaming, and could not help but smile as she thought of her blossoming relationship with Bartlett. She was so happy she felt like she could holler right where she sat. She was constantly seeking God, and praying things would work out according to His will and plan. She hoped that this was the embarking of a relationship that was finally heading in the right direction.

She liked Bartlett so much, it scared her. She tried her best not to be pessimistic, but she was somewhat afraid. However, their relationship was very open and honest. They had established a wonderful friendship, and she was happy to share her life with him. She could honestly say that she had never felt that way about anyone. Perhaps it was because she was older and wiser, and was learning to wait patiently.

Since she had started helping him with his business, she appreciated and enjoyed the time they spent doing even the simple things. He lived about 60 miles outside of the city, so they usually met at his mom's house and ended up watching TV as they worked. Several times, they had even met over dessert. She had enjoyed their conversation, as they ate ice cream on the park bench outside of his office. And particularly there were the long conversations back and forth on e-mail—about everything, and yet nothing. They had also sat and talked for hours about her dreams and goals to start a community center.

She had even allowed him to use her extra toothbrush, which was an extreme form of sharing. While in college, she had dropped her toothbrush in the toilet. Her mom convinced her to use "a little baking soda." Since then, it was her custom to keep an extra one. Bartlett had left it at her house and teasingly hinted that it was in case she cooked him dinner, or if he forgot his briefcase again.

They had also had a wonderful time tutoring the kids from the church. She had called him at the last minute and he was more than willing to help. She handled English, Math, and Chemistry but she had not done well in Physics in high school or college. Bartlett, on the other hand, had taken two Physics courses as electives while in college.

"You're such a nerd-a-burger," she joked. "Who actually loves Physics?"

After the tutoring session they had stayed and talked. Lisa had admired how confidently he worked with the kids. "You did a great job. When will you be available again?" she had asked.

"You did great too. I don't think you needed me. You were doing fine without me," he replied. Bartlett told her that working with kids was her gift. "We don't need you wasting such talent away in Corporate America," he had joked.

Lisa and Bartlett had already discussed her goals several times. She told him that she had taken several steps toward starting a community organization. She had devised a business plan and Cliff had helped her complete the application for 501(c)(3) tax exemption status. However, she had encountered several road blocks for funding, and acquiring a building. "Things have just been so rough, especially lately. I mean, nothing's been handed to me on a silver platter, but now it seems the harder I work, the less I get accomplished."

Bartlett knew Lisa was implying that everything had been handed to him because his family was wealthy. But he had worked hard. He knew that anything worth having, would cost a lot of time and effort. He told her that she was facing an awesome task, but she also served an awesome God. "Lisa, tell me what's really holding you back? What are you so afraid of?" Bartlett had asked sincerely.

Lisa could not believe that he had read her so easily. Somehow it forced her to share with him, things that she had never really shared with anyone. "I've struggled a lot. For instance, right now, my finances are a mess. How can I help others when I can't seem to get my own life together? I just feel so unworthy. It seems like it'll take at least five to ten years to accomplish my goals at this point."

"Stop being dramatic. Listen, you're beyond intelligent so I know you know this, but I'll reiterate it—God doesn't require 100% perfection before He uses us. All it takes is our willingness to be used. That way He gets the glory and we can't take the credit for the insurmountable things we accomplish. And I'm sure God didn't mean for you to carry this burden alone. You just need to tap into your resources. Hand over to God what you do have, and watch Him perform a miracle. And stop saying what you can't do. You're not doing it anyway, you're just the vessel God's using to fulfill His purpose. You have to believe your gifts will make room for you and bring you before great men, even greater than any technical ability ever could."

"I hear you. But it's been a long journey. Whenever I take two steps forward, I'm pushed three steps backwards. So, it's like I don't want to start something else, only to be disappointed if it fails," Lisa said. "Okay, there I've said it." She was relieved. "I'm moving at a turtles' pace here. I don't know if I'll be able to pull it off. It's such a large task. I know God called me to do this, I just don't know how. I guess it might help if I stopped second guessing my abilities, huh?" She had unnoticeably poured out her heart to Bartlett in ten seconds flat.

"Exactly, especially if it overflows into second guessing what God can do in you. And you're not slow. You're hesitant. But it's okay I'm here to help. We're partners right?" He leaned over the table and hugged her.

Lisa had tried not to stare into Bartlett's eyes, but they were so inviting. She felt like she would faint. "Yeah, we're partners," she had said, hoping that he did not notice her hands and nose sweating. She quickly regained her composure. "I guess I just don't see what others see. I know the real me and my track record. And it hasn't been all that good. It takes me several tries to get things right."

"Lisa Hush. You Nerd-a-burger," he said, mocking her. "You wear multiple academic and professional hats in a synchronized fashion and you wear them well. You're a great engineer, administrator for my business, teacher for those kids, and you'll be even greater in full-blown ministry. So, connect with what God says concerning you and it'll change your image of yourself. If you have it, you just do!" Bartlett said. "You need to see yourself as blessed, which has nothing to do with stuff or things and everything to do with having the favor of God upon your life. All that matters is how God sees you! Period! Nothing else!"

Lisa had really appreciated Bartlett's help with her personal life, and with tutoring the kids. She told him that she liked the way he had handled little Tommy Parker, who could be mannish at times. He told her that it was no problem—he was used to dealing with knuckleheads. "I used to be one," he had said laughingly.

"Well, if you hadn't been here, I probably would've had to take him outside," she had said. "I wouldn't want to fight him inside the church building, you know."

"Who were you going to whip, as big as that guy is?"

"Oh, don't let my size fool you." She flexed at him, as if picking a fight.

"What a joke," Bartlett had said, shaking his head.

"Okay, I'll take you right here, we don't even have to go outside."

"How could God honor your requests if you fought in His house?"

"I know you've heard that God helps those who help themselves," Lisa had joked.

"You're in an extra silly mood," Bartlett said.

"Oh whatever! You've had your moments."

"When have I ever done anything of the caliber of your silliness?" He had a semi-serious tone.

"So, now you don't remember, huh?" Lisa quickly reminded him of the time they had gone to the warehouse club and picked up a cake for his mom's candle party. He had rode the shopping cart like it was a skateboard. Then, a foreign guy, who could not even speak English, began riding his cart also. He and Bartlett began racing their carts through the parking lot. The guys' wife and kids had stood there in amazement.

"Well, I'll admit that perhaps I was extra silly that day, but it's likely because I was with you. You make me wanna smile. You make me want to be a better person," he had said seriously.

Lisa had been elated, because many a day, she had felt that his presence in her life was such a soothing ointment to her soul. He constantly affirmed her purpose and divine destiny, and supported her in her endeavors.

That evening Lisa had prepared for bed and then knelt down next to her comfy chair in her bedroom to pray. She repented for her slothfulness and for not trusting God. She asked God to give her wisdom and to remove all doubt and fear regarding her purpose. She was maturing—allowing God to cleanse her as soon as issues surfaced. She was learning to pray according to the Spirit. She did not want to revert back to when she was a new saint and had not yet experienced God's delivering power. Since then, He had brought her through too much for her to forget or backtrack.

The night she had given her life to Christ, her burdens were lifted. But almost as soon as she left the gathering room where they took the new saints, she wondered if it was just another thing that would build her up, only to let her down. Yet she remembered wanting to run and holler to the top of her lungs, because of the freedom she felt after giving her life to Christ.

"Hey, Lisa you were supposed to meet me at the elevator. Let's go before I miss the guy from the eighth floor." Jasmine interrupted Lisa's daydreaming. Lisa had forgotten that she was meeting Jasmine for lunch, but Jasmine did not. She had broken up with her boyfriend and was not about to miss out on an opportunity to flirt.

I Wanna Holler

I really wish I could scream right now!
But it's kinda inappropriate to stand in the grocery line
and scream your lungs out.
Or sit in your office cubicle, and let out a shout!

But there's a feeling inside of me that won't go away.
Maybe if I Holler, I can make it fade.
If I Holler, maybe I won't have to admit that
I wanna reach that part of your heart,
that makes you wake up with me on your mind,
and fall asleep awaiting the next day,
when you can share with me how the sun came
beaming into your room as you awoke,
and tell me of the dreams and goals
that you've otherwise left unspoken!

This has to be more than just that initial spark
from which, even superficial relationships start.

I don't wanna just help you pass the time.
I don't wanna merely be your good friend that you can count on.
I wanna be what no other woman could!
I wanna do for you what a Virtuous Woman should!

And I just wanna Holler!
If you've ever felt for another what you feel for me,
Then my heart doesn't want to know,
Because, unmistakably
I know I never have given my heart this way before!
You told me that you love me,
and would do so for eternity!
I see you and I loving one another through our joys and hurts,
and I see you loving me as Christ loves the church!

And I just wanna Holler!!
'Cause I'm just hoping; praying,
that this fuzzy reception
that's coming from your heart to mine
is the real thing!

Chapter Twelve
One Day Soon

Krystal was turning 31 in a couple of months. *It seems like just yesterday Lisa and I were living in the dorms,* she thought. In actuality, it had been over seven years since she graduated. Tonya, Lauren, and Angie had arrived at her home to help her plan the big celebration she had been anticipating.

When they arrived, Krystal showed them her hand. "Jarrett and I are engaged. He proposed this morning." Krystal was practically screaming. "He came over before work, saying that he couldn't sleep because something was bothering him. When I asked what was wrong, he said he was anxious to start his new life with me. Then he grabbed my hand, got down on one knee and whipped this ring out. You know I started screaming, and running through the house. He just stayed there with this big giant grin on his face, and said, 'I'll take that as a yes.'"

"Oh my God!" Angie screamed in excitement. "I'm so happy for you."

"Congratulations! Yes!" Tonya threw her fist into the air. "Now we have to plan a birthday party and a wedding."

"Well, just a party for now, and a bridal shower later. We're not going to have a large wedding ceremony. We talked about going downtown to get married, going to Hawaii for our honeymoon, and then having a reception later."

"This is such a wonderful surprise," Lauren exclaimed.

"I know. I thank God. He's a wonder in my soul," Krystal said with tears in her eyes. "I never would've imagined that my life with Jarrett would be this great."

"Have you talked to Lisa?" Tonya asked as they all settled down from the excitement of the news.

"We had lunch together today, so I could show her my ring. You know, she couldn't wait. But I haven't spoken with her since about noon," Krystal said.

"Something's not right. Lisa's usually 20 minutes early, and she hasn't even called. That's not normal for a person with a Type A personality," Lauren joked.

Lisa finally arrived a half-hour later. "We were wondering where you were. Are you slowing down in your old age?" Krystal asked, jokingly, although it was evident that Lisa was not in a joking mood.

"Are you okay?" Tonya asked, as she rushed to hug her.

"Not really!" Lisa said.

"Do you want to talk?" Krystal asked.

"I don't know where to start!" Lisa said, as she sat down on the couch, trying not to cry.

"What happened? You were fine this afternoon," Krystal said. She was thinking that it likely had something to do with James or Paul.

"I just talked to my father. I thought our relationship was growing, but now I don't know. When I decided to get my Masters Degree, my parents said they would contribute. And I've been reminding him since the beginning of the semester. I think he only agreed to help because Mike told him that Robert was helping. Anyway, now all of a sudden, he doesn't have any extra money. Yet he and Theresa are going to Cancun next month. I don't know if I'll ever understand that man. I just started catching up on my bills and was saving money to do some much-needed repairs on my condo. Oh Well!" Lisa was clearly upset.

"Did he say he definitely wouldn't be able to pay?" Tonya asked.

Before Lisa knew it, she had cried and let out things that she did not know she still carried in her heart. "It doesn't matter. I can't wait on him like I did when I was thirteen waiting for a new pair of gym shoes. He keeps promising stuff, but when it's time to deliver, he comes up with a million excuses. From now on, I won't expect anything. If he does it, I'll appreciate it, but if he doesn't that's fine too. As he was talking, I could just feel the anger rising up in me. And I prayed, 'Lord take this out of me.' I don't want to keep failing at love and trust from dealing with his foolishness for so long. It's like I've conditioned myself to anticipate neglect and hurt."

"You've turned it over to God, all you have to do is trust Him," Tonya said.

"I love my father, but he has really jacked me up because of his empty promises, for far too long. I've put a lot of emphasis on being accepted and gone from one extreme to the other—from walking away to avoid abandonment, to clinging too tightly. But I won't treat him like the back-stabber he is. From now on, his foolishness is his problem. It would behoove me not to blame my past for my present. Enough is enough."

Krystal told Lisa that whatever fatherly love she lacked, God would provide. Tonya's input was not as to-the-point. "It's hard to learn that people will treat you harsh, betray you, and lie—until you're almost wounded beyond recovery, but you still have to love them. You have to kill that part of your flesh that wants to raise up in revenge. That's why we need to be taught how to forgive and move on in love."

"I'm just glad you finally got that off your chest. I know how difficult it can be to open up and share your innermost feelings, especially as it relates to family," Lauren said as she hugged Lisa.

"Yeah, and pain from those close to us, usually spills over into every aspect of our lives," Krystal said.

"Right. I can't believe how vulnerable I've been. And to think, I was considering marrying John, and then James, knowing that I had trust and communication issues. At this point, I realize it's unfair to expect others to bear the burden of solving my problems. I keep hearing in my spirit that it's time to let go and move on, without condemnation, and without looking back."

"Well, it's not necessarily bad to revisit your past. It's good to have a mental map of it, so you can make better choices in the future," Krystal said.

Lisa felt better. "Hey! I feel the poetic flow coming. Audience gather around closely." She motioned for them to appease her and stand in a circle for her performance. "We *aren't* grieving to announce the death of Lisa's flesh, as her Spirit goes on to be with the Lord. Yes, the death of the flesh is precious in the Lord's eyes. And as we're standing here, heads bowed, I'll reveal why." She spoke in her preaching voice. "It's because the mind of the flesh is enmity against God. Flesh shouldn't glory in His presence. He can't move where flesh is being glorified—where carnal desires take precedence—excluding faith. It's faith, sincerity, and repentance that catches God's attention. So today we bury her flesh. May it rest in peace." She moved her right hand as if sprinkling holy water. "We now commit these fleshly, carnal attributes back to the ground from whence they came. Ashes to ashes. Dust to dust. And the next time someone tries to offend her, she won't notice because dead men can't feel." She bowed her head, with her fist raised. "Let all of those who agree with this prayer now say..."

"Amen!" They all exclaimed as they had a group hug and cheered loudly.

"You're so talented," Lauren said. "One of these days I'll convince you to do poetry readings or publish a book."

"Hey, I like that—The Death of My Flesh. That was awesome," Tonya said.

"Yeah, but enough about that. We're here to celebrate!" Lisa said.

After discussing the party for a while, the conversation shifted to relationships, as it always did when they got together. They all inquired about Lisa's status with Bartlett.

"We're just friends!" Lisa exclaimed.

"That's the same thing you said about Paul when you guys started out," Tonya said.

"Look, I'm done with that and all the men in my past. If I never see any of them ever again, I'd be just fine," Lisa said.

"Well, what about the man of the present?" Krystal asked.

"I'm just helping him with his business, that's all."

"Oh, so you're like a help meet," Tonya joked. "Well, it's about time you started dating again. You've had a good break and I definitely see the growth."

Lisa bowed down as if paying homage. "Thank you, my spiritual advisor!"

Tonya pushed her. "And we're still praying for Lauren, because that last little victim you created was a big mess."

"Hey, I still have plenty of time. I'm young," Lauren said.

"The problem with youth is that it's wasted on the young," Tonya said.

"Look guys seriously. I wholeheartedly agree and I've changed completely. And now that I've had my lecture for the evening, let's get back to Lisa." Lauren was only 21. The rest of them were in their late twenties or older. They loved to gang up on her and her philosophies, which they considered immature.

"Okay, Lauren. You're off the hook for now. Listen ladies, Bartlett is *so* very sweet. But I really don't know what direction our relationship is headed in. Plus, that's not my focus. I'm just enjoying what we have now."

"Oh, you're so deep!" Krystal said.

"Deep in denial," Angie said.

"His mom is the one who pressed the issue of us being a couple. So we addressed it and his exact words were, 'Friendship is very important, and I wouldn't have our relationship start any other way.' The next day I got a dozen yellow roses with a card that said, 'I appreciate the friend I've found in you.' We understand one another fully. There's no pressure at all."

"Yeah, I caught that. He said he didn't mind starting as friends, but I bet he knows how he wants it to end," Angie joked.

"Guys, let it go!" Lisa rolled her neck, as she did in grade school.

"Well, my definition of dating is a male and female setting an appointment for one-on-one contact. Whether you label it as a date or not, it is. You're spending time with the person and getting to know them," Tonya said.

"Our one-on-one sessions are business-related. Thanks, but no thanks, for your philosophizing." Lisa stuck her tongue out at them. None of them were buying her story. "Well, I won't deny that I think he's a nice, accomplished young man. And yes, I like most of what I've learned about him. But I don't believe there are any shy men. So, until he makes his move, we're going to be friends."

Tonya interjected, "Well, I guess that's true. If a man likes you, he'll let you know. He could be as dirty as he's ever been in his life, get off the bus, and walk over to a woman in a Mercedes Benz, and say Hey, Baby, can I call you sometimes?"

"Right. So I haven't been flirting, or anything." Ignoring Tonya's raised eyebrow, Lisa continued, "Well, maybe a little, but for the most part everything's been strictly business." She rolled her eyes. "And based on my experiences with David, I've learned not to let outsiders push me into something that's not there. That can ruin a relationship."

"You want us to start on David?" Krystal asked. "I can't believe you guys' relationship, as much as you preach against men and women being friends."

"Yeah, well he slipped in there while I was still forming that opinion…"

Tonya cut in before Lisa could finish. "I know we're joking, but seriously, be careful that you're not falling for someone who doesn't have mutual feelings."

"I'm clear headed. I'm fine if nothing happens and if it does, well, I think that could be nice, too." Lisa knew she was stretching the truth.

"Yeah right, that sounds good." Angie was doubtful. "Men are too slow on their own. So, it's not against the rules to give them a nudge here and there."

After John, Lisa decided that she would never again allow a man to string her along. Yet she did not want to make Bartlett pay for John's sins towards her. So, she asked God to give her patience until he made the first move. She would feel 100% better if she did not have to coerce him into the next phase. "Seriously! How can I be so attached to him, if he's never told me he's interested?" Lisa and Krystal smirked, remembering a conversation they had with Cliff, as he was on a mission to prove that women have unprovoked expectations of him. "Anyways, I can't wait to tell Saiheed about this conversation. He says we think we're the number one authorities on relationships."

"We're no different than any other circle of friends, when it comes to being experts on each other's lives," Tonya said, "Hey, I only speak on what I know!"

"Exactly, I know basically everything that I claim to know," Angie said.

It was after midnight, when they finally said their good-byes and finished planning Krystal's party. It was going to be a spectacular dinner party with 100 of her closest friends, at a five star hotel downtown.

The next day was Saturday, and although she had stayed out late with the ladies, Lisa felt revived. She had a wonderful time of prayer and devotion, and felt invincible. If only she had discipline to start off every day that way. As she fixed her breakfast, she hummed the chorus to her favorite hymn, "Oh what peace we often forfeit! Oh, what needless pains we bear! All because we do not carry everything to God in prayer! Everything! Everything! Everything!"

For several months, Lisa did fairly well reestablishing her prayer life. She even cut out late night phone conversations, which helped her to get to bed early. Tonya told her that she was in hibernation, because they had not spoken since Krystal's birthday party, but Lisa was enjoying her newly structured life. Soon, however, she slipped back into her lazy morning routine of getting up late and rushing through her prayer time. It took a few months, but again on a Saturday morning, she spent over two hours praying and reading her Bible. After she ate breakfast, she read two chapters for her E-Business course.

She eventually checked her e-mail and saw that Cliff was online. Tonya was online, too. This week, her screen name was "Who is the MAND of God?" She was mocking her husband's uncle, who was a Pastor. He always said "man", as if it ended with a 'd'. Lisa sent her an IM, but Tonya never responded. More than likely she had unknowingly left her computer on. So, Lisa started talking to Cliff.

Mona Lisa Says: Top of the morning! What are you doing up before noon?

The Righteous are Bold as a Lion Says: I should be asking you that. I've been up praying and studying. Now, I'm surfing the net for a couple of old CD's.

Lisa sent him an icon with its tongue sticking out for implying that she was not an early riser.

Mona Lisa says: I've changed my ways AGAIN. What's been going on?

The Righteous are Bold as a Lion Says: Ahnna and I are slowly getting ourselves together. (SMILE)

Lisa sent him a thumbs up icon.

The Righteous are Bold as a Lion Says: I'm grateful that she didn't give up on me. I was selfish, but I decided I wanted to spend my life with someone who I know loves me. And she was the first person to come to mind. I love her with all my heart. So, I told her, "I know I'm a mess and I can't promise you a lifetime of perfection, but I want us to be there for one another forever." I enjoy having her in every phase of my life. So, basically I begged her to take me back. I realize that I don't want to live without her. Believe me, I tried. I told her to overlook my stupidity and show some mercy. (And I know you're getting a kick out of this).

Mona Lisa says: Yes I am!

The Righteous are Bold as a Lion Says: She said she wanted me to take some time to remove myself from that old image. So, I got rid of my black book. (SMILE) But she agreed that if we took things slow, we could have a great future together. She basically put me on "house arrest" for the next few months. And of course, I agreed to her terms.

Mona Lisa says: I'm glad to hear that!

The Righteous are Bold as a Lion Says: We're working through our differences. She wasn't exactly an angel either. You'll recall she tried to pick a fight with me that time at breakfast. She also sent me a nasty e-mail and told me I wouldn't know love if it bit me in the butt.

Lisa sent him a smiley face icon.
He sent her an angel icon, signifying that he was always a perfect angel.

Mona Lisa says: I remember her saying that you had started blowing her off. So I told her to stop calling your tail. 'Cause men can only take so much talking in a given day anyway, and they're definitely not going to put forth any extra effort if there's no commitment involved.

The Righteous are Bold as a Lion Says: I don't remember blowing her off!!!

Mona Lisa says: Don't play dumb. You know you're famous for getting tired of folks and using those painful words that no one wants to hear. "I'm busy. I'll call you back. I'm on the other end." I know how it feels to share life with a man that's all over you, calling three and four times a day just to say he misses you, surprising you with electronic cards, and showing up at your door with flowers, etc. etc. When that stops abruptly, it's devastating.

The Righteous are Bold as a Lion Says: Hey, the relationship just wasn't a priority at the time. But it's very high priority now, and that's all that matters. You know my mom isn't happy. But I figure as long as I'm sure she's "the one" and as long as she's willing to be "the one", no one can make the final decision but us.

Mona Lisa says: I hear ya, dude. Aunt Ellen means well, though.

The Righteous are Bold as a Lion Says: Wow! I looked back at what happened and I was saddened. I was a knucklehead. I kept saying that I was satisfied with Ahnna and I being friends, but I guess I didn't realize that meant she would be out of every area of my life eventually. I just imagined her always standing on the side lines for me.

Lisa's smile was as wide as ever as she read Cliff's response. She remembered that not too long ago he would not have expressed his feelings so openly about wanting to be with Ahnna, or anyone else. Cliff did not usually show any hint of adverse emotions.

Mona Lisa says: Well, it happens to the best of us. (SMILE)

The Righteous are Bold as a Lion Says: Well, I had a great

wake-up call that time I called her and asked her to help me do some flyers.
Mona Lisa says: Oh yeah, I heard about that briefly. What happened?
The Righteous are Bold as a Lion Says: That morning, I went over her house to do the flyers. Well, Melvin and I saw her at church later that evening, and while we were telling her how much everyone liked the flyers, she was like, "Hey we should go get something to eat." Well, I told them to go ahead, because I wanted to go home and rest, so she and Melvin went together. Instead of going home, I ended up going to a movie with Andrea. Well, somehow, she found out.
Mona Lisa says: Oh no! Not good, Cliffy!
The Righteous are Bold as a Lion Says: Exactly! She called me and said, "The same bubonic plaque that I had when you lied and said you were tired, is the same Bubonic Plague I had when you came over my house to use my computer." I felt really bad. I really wasn't trying to use her, but I see now that's exactly how it looked. I guess I had to learn that lesson the hard way. I really did some stupid things.
Mona Lisa says: Well...
The Righteous are Bold as a Lion Says: So, you're just going to let me put myself down without consoling me, huh?
Mona Lisa says: Well...
The Righteous are Bold as a Lion Says: You have to tell the truth, right? This sounds like the conversation I had with Melvin. He was badgering me, too.
Mona Lisa says: Cliffy, you had to realize all that for yourself. I don't think you purposely tried to hurt Ahnna, or had ill intentions. I think you just weren't ready, but I always say that once a man's ready to marry, then he'll give his all.
The Righteous are Bold as a Lion Says: At the men's seminar several years ago, Pastor Lindsay told us that the worst thing we could do was hurt a sister who was seeking the Lord. When I first heard that, my slate was clean. I've been through a lot of women since then. I've realized that

preventive maintenance is the key. You can't just be a hearer of this Word. We must also apply it. It's what keeps us safe, and in the will of God.

Mona Lisa says: Well, I'm glad to hear that you've gained knowledge and are applying it. That's a trial we all must go through. And it seems like just when we're getting ourselves together, the enemy throws up a smoke screen to try to blind us, but you've passed the test and you're being promoted.

The Righteous are Bold as a Lion Says: That reminds me, Katie wrote me a long e-mail the other day. I started to forward it to you, but I deleted it. She said she wanted to know if I had been thinking about her. You need to give her your spiel about women pursuing men. (SMILE)

Mona Lisa says: It's okay to ask about a guy's intentions without stepping outside of your role. That doesn't change who's pursuing who. It helps to clarify the pursuit. Sounds like she put herself out there, though. I hope you were nice.

The Righteous are Bold as a Lion Says: You need to teach that lesson to every woman in the world. Because, I wonder sometimes how they come up with this stuff.

Mona Lisa says: Well, some of you guys can be pretty confusing. You wine and dine to satisfy your physical needs, and then when the woman thinks you're "the one", you want to pull the "we're-just-friends" card.

The Righteous are Bold as a Lion Says: Don't start. And don't act like only guys initiate the wining and dining.

Lisa was cracking up at this point.

Mona Lisa says: Well, that's probably true. And anyway stop letting women take you out in the name of friendship. As a matter of fact, send them to me first. I got a questionnaire for them. And my first question—Why in the world would you want to have a grown man as a "hanging buddy?"

The Righteous are Bold as a Lion Says: Right! Right! I see what you're saying. Well, you know what I always say, it's not in the clothes I wear, or the way I style my hair! When you got it, you just got it.

Mona Lisa says: As Aunt Josie says, that's the kind of arrogance that makes women blow up houses and cars.

Don't let the devil sublease your soul, dude.
The Righteous are Bold as a Lion Says: Okay, so I took her to dinner twice, and a movie once. I didn't say that I wanted to spend the rest of my life with her.
Mona Lisa says: Women are always one step ahead. (SMILE) When a guy asks for my number, I'm thinking he could be "the one", especially if he calls often. And after we've dated for a few months, I'm ready to start the wedding planning.
The Righteous are Bold as a Lion Says: Yeah, but, I can't understand how a woman can be so into a guy that's never told her "I like you!" Not even once.
Mona Lisa says: Here you go with that again. Hey, we can't help the fact that we're not interested in a bunch of superficial relationships.
The Righteous are Bold as a Lion Says: Okay, I see your point. We're adults, not high schoolers. And I'll admit that in some instances, I did cross the line of friendship. But I don't get Katie, how can you put such pressure on someone when everything was strictly platonic, and nothing physical ever happened?
Mona Lisa says: Maybe a couple of dinner dates and a movie is sufficient to become attached to a guy you really like. I've started off friendships wondering if there was more. Yet men seem to have the uncanny ability to distinguish between friends and lovers. And then some don't know what they want, so every woman who crosses their path becomes a statistic. It amazes me that Ahnna was always the first person to pop into your mind when you needed help with your business from "someone you could trust", or flyers, or even when you were contemplating buying a timeshare, but you could not take that as a significant indication that you wanted and needed her in your life. Men! (SMILE)
The Righteous are Bold as a Lion Says: Okay! You win! (SMILE) But if we agreed that friendship was best, why'd Katie keep her hopes up?
Mona Lisa says: Listen, when emotions get involved and you spend time with someone, initial agreements are liable

to go out the window. I think her feelings changed first and then she held on, hoping that yours would change.

The Righteous are Bold as a Lion Says: But maybe I spent time with her, as a friend, every now and then, instead of going out with the fellows, just to be with someone who has a soft voice, soft legs (HA) and smells nice.

Mona Lisa says: Yeah, and see how much confusion that caused?

The Righteous are Bold as a Lion Says: Hey, I'm finally concluding that men may never ever understand a woman's point of view. I wonder sometimes if God even gave us the ability to. Nonetheless, two dinner dates, a movie, or a few drips and drops of compliments, don't constitute a committed relationship.

Mona Lisa says: I agree wholeheartedly. But Cliff, save your drips for the one you want to saturate. Okay!

The Righteous are Bold as a Lion Says: I got you, but women hold on to fruitless hopes and dreams too much. I bet you every man has to hear, "You don't have time for me," at least once a day. And when you make time, you still get in trouble. Women are so crazy sometimes. I'm glad I'm a man.

Mona Lisa says: On that note, it could be said that men always overextend themselves with work, or use something (outside of their women) to validate themselves. I'm glad I'm a woman. (SMILE) We're blessed to be emotional, yet strong. There's a risk, but there's also a reward. And most of the time it's worth it.

The Righteous are Bold as a Lion Says: WHOA! Is this Mrs. "I'm never getting married?"

Mona Lisa says: I knew you'd eventually bring that up.

The Righteous are Bold as a Lion says: That's such a controversial issue—Can men and women be friends? Some say they can, if there's no physical or emotional attraction. I say, they can if they want, but I'm not interested. From now on, I'm sticking to my baby, and keeping the rest at a safe distance—leaving no room for confusion.

Mona Lisa says: David and I are the perfect example of a man and woman who can remain friends without crossing the line.

The Righteous are Bold as a Lion says: You're the exception, not the rule. And Lisa, I appreciate you bearing with us. You've offered sound advice. Thanks for loving on the brethren. You do still love me, right?

Mona Lisa says: Hey, I still think you're the greatest thing since Sweet and Quicky Cornbread mix. We just needed to alter your ingredients a little (SMILE)—more Jesus, and a lot less of your old, unconsciously womanizing ways.

The Righteous are Bold as a Lion says: Thanks, I think. I realized that once I decided to let all that stuff go, life got easier and things began to flow smoothly.

Mona Lisa says: We all need each other, and we all need God's grace.

The Righteous are Bold as a Lion says: I'm grateful that where foolishness and sin abounded, grace did much more abound. HA! Hey, switching subjects, are you coming to Charles' backyard barbecue thingy.

Mona Lisa says: Of course! David's coming home and he'll finally meet the other special man in my life.

The Righteous are Bold as a Lion says: Yeah, David's a great guy. I owe him a world of thanks, too.

Mona Lisa says: What did he do?

The Righteous are Bold as a Lion says: Push me into my destiny (SMILE)...

Mona Lisa says: Well, pray for me. This is Bartlett's first major family function. I'm hoping the clan will be on their best behavior, if that's possible.

The Righteous are Bold as a Lion says: You're finally admitting that you're more than friends, huh?

Mona Lisa says: Previously there was nothing to admit. I'll give you the details later, though. But, I have to say I love that man! He's great!

Cliff sent Lisa a heart icon.

The Righteous are Bold as a Lion says: Sounds like someone's in love.

Mona Lisa says: Who me? (SMILE)

The Righteous are Bold as a Lion says: Well, it'll be all over once Aunt Josie drinks, and starts male bashing, and cursing at Uncle Tom and all that jazz. I don't know why she's such a hurt, bitter, man-hater. Too bad this function's at her house. When she gets excessively drunk, no one will be able to convince her to leave, like at all of the other family functions.

Mona Lisa says: She is not a man hater. She's just expressive. And do you know a woman who hasn't been hurt by something some man has done?

The Righteous are Bold as a Lion says: That's my cue to sign off. (SMILE)

Lisa was tickled at Cliff's eagerness to deviate from that conversation.

The Righteous are Bold as a Lion says: Well, I'll see you there. And I'll have my sweetheart by my side. (SMILE)

Mona Lisa says: Alright! See ya. Love ya dude.

The Righteous are Bold as a Lion says: I love you, too, dudette. GBY.

Lisa knew that meant, "God Bless Ya." She signed off and decided to take a late morning nap. She needed strength to deal with her rowdy family for the evening and she had several hours before Bartlett was due to pick her up.

As she lie in bed thinking, she prayed, *This is the day that You've made, and I'll rejoice and be glad in it! Thanks for Your goodness, mercy, and grace. You're great! And greatly to be praised! Lord, I pray that You strengthen...* Lisa started drifting off to sleepy-sleepy land. The last thing she remembered thinking was, *I must believe that God's going to do what he promised—and soon.*

One Day Soon

One day soon,
I'll wake up and this won't even be an issue.
the Lord is working it out
so that I don't need anyone but Him;
so that I don't yearn for any presence,
other than His presence.
One day soon,
My thoughts will be toward Him,
and His goodness solely,
for that's where my true happiness lies.
My mind will be free
no more to wonder
who did what with whom, when and where.
But it will focus on His glory,
His goodness, His mercy
and my thankfulness to Him.

One day soon,
I'll rest easy.
There'll be no more anxiety;
no more anger.
One day soon,
I'll look back at these issues, as things of the past.
I'll love everybody.
I'll treat everybody right.
And it will extend from the root of my heart.

Many are the afflictions of the righteous,
But the Lord delivereth him out of them all…
And I just have a feeling
(way down DEEP on the inside),
that for me
it's going to be
ONE DAY SOON!

Chapter Thirteen
The Potter

Lisa was hesitant about attending Charles' bon voyage party. There would be lots of food, folks (including her half-crazy relatives), and hopefully fun, (after she got pass questions about her personal life, and the gossip hotline of aunt Josie.) Uncle Tom and Aunt Josie were wealthy. They loved sports, and had their home built with a bowling alley, and basketball courts. They had a heated swimming pool which was enclosed with glass walls so they could enjoy it year round. Lisa enjoyed being served by their hired help. Yet she understood why Cliff had wished that the party were elsewhere. Aunt Josie was known to get drunk and liven up parties more than most of the family could tolerate.

Lisa was nervous. Yet she was reminded that she and Bartlett had shared several special moments that week. So by the time they arrived at the party, she was on cloud nine, and was determined to have a wonderful day. They walked in an hour late, as Lisa had perfectly planned. Everyone was mingling. The party was well underway with the older crowd playing board games, while the younger folks bowled, shot pool, and swam. Krystal and David were there. They, along with Charles and his fiancée, greeted she and Bartlett as they entered.

After Lisa introduced David and Bartlett, the two hit it off really well. Lisa and Krystal separated themselves by a few yards. Lisa wanted an update on

Krystal and Jarrett, without David's overprotective input. Both pairs were engrossed in conversation until they lined up for the dinner buffet.

After dinner, Lisa left Bartlett with her parents to refresh herself. Upon her return, Aunt Josie beckoned for her to join in on her discussion with David. As Lisa approached them, she could hear that, as usual, Aunt Josie's conversation was a succession of curse words, with a few other words thrown in between.

"Aunt Josie, stop all that cursing," Lisa said. Aunt Josie had been drinking already.

"Oh, I'm sorry baby. I forgot how delicate your ears are. I just want to know how long you and curly top here have known each other."

"Uh, I guess it's been about 16 years, right David?" Lisa asked.

"Right!"

"And so, when are you all going to stop playing these friendship games and get married?" Aunt Josie continued, "Girl, If I were you, I'd have been running my fingers through those natural curls 10 years ago."

Lisa was embarrassed. "Aunt Josie please don't start that again."

Aunt Josie rubbed David's arm. "You're what I call wife-beater fine."

David looked puzzled. "That doesn't sound too good, at all."

"Well, most men who look this good are crazy and conceited and treat their women like slaves. But I have to say, you wear it well. I don't think you know how hot you really are." She was still rubbing David's arm. "But that curly hair and those brown innocent eyes could make a woman's mind play tricks on her."

David was a nice guy, with good looks, and naturally curly hair. Women approached him a lot, offering to take him out, or buy him things, but he never let it go to his head. He considered himself an average guy.

Lisa wished she could evaporate. *Lord, help her mind, right now, and please save her soul while you're at it,* she prayed. Tonya and Mark had walked in and diverted Aunt Josie's attention, so Lisa quickly grabbed David's arm and took him over to what she thought would be a less feistier group.

"Why would you call them Hosea and Gomer?" Angie was saying as Lisa and David approached them. "Is that nice?"

Melvin tried not to laugh but he loved to clown. "You shouldn't use the Word of God to insult people. That's too funny!"

"Ha! That's a perfect description, though," Candice said. "He's probably acting like it's his Christian duty to rescue her."

"Stop that. She seems nice. I met her at church on Sunday. She goes to Pastor Williams's church," Angie said.

"What are you guys talking about?" Lisa asked.

"Nothing but a bunch of vain jangling!" Cliff said. "I can assure you of that."

"Yeah! She goes there on Sundays, right after she leaves the bar on Saturday nights." Lauren was furious. She barely acknowledged Lisa and David.

"It doesn't sound like you guys are dishing out compliments," David said.

"They're talking about Minister Taylor," Melvin said.

Jeff Taylor was Charles's good friend. Lauren was upset, although Charles had told her that he had a new girlfriend.

"I know for a fact that she's wild. She curses and drinks and everything. One of my lab partners, Linda, lives across the street from her grandmother," Lauren said. "They went to the Sexy J concert last weekend."

"So, just because she went to the concert doesn't mean that she doesn't know God. Right, cousin Lisa?" Candice asked.

"Well, Candice, that's not exactly the exemplification of a Christian lifestyle. And most people who listen to secular music usually dibble and dabble in other stuff like drinking, and fornication. Those types of unclean spirits usually travel in groups. Misery loves company. That's why you have to be careful what you allow to enter into your heart and mind. But, as Angie said, maybe she's changed."

Angie agreed. "People said similar stuff about me when I had a child out of wedlock."

"Angie, please. You made a mistake, but she's a mess." Lauren was so frustrated. "I can't believe he would talk to her. He's such a loser."

"Cousin Lisa, you remember that girl he's with, don't you?" Candice asked.

Candice was Cliff's younger sister. She was growing up fast. Lisa was used to seeing her in jeans and a T-shirt. Today she had on a cute little skirt and cardigan. Candice had likely tried to come dressed in her swimming garb, but Aunt Ellen was too spiritual to let her child walk around "half-naked" in public.

Lisa looked over at them. "She does look familiar." Lisa shrugged.

"She's Mrs. Tinsdale's granddaughter," Candice said.

"Oh, yeah! She's cute." Lisa remembered mean, old, Mrs. Tinsdale who sat on her porch to make sure the neighborhood kids did not touch her lawn. "So, that's who he's dating, now?"

"Maybe she's changed," Angie said again.

"Yeah, I bet she changed overnight— her skirt length from short to long, her drink from beer to communion wine, and her conversation from profanity to praise and worship—from Saturday to Sunday she was a brand new person."

"Do I detect some bitterness or what, Lauren?" Tonya had walked up.

Lauren had a snooty look on her face. A few months back Jeff told her that he was not looking for a serious relationship. He had said that it would be against God's will and purpose at that time in his life. Lauren had not appreciated him labeling her "anti-God's purpose." He may as well had called her the Antichrist. Tonya was about to comment when Mark called her into the kitchen.

"I pray that she changed before they started dating, and isn't trying to impress him. She needs to do that for herself, because if their relationship doesn't work out then she may walk away from God also. I'm hoping she went to that concert on Saturday, and on Sunday went down to the altar and got delivered." Lisa was trying to remain optimistic. "Anyway, it's his choice who he wants to be with, so leave him alone. Perhaps he's found true love."

"It's his choice? Is this the same person who preaches to me about my choices in women and told me not to lower my standards?" Cliff asked.

"That's because your standards were already very low, back then," Lisa said laughingly.

Cliff glared at her. "Right! Right!"

"I'm sorry, you left yourself wide open for that one," she said.

Lauren was determined to plead her case. "Yeah, it's his choice, but based on what he told me, she doesn't possess any of the qualities he's looking for."

"Well, most of the time we don't know what we want until we meet someone and decide that they fit the bill," Lisa said. "Anyway, maybe he changed his mind, or maybe he fell in love and it softened his heart."

"Or lowered his standards," Lauren mumbled.

"Yep, and I can see why. She's gorgeous," David said jokingly.

Melvin agreed, "Yeah! She's hot, if I must say so myself."

"Such potential, if only he'd chosen the right woman to stand by him and…"

Angie cut her off, "Oh please, Lauren, as bad as your mouth is, I know you're not insinuating that you're the right woman to be a Minister's wife."

"Hey, I know how to act right when I need to."

"Too bad some of us have to act!" Angie teased.

"Apparently so does she." Candice spoke at the same time as Angie.

Lauren kept going. "I can only imagine what their conversations are about. He probably talks about God, while she thinks about her next skimpy outfit."

Lisa was tickled, but refused to laugh. They needed a role model. Lauren had called them Hosea and Gomer and Lisa assumed she was mocking Pastor Lindsay who told them not to missionary date—try to get someone to confess Christ in order to justify dating them. He was adamant about his parishioners dating those who did not profess Christ. "God only told one prophet to marry a woman who turned from the things of God, to prove a point about the backsliding of Israel," he had said. "She deceived him, and he was told to love her anyway. I know God won't use y'all like that, cause y'all get mad and will take a teddy bear back, if you feel like someone's crossing you. So, for the rest of us Paul wrote, 'Be ye not unequally yoked together with unbelievers—for what fellowship hath righteousness with unrighteousness? And what communion hath light with darkness?' Young people, let it go, unless God is using your anointed self to help save a nation. And if you feel that he is, please call my secretary and make an appointment with me. And we'll also need to contact the news station with that breaking story."

"I'm sure their conversation is limited. He wears "S.S." on his chest, and is the "Super Spiritual," super hero of all times. He has a scripture for everything." Candice was still ragging on them. "Almost to the point where it gets on your nerves. So, I don't see how he justifies that, but you know how men are, even Bible characters. As many wives as David had, he still stole Bathsheba. And as wise as Solomon was, even he couldn't narrow it down. There's a guy in my History class that still thinks men weren't designed to be with just one woman."

Cliff played the peacemaker in his own, rough way. He was frustrated enough, because not everyone was pleased with his choice. "You know what? Kill all this! David and Solomon were successful because even though they had issues, God used them mightily. As badly as we want to, we can't choose folks' mates. Stop being judgmental. We don't know every detail of their situation."

"That's enough!" Lisa said. "Maybe she's changed, or maybe he changed and wants a less accomplished woman that's more willing to submit—someone who he can grow with. Right, Cliff?" Lisa teased.

Just then Ahnna walked up. "What are you guys talking about?" she asked.

"Absolutely nothing!" Cliff said. He grabbed her hand and walked away.

Melvin left shaking his head. "This conversation's too heavy for me."

"Yeah, Lisa. You need to help these young ladies out," David said.

"Men! They're just mad because we're telling the truth," Lauren said.

Lisa corrected them in love. "Look, I know you weren't trying to be vicious, but be careful about bashing people, as Cliff so eloquently said. Don't look down on others, or act like you'd never do what they've done. You don't want to judge others and set a standard so high you can't even reach it. The Bible says that what you mete will be measured to you. In other words, God will use that same measuring stick on you. There's life and death in the power of the tongue. And you can't sow seeds of discord toward others, and think you'll reap joy and peace."

"We were just clowning around and having a good laugh," Candice said. "Don't act like Cliff—always getting on us like he's perfect."

"Well, you can't keep doing the same detrimental things thinking that God's grace will keep covering you. You got to stop all of this gossiping and backbiting."

They apologized and Lisa assured them that she still loved them. She blew them a kiss as she walked away. *Like mother, like daughter!* she thought. Lauren was usually sweet and friendly, but since she was of Aunt Josie's seed, it definitely meant that she could also be harsh and unruly at times.

Although she was never quite as high strung, there was a time when Lisa would have gladly joined in to help them bash Jeff on his date with an alleged heathen. Those were her "glory days"—when she thrived on cutting folks up; exposing their wrongdoing. Her big mouth, which had gotten her into a world of trouble, was one reason why she felt she was light-years behind. If she had learned at an early age to hold her tongue, and allow the Lord to fight her battles, she could have advanced much further. She was glad that God was teaching her about Christian love. Joking or not, she was not going to fall into that trap again, and she was going to do everything within her power to help her cousins. There was no need for the generational curse to continue. "And be glad I didn't sick Tonya on you," she had warned them.

Lisa finally met back up with Bartlett, who was enjoying a game of Chess with her stepfather. She apologized for leaving him. She never could play very well, so she finally got bored watching them, and excused herself to go talk to Krystal, Tonya and Ahnna who were watching Cliff and his dad play a game of pool.

After having her usual sessions of chastising Aunt Josie and Lauren, the party was quite enjoyable. It was an opportunity to spend quality time with all of her favorite people. She briefly told the ladies about her week with Bartlett, which reminded her that she was supposed to have a good day, no matter what.

She had even spoke to James and Elaine as they pranced in, holding hands. She wondered if Elaine knew about his pop-up visit to tell her how much he missed her. She shrugged it off as a dude being a dude—carefree and freely weighing his options. She liked Elaine, and hoped and prayed that James would treat her well. Perhaps they would be good for one another. She knew it would be awkward, but she had walked over to them, and greeted them both with a smile and hug.

At the end of the day, they all got the opportunity to tell Charles how much they loved him and would miss him. It had become a very sentimental time for the whole family. In spite of all the initial hoopla, Lisa was glad that she had come and glad that she had survived yet another family event.

The weekend after Charles' party, Lisa drove him to the airport. Uncle Tom, Aunt Josie, Lauren, and his fiancée, Shelly, had left the morning before driving with his belongings. Shelly had actually volunteered to go with his parents so that they could "bond." Lisa prayed that Aunt Josie and Lauren would be on their best behavior and not talk her ears off too badly. Charles had stayed behind in order to tie up some loose ends with his old job.

After Lisa dropped Charles off and sent him away with several hugs and kisses, she sat and watched several flights take off through the departure gate. She cried as she thought that this was not just an ending and new beginning for Charles, she was also starting off afresh. She was leaving in the past her slothfulness and fear of doing what God had called her to do. Within the next nine months her life would change drastically. She was embarking upon her role as a leader in church. She was receiving her master's degree. She was preparing for her career as program director of the community center. She was leaving her excuses in the past.

Lisa felt, in her spirit, that it was time to walk in her divine purpose. Her preparation had seemingly gone into over time, but she still felt that it was time she moved outside of her comfort zone, and allowed God to use her to advance his Kingdom. She was reminded of Romans 12:6-7, "Having then gifts differing according to the grace that is given to us, whether prophecy, let us prophesy according to the proportion of faith; Or ministry, let us wait on our ministering—or he who teacheth, on teaching;." Lisa had waited with patience for teaching to be imparted, and now it was time for her to activate her faith. It was "show time" and God was moving things along quickly. She had received God's Word for years through pulpit sermons, Sunday school lessons, and her own personal study. It was her turn to give back. Whenever she studied and received revelation knowledge of God's Word, she automatically visualized herself relaying the revelation to others. It was so vivid and real she could not escape it. Lisa had allowed her dreams to lie dormant for many years, but now she could not rest until she fulfilled her divine call. And she was more equipped now, than ever. She knew that she was the most unlikely candidate to teach the young ladies who would visit the community center, yet she thanked God for seeing in her, what she could not see in herself. She was looking forward to the weekly "Girl Talk" sessions.

Lisa had shared her vision with Bartlett many times. He finally told her that he also wanted to give back to the community that had nurtured him as a child. He said that when they initially talked about their dreams and goals, it had blew his mind because, before that, he had only thought of her as a typical business woman trying to make a name for herself.

Bartlett, Uncle Theodore, and his brother, Barry, had decided to combine their efforts. Seeing the passion in Lisa's eyes as she spoke about her dreams, assured them that she was the person they would use to bring the vision to fruition. "You have a business plan, you've gotten tax exemption status, and now we're going to provide the building and funding that you need," he had told her.

Lisa appreciated Bartlett's stance on education, and his dedication and commitment to the community. She told him that he had officially earned his nickname, "Brave Heart!" When they met to discuss the plans in detail, Lisa presented them with the program curricula and budget. She told them that she was interested in having a building with classrooms for tutoring and adult courses, a computer lab, a gym for extracurricular activities, a food court, an auditorium where they could hold drama presentations, a day care, and offices for the administrative staff. She requested a 100,000 square foot building. Their response was, "No problem." The building that Uncle Theodore donated was just right, and his friends in the construction industry gladly helped renovate the old warehouse at minimal cost.

Things were finally falling into place. And they happened all of a sudden, just as Pastor Lindsay had prophesied. Lisa and Bartlett worked on devising the vision and mission statements. Cliff became the Board's legal consultant. Uncle Theodore knew several educators and community leaders who were a great asset to the Board of Directors.

At their first board meeting, they had loved Lisa's suggestion to name it the Hart to Hart International Networking Community Organization; "The I.N.C." for short. Lisa remembered the first official quarterly meeting, very vividly. When she had arrived, the only empty seat was between Uncle Theodore and an elderly woman. Uncle Theodore introduced her to Mrs. Starchill who was an educational consultant and had helped several charter schools in the local area with their curriculums. Then Uncle Theodore pointed passed her at Bartlett and said, "And I'm sure you know this gentleman."

Lisa smiled. Bartlett had nodded his head at her as if she were a total stranger, and they were meeting for the first time. When Mrs. Starchill excused herself, Lisa slipped him a note with a smiley face, which read, "Oh, now you want to pretend like you don't know me—like you don't have a toothbrush at my house?"

Bartlett smiled. "Ma'am, I must say that your beauty is deterring me, Nonetheless, Ms. Wilson, is it? We shall remain professional."

"Yes, sir," she said. Throughout the rest of the meeting she had purposely ignored him.

When they took another break, Bartlett whispered to Lisa, "Uncle Theo thinks Hart to Hart refers to him and me, because he contributed the major funding, and I'm providing the manpower. But just between you and me, we're Hart to Hart." That was his way of getting her to soften up. It had worked wondrously, and had kept a smile on her face for the rest of the evening.

Lisa had lost track of time, and before she knew it, she had sat for an hour thinking about her life. "Charles is probably over half way to New York," she said aloud. As she drove off, she was so happy that she was finally moving forward, after constantly seeking God to change her. "Lord, please continue to cast the devil out of my will and out of my mind", she said, mocking her old Sunday school teacher. Lisa felt such a sense of growth, progression, relief, resolve, and victory. There was the ongoing saga with her dad, but she felt that the mere fact that she could speak to him without being bitter meant that she was progressing in that area, as well.

She had called him to apologize for their last conversation, and he basically blew her off and said it was no big deal and he had forgiven her. *You forgive me?* she thought. After all of these years, her father had never hinted that he was even slightly wrong for the role he played, or did not play in her life. Nonetheless, she was determined to have a working relationship with him. No matter how hard, she planned to call him again, once he and his "shack mate" returned from vacation.

Lisa was amazed at the impeccable timing of God. There had been many roadblocks, mostly that she had caused for herself, but God had moved in her life and made things work out perfectly in His time. She felt that she had failed miserably and wished that she had gotten to this point at least five years prior. Yet she knew that she had been anointed for the present time and purpose. She felt as if God had wiped her slate clean and given her a new beginning.

In spite of all of her downfalls and obstacles, she had seemingly stayed in place. She had worked diligently in the church and had not given up, even when she thought she could not live another day in her current state. And she had gone through the leadership class and her Master degree program simultaneously, and had received an A average on all of her work.

Tears began to swell up in her eyes as The Lord once again directed her to Isaiah 66. *Lord, you're so faithful. Even when we're not faithful, you don't allow us to abort the gifts that you've placed in us.* She realized, now, more than ever, that she could trust God and give him complete control over her life. He was not the kind of God to leave, or take advantage of those who were obedient and committed their lives to him. He stuck with His promises until they were manifested. He used her shortcomings and mistakes to help bring her to an appointed time of ministry and just as in Job 14:14 she vowed, "All the days of her appointed time she would wait until her change came."

Lisa recalled that her Psalms and prayer journal was previously filled with requests. Requests were now coupled with praise reports. She had sought the Lord to cleanse her, give her a fresh anointing, move her to the next level of ministry, and give her a closer relationship with Him. He had given her these things and more. She was grateful for the spiritual blessings, as well as the natural. A few weeks prior, her boss had unexpectedly offered her a management position, and a $25,000 annual increase (retroactive to January of the previous year). One of the perks was that her educational allowance increased. She was elated that she was finally getting a financial break to push her over the top. Yet she kept her promise to God by cutting her spending and increasing her giving.

She estimated that she would likely spend six more months in her current position, while transitioning to director of the community center, which would be just enough time to collect her bonus, pay off other bills, and start off her new career with a clean slate. Although she knew that she would not be in that position much longer, she was very grateful that God had continued to prosper her while she was there. She had been confused and torn about her career. On one hand, she felt that she was doing well, but on the other hand she often felt like she should leave before she got fired. She was still growing and progressing, but not as fast as she could if she were "giving 110%" as she had done in the beginning. Perhaps no one could tell that she was slacking, but she could tell and it did not feel good.

Lisa had met with Pastor Lindsay and he had told her that although she had not been designated to preach in a pulpit, she must walk in her ministry at all times, and find the pulpit or forum where God would use her to fulfill his plan. He told her that although there would be times where she would teach at the church, most of her ministry would be outside of those four walls.

The Lord had proved Lisa and since she had not given up, He rewarded her as promised. If the devil had had his way, she would have been strapped in a straight jacket, in a mental ward losing her mind, but she had such peace. There had been times when she wanted to give up, and stay in the bed and sleep her life away, but God had strengthened her. And now she could proclaim with certainty that she would never, ever give up. She could not imagine herself ever walking away from the things of God.

As she lay in bed that night, she chuckled aloud, "Lord, if you were going to get rid of me, you should've done it before I got the 'can't help its' towards you."

The Potter

I thought I was molded together and progressing perfectly,
but the potter saw a flaw that would ruin the masterpiece.
I began to wish things were different and remembered when they were better;
I began to wish things were easy, as it was when nothing really mattered.
I remember that as a child life was full of days without struggle; purely simple.
I recall my biggest worry then was whether or not I had a pimple.

All I really want is to live peaceably and be righteous as The Bible says.
My uncomplicated request for adulthood is that my good days, will outweigh
my bad days.
I desire to love and respect everybody, but for me it's just not that easy,
as I try to forgive and forget all the things people did to hurt me.
I want to learn to walk in God's Spirit boldly and with no remorse.
I want to go through life's tests with flying colors, even if violently by force.

I'm learning that what's going on may hurt so bad that I want to die
But God provides strength and power, and hears even my faintest cry.
When rebuilding, God renovated my mind and literally broke me down.
I was purged, cleansed, and cut, in order to reach higher ground.
And the end result is constant, and even when I'm closer than ever before,
I realize that I'm still being made into something that is as pure as gold.
I know that finer things have to be made with fire, or they will not last,
And I thank God for keeping me and not alleviating me as a useless task.

I press on, singing psalms and hymns, constantly giving all my might,
making melody in my heart unto the Lord, and speaking healing into my own life.
This time instead of whining, and instead of trusting and retreating within myself,
I allowed the potter to make me into a vessel to be used by someone else!

Chapter Fourteen
You're Still My Choice

Lisa was on her way to Bartlett's home. She was looking forward to the evening. Although she loved the scenery, she dreaded the long drive out into the country area that he called home. Things had gotten pretty serious, and she wondered if he would consider moving closer to the city if they got married.

Lisa had been afraid that their relationship would not work because it had not initiated with them admitting to their attraction for one another. On the other hand, the relationship seemed to have a head start because neither of them had ever had to try to impress the other. Bartlett had called it their bricklaying stage—saying they were unknowingly building a strong foundation.

Lisa had called Cliff after she got dressed, but he could not talk long because he was working on a huge case, but he had made Lisa's day when he told her that he believed she and Bartlett had something special. "One day we were friends and the next Bartlett confessed that he was having feelings for me that he hadn't expected to have," Lisa had told him. Things with Bartlett were unveiling perfectly.

In order to make the long drive go quickly, Lisa called Ahnna, whom she thought was such a strong-spirited young woman. Lisa was happy that Cliff had finally recognized her value. Ahnna was relieved, too, although she wished he had done it sooner. "I know women supposedly mature faster than men, but geez. Yet somehow I don't think he's insincere, just slow," Ahnna said.

Lisa had once again indulged Ahnna, and let loose on one of her "joking spasms." This time she mocked the elderly lady who did the announcements at their church. "Next Sunday we'll host our Ninth annual Mighty Men's seminar. The topic is "I'm Slow, but Anointed!" Our power-packed Saturday features a theatrical performance, "Slow Men Need Love, Too!" We're flying our guest speaker in all the way from Italy. His anointed message has delivered millions." They had a great time laughing at Lisa's commentary on the snail's pace a man seemed to have regarding commitment. Lisa decided to quit while she was ahead. She did not want to be in too silly of a mood when she arrived at Bartlett's house.

"Lisa, at Charles's party, you never did give me all the details of 'Wonder Week with Bartlett,'" Ahnna joked.

"This is going to take a while," Lisa said, as she began sharing she and Bartlett's brief history with Ahnna.

The Sunday before Charles' shindig, Lisa had caught Bartlett's eye from the balcony, where he usually sat. He insisted that he needed emergency assistance with his handheld computer. He offered to take her to dinner, but she was happily compensated by the four hour conversation they had in his car afterwards.

She remembered the exact time he had showed up at her door the next day. It was 9:03 p.m. He stated that she must have drugged him with her charm and that he was just stopping by to say hello. He had been yearning to see her "beautiful face all day." He had surprised her with a caramel apple, her favorite gourmet snack, from a specialty shop out by his home. Earlier that day she had also mentioned that she had a lot of trash to dispose of because she had finally cleaned out her basement. She recalled that he had a very serious look on his face that evening, as if he had something on his mind. However, he had only stayed long enough to take out her trash, and give her the apple, and an extra long hug. Lisa had felt so special.

The next afternoon, he e-mailed her saying that he wanted to talk to her, but she had already made plans to go to dinner with James's sister, Bonnie, and did not want to reschedule because Bonnie was experiencing a lot of stress, and was on the verge of divorce. So, they postponed their date.

On Wednesday, he called her after church. She remembered looking at the clock when she got home. It was 9:47 p.m. when she walked in the door, and

10:14 p.m. when he called. They started off talking about God's goodness, and each shared their testimonies. Bartlett told Lisa that he had grown up in a very dry church. The choir was dry, the parishioners were dry, and even the Pastor's preaching was good, but dry. His relationship with Christ had flourished once his college buddy invited him to a Pentecostal church, where he received the baptism of the Holy Ghost. Then, he learned to incorporate God into his everyday life. "I had a strong foundation of The Word, growing up, but there was something missing. There's no way around it. We need to seek God for the indwelling of his precious spirit, or we won't make it. We need to become one with Him, and possess His spirit continually. It's kind of like expecting to drive for weeks without refueling, or trying to talk on your cell phone for hours on end, without recharging it." Bartlett was in an extra talkative mood. "For instance, let's say you and I get married and become one, we can't expect our love to continue if we're not constantly rekindling it by protecting and cherishing our intertwined purpose." Lisa had blushed hard when he used their love for one another as an example.

Finally, on Thursday, he had the same serious look that he had worn on Monday. He had placed a dozen roses on her mantle, with a small note card that read, "I'm looking forward to our future. I love you." Lisa had remained calm, although she wanted to scream. Bartlett had sensed her hesitation. He had been hoping for more visible elation. Lisa had not said much, but she recalled what he had said verbatim, "I don't want you to think that I'm trying to run a line on you or play games with you. I want to be with you. Everything I know about you thus far, is wonderful. Or should I say, there's nothing that I know, that I can't handle." He had smirked and playfully pulled her hair. He continued with, "I've enjoyed spending time with you and I want this for the rest of my life. I see it. I want it. I want it with you and I sincerely hope you feel the same because it's time for me to sweep you off your feet." Lisa had placed her hand over her mouth, to hide her excitement. He had gently pulled it away, and kissed it. That evening, he took her to dinner at her favorite restaurant.

That weekend, Lisa had three assignments due for her last online class. Thus, they agreed that they would not see each other again until Charles's party.

"Ahnna, for several weeks I had felt our relationship shifting. I was nervous because I knew Aunt Ellen, and perhaps others, wouldn't approve," Lisa said, as she continued reminiscing.

Lisa told Ahnna that she was not interested in pleasing others, at the expense of making herself miserable. She consciously and willingly chose to be with Bartlett. He possessed her top three qualities—He had God's Spirit down inside, he "could not get enough of her," and had a great sense of humor.

It had become like clockwork. Every day, he would get to work at 8:00 a.m. and call her at 9:00 a.m. That Friday, he had also gotten up extra early to surprise her by installing IM software on his home computer.

Mona Lisa says: Top of the morning to you! I'm shocked! (SMILE)

Brave Hart says: You weren't supposed to tell me first. How are you, Ms. Wonderful? You're so wonderful. You're so amazing. You're the love of my life.

He sent her a musical note icon to remind her that these were the words to a song that he had heard in the barbershop and told her about a few days before.

Mona Lisa says: When I saw that you had signed in, I couldn't resist. And if I'm wonderful then you're more than wonderful. I love you!

Right then Lisa decided to change her screen name.

The Wonderful Mona Lisa says: I LOVE YOU SO MUCH

Brave Hart says: Whoa! Who is this?

The Wonderful Mona Lisa says: I knew that'd take some time to swallow.

Brave Hart says: Right! I need some time to recover. But I'm not complaining. This relationship has evolved into something wonderful. He's a Mighty God! He gives us richly all things to enjoy! (SMILE) I LOVE YOU, TOO!

Brave Hart says: Yeah! Yeah! I Love You! Yes I do, Love You Darling!

He was now singing one of the oldies but goodies songs.

The Wonderful Mona Lisa says: This is not the time for your singing career debut. Get to work, young man. "It's time to make that money!"

Bartlett had told her that his 5-year-old niece had picked up the saying from the lyrics of a popular song. Lisa thought it was hilarious.

Brave Hart says: Yes Ma'am, good-bye. God bless you and I love you. Oh yeah, did you call the restaurant and make reservations for next week?
The Wonderful Mona Lisa says: Yes, one more question, though. Is this what real love feels like?
Brave Hart says: I hope so. How do you feel?
The Wonderful Mona Lisa says: YES! This is the real thing!
Brave Hart says: Are you sure?
The Wonderful Mona Lisa says: Definitely!
Brave Hart says: AMEN! You've been Engrafted into my world. How will you handle it? (SMILE)
The Wonderful Mona Lisa says: By enjoying every second. It's now my life's goal to keep a smile on your face.
Brave Hart says: Well, I'm definitely smiling right now!
The Wonderful Mona Lisa says: Good-bye for now, ma lawd!

Lisa decided to practice her English accent in writing.

Brave Hart says: Ha! I got you calling me, Lord, already (SMILE). Now how can I cope with that closing? Bye, My Queen!

Lisa wished that fairy tale moment could have lasted forever. On Saturday, to put the proverbial cherry on top of the whole week, he had stopped at the convenience store to purchase a card for Charles. They had sat in the car for a few minutes while he signed the card, and wrote Charles a check for $100. After their brief argument because Lisa thought it was too much money to give someone he was just meeting, to Lisa's surprise, he pulled out another card . The card read, "Some things are meant to be! I know that each morning the sun will rise, and each morning I awake, I know that the sky will still be blue." She opened the card. On the inside it read, "And I know that I am supposed to be in love with you!" Lisa screamed with excitement, as she read it. She hugged him tightly, as if she would never let him go.

Bartlett grinned, nodding arrogantly. "That's the reaction I was aiming for."

After Charles' party, he told her that he found himself wanting to spend every waking moment with her, but since they both had other obligations, it was time for them to slow down. "I haven't been in a serious relationship in a while, but I do know that most of them start off with both parties being consumed with each other, and inadvertently neglecting other responsibilities as they transition into a new life, which includes one another. Now, I'm not saying I want this to fizzle out, we just need to stretch it out. We have a lifetime to be together," he had said. Once he had made that point, Lisa was sold on everything else he said.

It had been two months since then. Lisa smiled, thinking that things had only gotten better. She was looking forward to Bartlett "wining and dining" her that evening. It was more like her favorite, clear, caffeine-free drink, and grilled pork chops, with his famous fried rice, but she was excited, just the same.

As she hung up with Ahnna, Lisa could not help but wonder if he would "pop the question." She had finally shared her John Davis madness with him. His reply had been, "You're too special to be kept waiting. And I don't plan to go through the dating phase very long because it only complicates things and somewhat forces me to put my feelings for you on hold. A person could explode trying to suppress all of this love," he had joked. She wanted to tell him that her schedule was wide open, and she was available immediately, but she withheld her "joking spasm." She did not want to scare him away.

In preparation of their date that day, Lisa went to the salon and got a perm, and fresh eyebrow arch. She even sat through two dreaded hours for a manicure and pedicure. She wore one of Bartlett's favorite outfits, (a mauve blazer, with a slightly fitted, knee-length skirt, with black, mauve and gray stripes). She added a touch of sass by concluding it with knee-hi boots which fit her calves perfectly.

Bartlett had seen her in the outfit and could not stop commenting on how nice she looked. The next week, he had come over for a business meeting and noticed it hanging on her closet door. She had watched him pick up the skirt by the hanger and smile. "For some reason, I really like this skirt," he had said.

Although Lisa did not want to entice Bartlett, she wanted to look her best. They had several lengthy conversations regarding avoiding focusing on each other's physical attributes, particularly when they were alone. They did not want to do anything that had even the slightest hint of sexual flirtation. Bartlett had said that the key was to discuss the issue before it ever became an issue. And they had already squared that away. She told him that she was determined to wait until she was married. "Hey, this is as important to me as it is to you," he had told her. "But if I lose my mind, I need you to be strong for both of us," he joked.

They decided that a simple kiss here and there was sufficient until they married. She did not want to violate him, and she definitely did not want him to violate her in any way. She had successfully escaped fornication with her most recent beaus, yet she had done impure things that made her feel spiritually separated from God. She was not interested in ever traveling that road again.

As Bartlett greeted her at the door, she was trying to ignore how nice he looked and smelled. Her biggest downfall had always been a nice guy, with a charming smile, a nice hair cut, well-groomed facial hair, and a fresh scent of cologne. At the moment, Bartlett had all of those things working in his favor. Bartlett welcomed Lisa into his home and gave her a huge hug. "Hey Wonderful, I've been missing you. And I must say you're looking as wonderful as ever."

"Hello, Mr. Brave Heart," she said. Bartlett bent down and kissed Lisa lightly on the lips. Their lips were only locked together for a few seconds, but for Lisa it seemed like forever. Lisa blinked and tried to regain her composure. It had been a while since she had enjoyed a kiss other than a peck, and it felt nice.

Bartlett grabbed her hand and lead her into the dining room. "Oh, my goodness, you smell so good," she mumbled.

"Yeah, the food does smell good, if I must say so myself," Bartlett replied. He was focusing on reminding himself that they were not married and forcing his feelings to stay in reserve. He had prepared his mind for this battle, and he was determined to win. He was having second thoughts about the romantic tone he had set with her favorite berry scented candles. As they walked into the dining room, he tried to unnoticeably adjust the dimmer to help change the ambiance.

Lisa noticed. "Yes, please let there be light," she said laughingly.

Bartlett chuckled. "Yeah, we do need some light. I didn't know that you were going to wear that today, geez. I thought I asked you to only wear that when we were going out to very, very, very public functions."

"Mortify your members and behave yourself, young man," Lisa joked. She knew that there could be some truth to his jesting, but that they could handle it hands down. She was determined to kill her flesh. She was tired of being carnal and spending all of her time repenting and feeling like God was not being honored in her relationships. The foolishness of fornication was not an option.

Lisa watched him from the dining room, as he finished cooking. He put some rice on a spoon and then tried to feed it to her. "Taste this," he said.

"The last time a man did that to me, he was trying to seduce me," Lisa said.

Bartlett smiled. "There's no need for me to seduce you. Whatever I want, I'll just ask for it," he said, teasingly.

After dinner, Lisa was anxious. They cleared the table, and although Lisa considered herself the automatic dishwasher connoisseur, they spent the next 20 minutes talking and hand-washing the dishes. "This is an opportunity for us to spend some quality time together," Bartlett said.

He finally led her back into the dining room so they could talk. Lisa had a brief flash back. James also liked to have major discussions at the dining room table. "Uh, can we go into the living room?" she asked.

"The last time someone said that to me, they were trying to seduce me," Bartlett teased. "And besides, I'm better able to read your eyes if we sit at the table."

After he pulled her chair out for her and made sure she was comfortable, he began. "Lisa, first of all, I love you and I trust you dearly, with all my heart. There's no question that I want to spend my life with you, and everything that entails. I'm looking forward to God bringing us to our expected end together. I wake up thinking about you. I've never given my heart to anyone like this before. I don't have all the answers, but I'm committed to this forever. I don't believe in divorce or separation or none of that. I've found my good thing. And I'm going to hold on to you forever. Even when you're in the worst mood. Even if you spend all of my money. Even when your breath stinks. Even when your hair thins..."

"...such a comedian," she mumbled under her breath, "...so silly..." She wished he would get to the point, but it was a fat chance of that happening. He flashed the charming smile that showed his dimples. At that point, Lisa's heart began to beat extremely fast. She took a deep breath.

"I take 'us' very seriously. It's my duty, as head of this relationship, to do what I deem necessary to preserve it." He paused. "I've thought long and hard about this. And I know that I'm about to reveal a side of me that I never openly discuss."

Lisa began to speak but Bartlett lightly placed his right hand in the air. "I love you!" he said, "Do you know that? I want you to look into my eyes and tell me that you love me."

Look Sucker, you ain't about to break me down, she thought. She rebuked her inopportune joking spasm. She looked up at him and grabbed his chin. "I love you. I love you. I love you," she said softly.

His heart melted, but he tried not to let it show. "Now, I know you think I can be extreme, and callous, but I have to do what I have to do. And I know this may cause friction between us initially, but I'm just going to say it bluntly, and we can discuss it thereafter. So here it is—your relationship with David has taken its course, and frankly, it's time out for him being an intricate part of your life."

Lisa could not believe what she had heard. Bartlett wore an expression of discontent that she had grown to dislike. His entire demeanor had changed, and he was no longer his usual charming self. He waited patiently for her response. She fought back tears. *Are you asking me to choose?* she thought. "Bartlett this is all a surprise," she began. "This issue has never come up. I'm speechless I don't know what to think or say."

"I understand."

She was so angry that he put her in that position. "So, does this apply only to him or am I too close to anyone else?" she asked, out of frustration.

Bartlett did not reply. He did not want to argue. He was praying that they would escape the conversation without too many bruises. He stood up and walked to the patio door. He finally turned back toward her, "Don't take this the wrong way, but, I do plan to be your everything, if that's what you're implying. I want to supply everything you'll ever need. I don't want you to feel like you need outside assistance emotionally, physically, spiritually, financially or otherwise. And I won't apologize for that. I have to be willing to die for you and I take that seriously. I want to be honest about inappropriate outside involvement."

Tears rolled down Lisa's face. He offered her some Kleenex, but she shook her head. She was too upset to care about wiping her tears.

"Am I saying that I don't want you to confide in your usual entourage of friends? No! That's selfish, ludicrous, and senseless. But I'm saying that if you confide in them instead of me, that would be hurtful," he said in his fatherly tone.

"Bartlett, you and I have never had a problem communicating..."

He cut her off, "Lisa, this goes beyond communication."

"Okay, but why do you think it's impossible for me to have a male friend and nothing happen between us?"

"I just don't!" he said firmly. "Now, I know he lives in Chicago, and I'm not jealous of you guy's relationship at all. I know who I am, and no one else can be me. Neither can I be anyone else. But you guys' relationship is not an asset to anything we're trying to accomplish. As a matter of fact, it's a hindrance. I'm not asking you to do anything that I'm not doing. All this friendship stuff is the very thing that's caused me so much mayhem in the past. And it would be insane of me to keep doing the same things, and expect different results."

Lisa was angry. She remembered taking his leather jacket to be repaired. She had found his ex-girlfriend's phone number in the jacket pocket on a Southern Grill napkin. She had called his office, and his secretary had told her that he was having lunch at the Southern Grill and had left his cell phone on his desk. She had picked the jacket up from him the next day. In her mind, she was the one who should question their trust, but she had given him the benefit of the doubt, and placed the situation in God's hands.

She sat quietly and thought about his request. She remembered speaking with Elder Peterson, and praying that God rectify both of their pasts regarding dealings of the opposite sex. Although it was a very hard thing that he was asking, perhaps it was the answer to her prayer. *So much for going home with an engagement ring!* she thought.

"Bartlett, this is not going to be easy for me." Lisa was trying not to deny his request, but she wanted him to know that she was not happy.

"Listen, I recognize that you're accustomed to your circle of friends, and I'm not asking you to give that up, for the most part. I'm just expressing..."

Circle of friends? She was offended. How dare he down play her friendships. Was he, like her brother, trying to imply that it was unhealthy for them to be so close? Did he also think there was some "hanky-panky" going on?

"I'm just asking that you consider my feelings. I'm trying to be honest. I can't live like that." His voice softened. "I'll understand if you need more time."

Lisa felt that he was wrongfully spurning her explanation. "Why do you want me to rid my life of him? He's like a brother to me and that is all. I promise you."

"I understand."

She hated when he said that. It meant that he was not budging. She cautiously continued. "Bartlett, I love you." She paused. "This has definitely been a blow to me, and I would be remiss in my responsibility to our relationship if I didn't admit that I think you're being extremely perceptive, here."

"Hey, where there's perception, there's forgiveness. Between you and I, anyway, right?" he tried to lighten the mood in the room. "Lisa, I've perceived too much foolishness and I just can't tolerate it. And I hope that you can clearly see things from my point of view."

"David and I are just friends. I wish you could see that clearly!"

Bartlett cut her off. He knew that it was time to share his testimony with her. "Lisa, he's like a brother, but he's not your brother. And I'm not saying that either of you have hidden feelings, but I don't like all of these one-on-one events, nor your habit of confiding in him. I want all that to cease. Hey! Would it be so bad if you afforded me the opportunity to become your confidant?" he asked.

"Whew!" Lisa sighed. She was extremely irritated.

"Let me share this… When I was in Junior High, my parents divorced. My father had an affair with his secretary. They married and moved to Europe."

Lisa did not want to pay for his father's mistakes. She tried to stay focused on the issue at hand. "I'm sure that was a difficult time for you," she said.

"It was," he said. "And the worst part is that a few years back I made the same mistake with my secretary. I constantly told myself that we were only lunch buddies and friends—Red flag number one. Well, one day she came over to watch a movie. One thing led to another, and I slept with her." Bartlett stood up and walked back to the patio door. "I don't think she told her husband. He was a good guy. And I made a mistake because I didn't take necessary precautions. It took me a long time to forgive myself. God has really dealt with me and delivered me from years of guilt and shame. I'm just hoping that you can forgive me, and we can move beyond our skeletons and start over together."

For several moments Lisa sat stunned. Her first thought was to run for her life. She was practically living her worst nightmare—lending her trust to a man that had committed adultery. God quickly reminded her that she and Bartlett had been through enough for him to qualify for her trust, and so she stayed. She walked over to Bartlett, and hugged him. "Thank you for sharing your story with me. I know how difficult it must be to discuss." As they stood at the door, she leaned her head into his shoulder. "You don't need my forgiveness. You've received God's forgiveness and you just need to actively forgive yourself."

Lisa knew that Bartlett's request was not unreasonable. She had preached against this very thing to others, and now she had to eat her words. At least Bartlett had given her fair warning. And since she did not want to be hypocritical, as painful as it would be, she knew that separation from David was inevitable. Until that moment, Lisa was not aware of how emotionally attached she was to David. She knew that it was very possible for men and women to be friends, if kept in its proper perspective. However, she also knew that any normal person which spent oodles of time with someone of the opposite sex, was bound to have a spark of emotion or attraction towards the other at some point. *Every sitcom in America has exposed the danger of this, and with just cause. So, if Hollywood can acknowledge it, I guess I can't ignore it,* she silently admitted.

The more she thought, she was flattered that Bartlett had taken the initiative. He could very well have kept his past issues hidden, but he was open and honest and she wanted to return the favor. Through her tears she explained to him that she and David had never done anything outside the boundaries of friendship, and that although it would be difficult, she would find a way to let their relationship fade. Bartlett assured her that he trusted her. "I knew you'd be upset, but this discussion was much-needed." He pulled her close to him.

On the ride home, Lisa called Krystal and told her the whole story. Krystal consoled her here and there, but Lisa could tell that she was distracted. Lisa forgot about herself and unknowingly turned her focus to Krystal. Krystal told her that she was just a little bogged down with her relationship with Jarrett.

Krystal had not told anyone that Jarrett had habits that she had initially overlooked. She had a huge argument with her mom who did not like the fact that he only went to church "once in a while." However, Krystal knew that Jarrett had confessed Christ. In her opinion, he just needed some help with making a stronger commitment to God.

Things really heated up in their first marriage counseling session when Jarrett said that he did not think he needed the Holy Ghost. Krystal knew that could be a huge issue. It had separated denominations of God's people for years, and Krystal was sure that her friends would not approve. They had all agreed that this was a necessary trait. So, she had kept her concerns to herself, and turned the situation over to God. Krystal had also known from day one that Jarrett was an avid smoker, but she had not told anyone that either. Things seemed to be piling up on her. She did not like feeling deceptive.

Jarrett had promised Krystal that he would try to stop smoking and would attend classes to learn more about being filled with the baptism of the Holy Ghost. However, Krystal was fully aware that she could not allow his promise to change to be the basis of her decision to stay in the relationship. She did not know what to do. All she could think about was how much Jarrett adored her. She really wanted to be with him. She did not want to give up on him, nor their relationship. She measured their ability to succeed based on principles that promoted longevity—love, trust, honesty, and integrity.

"Lisa, just pray for me," Krystal said before hanging up.

"I'll pray for you. And please pray for me," Lisa said.

The next morning Bartlett sent roses to Lisa's office with a card that read, "It's beautiful outside. God must have thought of you when he was making this day. I love you. And our love will take us to the other side of this issue."

For months he had wanted to marry Lisa, but he had been seeking God regarding their relationship, and was waiting on His perfect timing. Later that evening he called her. "So, do you still want to be with me, or what?" he asked.

Lisa could not help but laugh. "I'm going to love you forever," she replied.

Lisa was not aware that he had been on her porch the whole time. He finally asked her to come to the door. He was on one knee, surrounded by thirteen dozen roses, one for each month that he had known her.

Lisa had been so relieved. God had granted her request and saved her from another John-Davis-experience—waiting and waiting for the marriage proposal to be initiated, which never happened, then when she finally "forced his hand," he opted to walk away. Lisa remembered praying to God and requesting mercy as soon as she recognized how hard she was falling for Bartlett. She had felt that if he waited too long, things would go sour between them at an exponential rate.

Lisa was elated to get her ring, but even more so to find the thing she had prayed for with intensity for many years. She knew men who were looking for wives, and women looking for husbands. They often settled for the title, without the essence of the position, but Lisa was simply looking for love, trust, and life-long friendship, and she knew that she had found it in Bartlett.

You're Still My Choice

I know what you did!
I saw it!
I was there!

I know who you are!
I saw the masks removed!
I saw you naked!

You asked me a hard thing!
You took me by surprise!
You hurt me!

I cried!
I was devastated!
I forgave you!

I prayed to God!
I was shown myself!
I love you even more!

You were searching for love!
You chose me ultimately!
You changed my outlook!

My ego says leave!
My heart says stay!
My soul confirms that you're still my choice!

Chapter Fifteen
The Lover of My Soul

Lisa started Saturday morning by thanking God for renewing her mind. *I'm not perfect, but I'm glad you labeled me a seed of Your righteousness,* she thought. She repented of her sins, and asked God to help her walk boldly in His assignment for her. He had elevated her in the church and the community, and she could no longer apologize or tiptoe around her divine purpose. *Lord, help me uncover all hidden issues. I want a pure heart towards you and your people,* she prayed.

Immediately, as if at the movies, Mandy Redding's face flashed across the screen of her mind. She went to the file cabinet to get the note Krystal had given her at the Lewis's home. She dialed the number, but hung up quickly. She did not know what to say. However she had to surpass this roadblock on the road to her goal of obtaining freedom and peace of mind.

Lisa had loved Mandy as a sister. They had been roommates since freshman year, and did everything together on campus. However, after college, Lisa found out that Mandy had led a double life. Mandy had used her calling card without permission and ran the bill up to $800. When Lisa confronted her, she said that she thought it was hers, "…but don't worry. I'm expecting a lump-sum settlement soon," she had said. After trying to track her down, to no avail, Lisa heard from a mutual friend, that she had moved to Florida. Her great-aunt had left her in charge of her estate. He also mistakenly mentioned that it was Mandy who had lied to John about Lisa cheating on him. Lisa had promised him that she would not repeat what he had told her.

Mandy had also used Lisa's license several times. She used it to open an electricity account, because she had bad credit and a balance from the utility in Texas, where she had done a summer intern. Lisa had felt bad afterwards, but she had called and had the electricity turned off as soon as she found out. And the worst of all things she had done was use it in a gay bar, while trying to be incognito.

This instance hurt Lisa the most because after four years of living with her, she found out that Mandy was bisexual. Lisa had a low tolerance for bisexuals and homosexuals. It was a very touchy issue with her. While in high school, she had gone out with a guy who was very popular. When Lisa would not have sex with him, he spread a rumor throughout the entire school that she was a lesbian. Since then, Lisa had a hatred towards homosexual behavior. She knew that she was not a homosexual, but it had hurt her badly when people kept asking. She had a similar occurrence in college. When people found out that she was trying to uphold a standard of sexual morality, they had labeled her a queer. She was considered an outcast and it took her a long time to be confident in who she was, and ignore their slandering.

Lisa could not understand Mandy. They had grown up in church and learned that homosexuality was wrong, that Sodom and Gomorrah was destroyed because of such sin, and that it was the most abominable form of fornication imaginable. They defended their beliefs with Romans 1:27, "And the men also turned from natural relations with women and were set ablaze (burning out, consumed) with lust for one another—men committing shameful acts with men and suffering in their own bodies and personalities the inevitable consequences and penalty of their wrongdoing and going astray, which was [their] fitting retribution."

Lisa really wanted to reach out to Mandy, but she could barely look pass her bitterness and resentment for the conniving things she had done. The few times she had seen her, she had seen the hurt and despair in Mandy' eyes. Yet she had not forgiven her. Lisa had kept Mandy's secret, but she had also blanked her out of her life as if she never existed. Mandy had written Lisa and tried to apologize several times, but Lisa had thrown the letters out and never responded.

In Lisa's mind, bisexual and homosexual people had made an open choice to be the way they were, and there was not much she could do to help. They believed that their lifestyle was acceptable to God, and so she would not waste her time convincing them of otherwise. Lisa had never shared her pain as a result of her bouts of celibacy in high school or college. However, it was time she shared it with Mandy. When she finished praying, she dialed her number. Mandy answered on the first ring, as if she had been anticipating her call.

Lisa got right to the point. "You're forgiven. I've released you of any debt you owe me. And in spite of it all, I still love you and I want you to know that I'm still concerned about your well-being." Lisa really wanted to minister to her, but she was not sure of Mandy's mind set, or if she would hear her out. She knew that she was being somewhat harsh in her approach, but she wanted to be honest. "Mandy, I won't try to force you into believing that you're leading a lifestyle that's against God's will for you. I think you have your own convictions. And if you think that this is how God made you, then I won't waste my time. But if you know that God made you a woman, and has ordained a lifestyle that doesn't require you to be promiscuous and confused, then we can talk," Lisa said.

To her surprise, Mandy opened up immediately. "When the opportunity presented itself, I was hurt because of Derek and thought friendship and love with a woman was the answer. I hid my secrets and feelings behind bisexuality. I know deep down that I'm not pleasing God, and therefore I can't please myself. I have no peace. I can't sleep. As The Bible says, to be carnally minded causes torturous death, but there's life and peace in living according to God's Word." Mandy was crying. "The world tries to glorify this lifestyle. They don't talk about the anguish, and thoughts of suicide from trying to convince yourself that your abnormality is okay. It's like people are rooting you on to 'choose controversy', no matter how wrong, instead of what's going to ultimately bring peace. That's why you can't live life worrying about people. They have something to say no matter what." She sniffed. "I'm glad God gives every person a chance to get it right, even poor, little, insignificant me."

While talking to Mandy, God revealed to Lisa that *He* had ordained the physical and emotional differences and distinctions between men and women. Lisa told Mandy that she felt that society tried to make it seem as if there was no such thing as male and female, or right and wrong anymore; that the term "moral" was obsolete. "But God always has a remnant of righteous folks," Lisa concluded, "to help us admit that it's easy to become slaves to our weaknesses. For the most part, people want to be free, but they don't want to acknowledge that its Jesus that makes us free. We're worried about being exposed, when we should be focusing on freedom. That's why I like to talk one-on-one, people are less defensive and more receptive and honest."

"Yeah, I definitely know a lot of confused people, male and female, that I've been trying to minister to. I'm thinking of starting an organization to reach out to these people," Mandy said. Before they hung up, Mandy said something that Lisa could really relate to: "I found out that we so easily accept a counterfeit of love because we never truly give ourselves over to God to experience the real thing."

Lisa was so glad to have had that conversation with Mandy. She felt so free afterwards.

Around that time, Pastor Lindsay started preaching about the importance of tithes and offerings. He admonished them to view money as an opportunity to sow into God's kingdom, not just income to pay bills and buy stuff. "Leaders must know how to give," he said. Lisa was a faithful giver, although several times she had missed paying her tithes. She had felt awful. Her mother had taught her it was like "robbing God." She prayed that God would make her a tither in her heart. While praying, God told her to stop borrowing if she wanted to get ahead. So, for several weeks after paying bills, she could barely afford to put gas in her truck, but she cut up her credit cards and waited for God to bless her obedience.

Within that same period, a visiting evangelist came and cosigned practically everything Pastor Lindsay had been preaching. She prophesied that God would do some things "suddenly and mightily" if they kept trusting Him. "That's just how He works. It doesn't take Him a long time to break the yokes of bondage," she said, "The way to receive is to give. The Bible instructs in Luke 6:38, '*Give*, and it shall be given unto you; good measure, pressed down, and shaken together, and running over, shall men give into your bosom.'"

In obedience, Lisa bagged up four coats, 19 pairs of jeans, 12 sweaters, 13 dresses, and 17 pairs of shoes, and took them to some twin sisters that attended her church. The look on their mom's face when she gave her the clothes had made Lisa feel so good. Lisa was learning to involve God in her finances by trusting Him with her money, which was not always an easy task. And just as the prophecy came forth, as she continued to sow seeds, "suddenly" God showed up and blessed her.

She received a call from the CEO of a huge civic organization. Mrs. Starchill, an I.N.C. Board member, and long time friend of Uncle Theo's, had recommended Lisa to help her do research on educational programs in the inner city. Lisa had gladly helped her without charge. The CEO said she was very impressed. "Your work was very outstanding and professional work. And since you're a director of a non-profit organization, I'm going to authorize a grant. This is usually only done for Perkins loan recipients, but I have extra money that I must spend within this fiscal year, so, I'm going to make an exception for you," she told Lisa. The next week, she wrote a check to Lisa's Stafford Loan lender for $66,664.44. Lisa knew it was a gift from God, not because of what had happened, but because of how it had happened.

Lisa was finally at a point where she did not want to do anything to jeopardize God's grace or trust, nor the trust she had established with Bartlett. So, on the ride home from their second marriage counseling session, Lisa released all of her issues to Bartlett. She finally gave him details about her past financial woes. She told him that by the time she graduated from college, she had racked up over $50,000 in credit card debt, in addition to her student loan debt. She had considered filing for bankruptcy, at the advice of a friend of the family. Yet she had been cursed enough in her finances, so she began to slowly but surely work on relinquishing her debts. It had been over six years, and she was almost halfway there. "I don't want you to have to pay for my mistakes," she told him.

Although Bartlett had never had to struggle financially, he had been very sympathetic. He told Lisa that he would not hold her to the mistakes of her past, but that he would teach her how to be a good steward over her finances. His credit history was perfect. He was practically debt-free. He had paid off his home, and owned several rental properties and a vacation home in the south. He told Lisa not to worry because together, they could handle her current bills without a hitch. "I'm not going to be judgmental. I think at some point in life, we all get tired of working hard and not having anything of substance to show for it. And I think you've finally learned your lesson. How about I'll agree to teach you everything I know, if you're willing to learn, that is. Just promise me that I won't wake up one day and all of my money will be gone," he joked. "Although if I had to choose between you and money, you'd be my choice hands down," he assured her.

Soon afterwards, Bartlett made Lisa prove her willingness to change by sending her to a 12-week financial workshop. Lisa learned a lot about eliminating and reducing the use of credit, and establishing short-range and long-range savings plans. Through attendance, she re-established her 401(k) savings, and began contributing to a mutual fund. Lisa was so grateful that Bartlett had been supportive, but she did not want him to think that she was trying to take advantage of him. "I don't want you to think that..."

Bartlett cut her off. He would not let her throw a pity party. "I think God says, 'Hey, since this is your downfall, I might as well use it to prove you and draw you closer to Me'. If you'd never had financial issues, you wouldn't know, first hand, how it feels to be free from them, and what Christ can do in your finances. That's why I'm a firm believer that the Bible is the best-seller of all time. And Jesus is the best storyteller. Just consider how the old testament shows us so many times the foreshadowing of Christ's coming. That let's me know that He's not an after thought, or plan B. But He was in the original plan. God did all this to show man that it's impossible to become clean and pure through the sacrifices and rudiments of the law, but that we need Christ's one-time blood sacrifice to make us pure. Now, He could have come right from the beginning, but when there's a delay with our reward, we tend to have a greater appreciation."

After Lisa completed the workshop, she was still somewhat hesitant about her financial stability, although she was grateful that she and Bartlett had confronted it before they married. She was glad to have found someone to love her; someone who new her mistakes and still chose to stick by her side. "I know it's not easy to trust someone or share your finances with them when they haven't had a very good track record," she said. "I love you. Thanks for not giving up on me."

He hugged her tightly. "Hey, I feel like you've done the same for me and my issues. That's why we make such a great team," he replied.

Bartlett later gave her a card which read, "If I could, I would take your place and not allow you to experience any sorrow. But since I cannot I will do my part by helping to share your load." He told her that she should not look at her struggles as hindrances, but opportunities to grow. "After all, the steps of a good man are ordered by the Lord. God is a Wonder. He uses all of our experiences to bring us to an expected end of victory and peace. And I want you to walk boldly in His promises. There's a certain posture of confidence and faith you should have when you trust in this great God."

Shortly thereafter, Lisa went home from a long day of reviewing reports and preparing another technical presentation for her boss, and sat down at her computer to type up her letter of resignation from Corporate America. She had been working two jobs long enough. She felt kind of sad that this chapter of her life was coming to an end, but at the same time she was elated at what was evolving, especially between she and Bartlett. It was like a dream come true, and she owed it all to God. There were amazing things taking place, and she was at a huge turning point in her life. *Lord, why do we make this love thing so hard. All we have to do is turn our dreams and goals over to you,* she thought.

That evening, she also spent time tying up loose ends for "The I.N.C's" kickoff fundraiser. Afterwards, she was fairly tired. She prepared for bed, and then called her mom who was very encouraging, as usual. Her stepfather, was in the background teasing her, as usual. "Who's the "Boyfriend of the Week, Mona Lisa? Kareem, or is it still Baritone, or something like that?" Lisa realized it may take him a while to realize that she was finally settling down.

She was tired, but excited when she got a call from Tiffany and Kanisha, two of the young people she tutored. They called about math, which somehow led to inquiries about James. "He's cute. I think he still likes you, even though Elaine's always in his face," Tiffany said. Lisa ignored her. Kanisha insisted that he was dating the "light-skinned lady that we saw him at the mall with." Lisa figured he was probably dating both of them.

Kanisha commented that she "heard" that Lisa went to Krystal's party with Bartlett. "Oh yeah, that's right! That's that guy I saw you whispering and caking with after Bible Study," Tiffany said. Although they had inquired about James, Lisa knew it was just a matter of time before they brought Bartlett into the conversation, and whoever else they could pin on her.

"What is caking?" Lisa asked.

"You know what caking is—two people drooling all over each other like they have to be together 24 hours a day, 7 days a week," Kanisha said.

"Right, like they can't breathe unless they're together. I saw the way he was looking at you, too," Tiffany said.

"And you like him, too," Kanisha said.

"Let me tell you something, if I'm ever with a man, you can rest assured it's not because I like him, but because he's consumed with my being," Lisa said. "And on that note, goodnight." She remembered being a teenybopper. No need to get them more roused up than they already were.

Before they hung up Tiffany said, "Sister Lisa, I want you to know that I love you and that I kept our promise!"

Lisa was elated. Previously, Tiffany had asked for her advice about contraceptives. Lisa knew, all too well, the prompting of the enemy regarding fornication and the sexual schemes he used to trick even God's people. Lisa told her it would be best to wait. "Well, what if we only…" Tiffany had begun to say.

"Let me help you out," Lisa had cut her off. "I have an equation for you. Sex organs being involved equals sex."

"Oh, well never mind. I guess that answers my question."

Lisa told her that she was not missing out on anything, and that fornication was overrated. "Sex only complicates things. Playing with the idea will only take you farther away from God than you've ever thought you could be. It'll make you feel dirty. It snatches away your innocence and forces you to deal with stuff that God ordained for people in covenant with one another, not people who *think* they're in love." Lisa told Tiffany that once she became sexually active, it would be very hard to stop. "It can easily turn into you guys using one another for sex. And I know that sometimes it feels right, but if you break up with him, then the next guy becomes the exception, and the next, until you end up with a string of sexual partners. And your intent was simply to show your love. And don't feel bad if you have to separate yourself from those who make you think it's okay to compromise your standards of holiness."

Lisa remembered that she had done things with James that she had promised not to do again until marriage. Technically, they did not have a sexual relationship, but it had been carnal, nonetheless. She finally had to tell James that if he did not stop asking her to sleep with him she would not see him any more. She point blank told him, "If I have sex with you I'll never marry you and I probably won't like you or respect you much after that either!"

Lisa told Tiffany to have a talk with her boyfriend. "Just tell him that you love God, that His Word teaches against such practices, for obvious reasons, and that you're saving sex for marriage. I mean people tend to think that teen pregnancy and contracting STD's is inevitable, but I'm here to tell you that it can be avoided. And furthermore, it's just not worth it."

After Lisa hung up with the teens, she went downstairs to fix a snack. When David called, she had eaten and was asleep on the couch. David sounded distraught. Lisa tried to pry unnoticeably. He finally told her that he and Susan had decided to go their separate ways.

"I knew Pastor Henry was talking to me when he taught about not settling until God answers your prayers," David said. "I had had to let go because

Susan's just too content with mediocrity. I admit that it was very hard to walk away but if I have to, I'll rebuke the devils of compromise and complacency every day. The relationship wasn't growing, and thus I wasn't growing as an individual."

Lisa remembered feeling the same way with James. Yet, although she had gone through a period of stunted growth with John, somehow she had still wanted to make their relationship work. "David, I've been thinking..."

"Don't hurt yourself!" he joked.

"Ha! Ha! Ha! You Clown, Listen. I've been in relationships that made me feel like I wasn't growing. One, I walked away from without too much heartache, but the other, I found it very hard to walk away, even knowing that things were going sour. That relationship literally cost me my emotional stability, but I was still willing to make it work. So, I'm just wondering what the difference was there. Do you think that our standards are too high and we expect too much of others?"

"No, I don't. Frankly, I think life is all about choices and responsibility. And it's important that we're honest about what we're willing to live with."

"I agree. I was hoping that it wasn't just me," she said. "I remember being in a prayer service, and this minister walked up to me and started rubbing my back. She prophesied that God was going to birth things out of me, and that it was time for me to walk in my purpose. And then all of a sudden she whispered very lightly, 'Don't settle. Not even a little bit.' At the time, I didn't know if she was referring to ministry or my personal life. I see now that the two go hand in hand. What she said stuck with me. And so, I agree with you. If you haven't found what you want, then by all means, don't settle. In fact, raise the bar even higher."

David agreed. "I have to wake up with this person. I have to be realistic. Susan had absolutely no motivation, no spirit, no drive to do anything but have a husband, 2.3 kids, and a dog, and then die. She doesn't have the 'oomph' I need. I kind of settled for her because she's pretty, and she's been in holiness a long time. I really wanted things to work out between us, but, I need a little more."

"I understand, completely," Lisa said.

"I'm wondering how she grew up in church and only attended prayer meeting after I suggested it, or stopped listening to secular music only when I told her that it was carnal and stunting her spiritual growth. Man, if I were on my death bed, I don't know if her prayers would save me or not. I've wanted to settle down for quite some time, but after all this time of sharing my life with her, I couldn't do it. I think I was mostly in love with the idea of having her around. And I recognize that's a serious problem. So, I have to move on. No, I don't think I have unrealistic expectations at all. Forget being unequally yoked. How can two walk together except they agree?" David was frustrated.

"Have you ever thought that maybe she sincerely wanted to do those things before, but you gave her that extra push she needed?"

"Or, maybe she just did it to make me happy, and one day she won't care, and she'll stop going to prayer, and start back going to the bar to be happy."

"Perhaps… But perhaps you think too much," Lisa said.

"So, you're asking me if I'm being unrealistic in wanting someone who fasted, prayed, and lived sold-out for Christ before we met? Well, I sincerely hope that's a reasonable request of the almighty God I serve."

The conversation ended shortly afterwards and Lisa knew that was likely one of their last conversations. She had mixed emotions, but she knew that it signified growth and her ability to walk into her new life with Bartlett, freely. Immediately after they hung up, Lisa called Bartlett and tried to relay the whole conversation to him. He kept assuring her that it was not necessary, and that he trusted her. He was glad that she was open. "Although, I'm not particularly interested in receiving every detail of the conversation," he said, jokingly.

Lisa remembered that she had often thought that she would never find the man of her dreams, but once she sat back and trusted God, he sent Bartlett her way. She had passed the stage where she pouted and gave up on God when things did not go her way. And He had proven Himself to be faithful.

There was still certain drama she wished she had alleviated. It seemed to take her years to learn what most learned in days, but it taught her to wait patiently on God.

Late one evening, Lisa lie on the couch thinking about Bartlett. *He is beautiful,* she thought. Lisa also felt good that she had found someone who her friends could be proud of. David and Cliff were relieved. Tonya practically preached about the importance of finding someone who qualified for her affection. She did not mention James, but Lisa knew that she was referring to him when she said, "The Bible teaches us not to cast our pearls before swine. They can't recognize anything's value—whether trash, or a 10 karat diamond, it's all going in the mud." Lauren reacted in her typical rowdy way, saying Bartlett was "the Bomb." Krystal said, "I always did appreciate a man who handled his business in a timely fashion." She knew that she did not need their seal of approval, but it still made her feel good.

Lisa was especially happy that she could trust Bartlett with her most sensitive issues. She was amazed at his confidence in her ability to overcome her past, and God's ability to use her testimony to deliver others. "I appreciate you as a virtuous woman and plan to treat you accordingly," he said. He was glad to have found love, trust and companionship in her—they could be there for each other in the good times, and support and encourage each other in the bad times. "I've heard that your relationship with your mate is God's way of showing you, in the flesh, a picture of your spiritual relationship with Himself. I plan to spend a lifetime reaching my goal of becoming one with Christ and one with you."

Lisa loved Bartlett's personality. Besides always having the right words, he was very manly, but never too harsh; and always calm and confident. He was everything she wanted—a "righteous, high-class, thug", as Krystal had said.

In the past, Lisa wanted to marry to be rescued, but now she knew it was about giving and ministry. She had felt that the mistakes of her past relationships would be the death of her. Yet at that moment, she acknowledged that a rough start only gives a mature individual a greater appreciation for a smooth landing. In retrospect, she saw that for various reasons, some beyond her control, things had not worked out with her past relationships. She also realized that there would not always be a clear, concise explanation for every decision made. Life was certainly about choices. This particular time her choice seemed easier than ever. She opted to marry Bartlett because she recognized her need to give away love to someone who loved her so much.

Lisa remembered Barb saying that in marriage counseling, Pastor Lindsay had asked the infamous question, "Is there anyone more suitable for you?" Lisa thought about what she would do when it was her turn to be put on the spot. She saw the results of Bartlett's labor. He spent time seeking God, and placed his goals and desires in God's hands. This was very important to her. She knew that he was the best choice. And she was looking forward to a lifetime of falling in love with her choice, over and over again. She concluded there was no other man more suitable for her and began to prepare herself mentally for their plans to marry the following year. Just as Christ was the lover of her soul spiritually, Bartlett was the lover of her soul naturally.

Lisa finally got off the couch and went upstairs to bed. She began her nightly prayer thanking the Lord for all He had taught her about love—it bears, believes, hopes and endures.

The Lover of My Soul

My love speaks to me in the midnight hour.
I hear his voice ever so clearly then.
When everything else is laying dormant,
his voice whispers to me like a calm wind.
His touch is ever so gentle.
His words are filled with grace.
When failure and anguish came to taunt me,
He humbled Himself and took my place.
So when I see others hurting,
and living lives full of anguish and defeat,
my heart goes out to rescue them,
as the lover of my soul does for me!

Chapter Sixteen
Being in Love as One

Lisa sat on the deck of the home she now shared with her husband and breathed in the spring air. Although life had been difficult, she did not give up, and her personal struggles had not prohibited her from prospering.

Besides the wonderful developments taking place in her life, those around her were also in the season of prosperity. Cliff and Ahnna were now in wedded bliss. Mark and Tonya opened a family crisis center. Mike and Dee were expecting Mike, Jr. Mr. And Mrs. Townsend were building a new home. Angie got a promotion, and she and Brandi were moving to Schaumburg, Illinois. Charles and Shelly had split up, but he had found a nice young lady in New York. Lauren was still happily being Lauren, as only she could. Even Jasmine and her boyfriend had reunited and eloped. David finally launched out and opened a business. Lisa teased that he broke up with Susan because Angie was relocating to the area. He insisted he was not interested in the drama associated with a ready-made family. Lisa was not discouraged. She had never informed David of Bartlett's concerns. She had simply cut their interactions significantly, and was hoping that someone like Angie would be good for him and could help distract things even more. Carefree Krystal had married Jarrett via a wedding ceremony in the Pastor's office, and was on her honeymoon in Hawaii. Lisa teased her for "making her man wait," but she was glad that he won his prize.

They all had a long talk with Krystal before the wedding, prior to which, Krystal had given "the gang" the silent treatment for months. Lisa had called her once during that time, and ended up wishing that she had not even bothered. She had asked Krystal if there was something specific that she needed prayer for. Krystal had been very curt and withdrawn, and had blown up at her. "I don't need your help or advice. Stop trying to solve the world's problems and concentrate on your own." Lisa had ended the conversation quickly and cried herself to sleep.

She wondered if everyone thought of her that way. She was only trying to be encouraging and helpful, not all-knowing or cocky. All she had ever tried to do was shed some light and help people see things from a clearer perspective. It had naturally evolved into her mission in life. Yet the more she helped, the more she was rejected. She figured everyone needed balance in their lives, which is why she constantly sought an outside voice of reason, without which, she felt she might only make rash decisions. Her brother had long since labeled her a tattletale— always telling on somebody, or telling them about themselves. He said she was more like a flashlight and that people did not want her always exposing their mistakes. Tonya agreed. "Folks know their actions are detrimental, and they usually don't want to hear it from someone else," she had said.

Lisa read what she had written in her Psalms booklet the night Krystal hurt her. "Lopsided viewpoints! We all have them! You and I got along wonderfully, until your streamlined thinking was interrupted by the light I shed. I carried the infamous torch of honor, yet I got burned. I was only trying to help! I'm sorry if I hurt you, but whenever I show up there's illumination. And I can only be myself. Hopefully, in the end you'll thank me for bringing you closer to the center! The view is better there anyway!" Lisa imagined herself saying this to those she had hurt by giving her unwanted opinion, and prayed for God's wisdom, sympathy and love.

Finally, when they could not bear it any longer, Lisa, Tonya and Cliff drove over to Krystal's. And without any pressure, she told them why she had been neglecting them. She said that she felt as if Jarrett did not measure up to their standards. She assumed that since they had all found mates that were strong in their Christian faith, they would be judgmental of her choice. She admitted that she had been hiding things from the very beginning. "I wasn't sure you guys would understand. I love him, and I want to help him work through his issues. That's a decision that I had to make on my own, without any input from anyone but me and God," she had said.

Tonya had told her that there was never a need to explain love because giving reasons only devalues it. She said, "I love my husband because he cares for me and our children, but if he stops, my love will still be extended towards him. Love just loves."

They were back to their normal, analytical selves in no time. They all seemed to be heading in different directions, but they still recognized that they needed one another. "I wish you'd given us the benefit-of-the-doubt. We've had numerous conversations and agreed that the packaging love comes in, is not as important as what's inside," Lisa said.

"You can't relate. You got everything you wanted in Bartlett," Krystal said.

Lisa consoled Krystal, while being sure not to uncover or expose her husband's weaknesses. "I don't think that's ever true as it relates to any relationship. It's give and take. I choose to love him in spite of, and he does the same for me. I mean, you know how hesitant I was about him because of his alleged history as a chronic womanizer," she joked.

"Oh, please! What man isn't a womanizer at some point in his life?" Krystal asked. She smiled, knowing Cliff would have a defensive statement awaiting her.

"And what woman hasn't been a 'mananizer', for lack of a better term, at some point?" Cliff jokingly gave her exactly what she expected.

"My definition of a womanizer or 'mananizer,'" Tonya said, looking at Cliff, "is someone who's at a point where their not serious enough to settle down."

"Or someone who's selfish and ornery," Lisa mumbled.

Tonya continued. "So, I guess I'm actually agreeing with Cliff, for a change. That's a problem for both men and women."

"Especially women. You know how temperamental you are."

"Women?" Krystal asked, shaking her head. Lisa, Krystal, and Tonya agreed that they would let that one slide.

Krystal had assured them that she and Jarrett shared mutual love and respect for one another. "I'm glad we met now. Why didn't anyone warn me about being 31 and single? 30 was nice to me, but 31 will try to turn you into a fornicating mess," she joked.

Tonya and Lisa totally understood. Lisa had only heard horror stories, and knew at least three women who lost their virginity the month of their 31st birthdays. Cliff covered his ears. "Please don't make me sit through this!" He did not want to hear about the intense sex drive of a woman in her thirties.

Bartlett poked through the patio door, interrupting Lisa reading and writing in her journal. "Mrs. Hartins, are you sending your husband off into the cold world without any loving?"

"No, I'm going to spoil my baby, as always," she smiled. She walked into the house, realizing that in just 18 months, her life had changed drastically. She had gotten married. She was teaching the church youth group. And they had been offering full services at Hart to Hart for about a year. She could not explain it, except that God had chosen it as her appointed season of manifestation.

The next morning, Lisa awoke to the sound of the local weather and traffic report on her clock radio. Bartlett was sleeping soundly. She opened her Psalms booklet and began to write. Reflecting on her life, which had gotten pretty hectic, and proven to be a long treacherous battle, she thanked God for having Bartlett to share her life with.

She was thankful to have her sanity after the many ordeals she encountered. Her struggle had been mostly mental. She often thought she was crazy for spending so much time talking to herself and God. However, she figured she was no different from any other person who lie in bed at the end of the day, reflecting on their lives, or stealing away to pray for change, at some point in their day. For a long time, she disliked the part of her personality which caused her to have "joking spasms" or constantly reflect on her past. However, she realized that although her reflections and "spasms" were a bit extreme, they had helped her press forward.

Her leadership teacher had said, "There are three voices that we hear—God, the devil and our flesh." Initially Lisa had envisioned a dangerous schizophrenic person, but later she had thought, *So, I'm normal for hearing voices.* Her failures had come from listening to the wrong voices—being obedient to the devil and her flesh, instead of her God. She was now learning to decipher which thoughts to keep, and which to ignore or shut out of her life forever. She was now victorious in the battleground of her mind.

The devil had fought her heavily, trying to make her ashamed of her past, present, and the future she had not even encountered. Yet God had taken her to a new level, as she had prayed many times, and she was learning to partake in His forgiveness daily through repentance.

She was thankful for her victories, and thus trials, which she encountered with each new level. She had used an analogy about levels to teach leadership to her teens. It was an ice-breaking discussion and her students had really opened up. They were discussing strategizing against their opponents of peer pressure, low self-esteem, doubt, and fear of failure. She told them about her favorite word game, which had an endless number of levels. "The most challenging part is reaching the next level. The higher the level, the more difficult the words become, yet the associated points are also higher." She was sure they could relate because most of them were experts on computer games. She was elated when one of her astute students raised his hand. "So, Mrs. Hartins, you're saying that the most successful people are those who defeat the most obstacles."

She told them that this was a principle they could apply to every area of their lives. She had picked up a lesson from each of her trials. And each test had only made her stronger—in her finances, prayer life, career, and divine purpose. She had been promoted from level to level even in her relationships, and now she was reaping the ultimate benefits—eternal covenant with Christ and Bartlett.

The devil had tried to discourage her from doing many things, including teaching, but with each temptation, God had given her a way of escape. Her enemy had tried to convince her that she had nothing of substance to impart or offer to the young people. But Lisa knew otherwise. She was no longer the "Princess of the Giving-Up Village", she was now the "Queen of Survivor Town", which she learned from the smaller children during Self-Esteem Week.

Lisa had stayed in place and survived. And now she could impart into others how to stick with the things of God without wavering. If she had never gotten to the other side of her issues, she would not have known by experience that she could defeat the spirits of distraction, torment, suicide, depression, fornication, and any others that came against her. If she had not defeated them, she would not have accessed the power to help others defeat them. She rebuked the devil, because after all, it was not her that they needed, nor her attitude or idiosyncrasies, it was the gift inside of her and she was ready to share it. She gave them what God had given her, anything more or less, would only be a counterfeit.

After teaching the "Girl Talk" class for several weeks, Lisa was so thankful of God's faithfulness to her. Those young ladies badly needed to be taught about self-esteem and self-respect, which boiled down to many discussions about boys. Lisa used her experience to teach them how to avoid the mistakes she had made, which made them even more willing to listen to her. She was glad to give away God's eternal wisdom through the gift of teaching.

The young ladies reminded her of herself as a teen. She had been strong-spirited academically, but very emotional about boys. Lisa thought about the discussion they had had when Natalie had dumped her boyfriend. "I love him, but I'm tired of worrying about him cheating on me," she had said. When she burst into tears, Lisa quickly ran and gave her a hug. "Natalie, it's okay, sweetie." She had gotten her and the rest of the class to laugh as she said, "And don't feel bad if you take him back."

"I just wish I could go three days without talking to him," Natalie had said. She could never bring herself to turn him down when he asked for her help with his homework and stuff. Lisa knew how it felt to want to cut someone off and not have the necessary willpower. "Well, don't worry about that. Honestly, it only causes more stress to convince yourself that you need to determine right now what you're going to do next week about him. Take it one day at a time," Lisa had said.

Even the smallest of Lisa's interactions at "The I.N.C." reminded her of God's goodness. She ran into an old childhood neighbor. Mrs. Mallory had twin, teenage daughters that Lisa had grown very fond of. She was glad to see their family doing so well, years later. Mrs. Mallory had just retired from teaching and was a volunteer at Hart to Hart. She and several of the other parents had enjoyed watching Lisa teach and tutor. They particularly enjoyed how she always included Biblical principles in her teaching. "When did you get your certification?" Mrs. Mallory had asked. They were shocked to find that Lisa's degree was in Engineering and that she had spent the bulk of her career in Corporate America. All Lisa could do was smile. She knew that it was not her natural ability they recognized, but a spiritual gift from God.

Lisa had also become bolder and wiser in her witnessing techniques for sharing the Gospel of Jesus Christ. There was the time she had pulled over and witnessed to a young couple. They had stopped at the light and saw her bobbing her head and using her steering wheel as the drum. They assumed that she was listening to the latest secular jam, but she told them that she was praising God and singing songs that would deliver her spirit, not just cater to the desires of her flesh. She had given them a card for the community center, and also invited them to church. The young man told her that he was glad that he had run into her because it helped him to realize that he needed to get back to his roots in the church.

It was after that incident, that Lisa and Bartlett made a pact to go out monthly to witness in the community. They signed up to talk to incarcerated youth and volunteered to teach on a college campus. It had been such fun sharing their stories of planting seeds, praying with people, and even being rejected. Lisa recalled witnessing to the man who was replacing their neighbor's windows. His truck was parked near their house and he was enjoying a cigarette when she pulled up. She told him, "You know I just made a new rule that since you get to stand near my property and smoke, I get to talk to you about the love of Jesus Christ." He said that he might try to come to church to learn more, but that he could not promise to stop smoking. Lisa did not mind, she was just glad to be able to share the gospel with him.

As Lisa dreamed, she had a marriage filled with lots of love and friendship. She and Bartlett were actively assisting in changing the lives of others, which helped bond them even closer. The time they spent working at Hart to Hart, with "their children" was invaluable. Almost weekly they took walks in the park or sat in front of the fireplace at home and shared their thoughts in accordance with their vow to keep the lines of communication flowing. They visited senior citizen's homes. They volunteered to pass out meals during the holidays. They both loved poetry and had done several poetry readings together in a café uptown. "With my wit, your charm, and our love for words, you and I make the perfect prose," Bartlett had said. Lisa thought that was so corny, but she was glad that he valued their togetherness. The most fun, yet exhausting thing they had done, was spend three hours putting together his mother's futon. Bartlett had finally admitted that he needed a "power nap", but Lisa was in handyman mode, and did not stop until it was finished.

They had also experienced some turbulence. There was the time that Bartlett stayed out until 4 a.m. with his college buddies. "We were just shooting pool," he had said. "I didn't plan to stay that late, that's why I didn't call, and I didn't know you called because my phone was in the car. Besides I didn't want to wake you." Lisa wondered if there were women there, and what else had taken place.

Bartlett had gotten extremely upset with her. She had told him right then, that she was trying her best not to be jealous or untrusting. "If you say that's all that happened, though, I'll believe you," she had said. "And I'll be done with it, but I'm not pleased, and I don't want it to happen again, so…"

"So, I won't have to hear about this again?" Bartlett had asked. "Speak now or forever hold your peace," he had teased.

"You were playing pool with the guys and lost track of time, right? You thought it not best to call, and I'll just have to trust your judgment, now won't I?"

After she said that, Bartlett had perked up immediately.

There was also the time they had their first major argument, which at the time, Lisa called, "The Fight of the Century." As she looked back, the ordeal seemed so minor. She had spent almost $3,000 on clothes, shoes, furniture, and house wares. She had not shopped in a long time and had gotten some very good deals she could not pass up.

They planned to renovate their basement, but Bartlett had been busy with work, and helping her run the community center, so she had taken the initiative. She had also hired a contractor for $2,400. Lisa thought she was giving him a great surprise, but when she told him about her purchases, the look in his eyes was probably the meanest look she had ever seen on his face. It was also the maddest she had ever been with him. "You have three business days to cancel that contract before it's binding," he had said.

Lisa could not believe he reacted so harshly. It was a great opportunity for them to finish their basement, change the blinds in their guest rooms, and replace the doors to their master bedroom. He had not given her a budget, and she thought he would be proud. The money she spent was only a small percentage of their savings. *It's my money that goes into the savings account, since you maintain the bills,* she had thought.

Almost in one breath, he had told her to return her items, and then tried to convince her that they should pay $6,000 in tuition for his cousin in California. "Her parents came up on some hard times," Bartlett said. "That's much better use of our money. And Lisa we both know the value of a good education."

"She's not our child, nor our responsibility."

"Yeah, but we have the means to be a blessing to her. You remember how tough things were financially when you were in college. And you also remember how unburdening it felt when Mrs. Langster relieved you of your student loans."

"Whatever! If that's what you want to do then fine!" Lisa was really upset. "It's obviously not my place to make such decisions anyway."

Bartlett ignored Lisa's direct slash at his ability to lead their family. He knew that she was responding out of anger. "Lisa, we have plenty of time to renovate. We discussed in detail that we'd do it over a period of months, and not with one lump sum. I don't think I'm being irrational. You went outside of our original agreement."

"But we planned to pay your cousin's tuition?" she asked sarcastically. "Did I miss something, here?"

"You don't need those clothes, nor were those repairs an emergency. We're still learning the lesson of delayed gratification. This stuff's going back! All of it! That's the bottom line." Bartlett's voice softened. "Wonderful, we promised God that we'd give to His people, and this is an excellent opportunity to be a blessing. And once you look pass all of your momentary hurt, I know you'll agree."

Lisa was tired of Bartlett seemingly pushing a button and a syncopated, recorded, response popping out of his mouth. "Can we have a normal discussion, please?" She was so upset she began to cry. She stormed out of the room, not wanting him to see her so distraught. Although the issue was borderline petty, she could not seem to calm down or let it go. She called her mother. "Bartlett and I are having a disagreement about money. What should I do?"

Mrs. Townsend consoled Lisa as only a mother could. "Lisa, I'm telling you this because I love you. When you think about it, you'll see that this is not worth causing division, and anxiety. Even when I'm mad at your dad, I try my best not to walk away. I need him by my side even then. And the reason I can say that after all of these years is because I keep my heart soft towards him. You can't let issues fester, and get blown out of proportion. Handle them immediately."

"Mom, I know but it hurts so bad! Bartlett hates me. I can't do this marriage stuff anymore."

"Yes you can, sweetie. He's the same man you were *so* convinced God had heavenly orchestrated to be in your life. In order to stay in love, you have to stay focused on the object of your affection. Lisa, people you love have the ability to hurt you deeply, but, you can't allow it to affect your love towards them. And at some point they have, or will have to do the same for you. Besides, how can you say that you love God, whom you've never seen, and can't stop bickering and fighting with your husband, whom you see everyday. It doesn't work that way. Things are first natural, and then spiritual. We must learn these lessons naturally, and then and only then, can we apply them spiritually. The benefit of marriage is found when all is said and done, and you're still happy, sharing, and giving selflessly. You'll be happy you stayed and endured. The end of a thing should be better than the beginning, just as the Word of God says. Happy endings aren't reserved for fairy tales. We just need patience."

"Easier said than done! I'm getting a divorce. He hates me," Lisa whispered.

"Sweetie, just go talk with him calmly, and I do mean calmly."

"I want to, but I'm upset," Lisa started crying all over again.

"It's okay to be upset. But if you constantly ignore that voice that's telling you to rectify things, the more you ignore it, the easier it'll be to take the stubborn route as time progresses. Let the truth be told, most of the pain is coming from your flesh, pride, and self-will dying. And that's a good thing. You're no longer an individual. You're a wife and you have to think in terms of what's best for someone other than just Lisa. Let him know that you're agreeing to disagree, that you still love him, and you won't allow anything to erase the years and months you've spent building this relationship. Now, that may seem extreme, but it's necessary and it works. No incident is greater than the relationship."

Lisa had really started bawling at this point. "I'm going to sit and pray, and then I'll go converse with him—if he wants to, that is."

"I'm sure he does."

"Lisa, it doesn't make sense to have God at your disposal, and turn to other alternatives. That's what's wrong with the world today—we turn to the media, the government, and the entertainment world, instead of the church—the birthplace of God's love. All we have to do is trust Him and access what He's given us. The difference between those who have Christ and those who don't, is that those who do have constant help. Every answer to every question can be found in Christ. I just wish more people realized that. And furthermore, women need to learn to throw sugar, not salt when flexing our negotiating skills. They'll work every time… but I'll teach you that lesson later," she said laughingly. Mrs. Townsend had prayed with Lisa before they hung up.

Lisa had learned a lot about the ministry of marriage, in a very short time. She had felt so bad. Before this instance, she was sure that God had changed her mind about money. So why had she felt like she was having a major setback? As she sat and prayed, she heard God's voice speaking to her heart, *You can't just say your attitude has changed. No one will know it, unless your actions change, too.*

By the time she got off the phone and prayed, Bartlett was already making his way up the stairs. He knew exactly how to make her feel better. Instead of giving her the silent treatment, (which is what she unsuccessfully portrayed that she wanted), he simply grabbed her and hugged her without saying a word. Then he finally said, "I love you and we're going to get through this."

"Bartlett, please forgive me. Please don't give up on me," she cried.

"Of course, I forgive you! I would never consider giving up on you, because that would mean I'm giving up on myself."

"I realize now that perhaps I went off on a binge and I'm so sorry because I really thought I was progressing."

"I don't think you're regressing. There's just more pressure now. You're more aware and concerned about our finances. And I appreciate that. You've grown a lot, so don't go back to the very things you walked away from. We both need to be a part of our financial decisions."

"I agree. And I really want to help your cousin. It's not a coincidence that her need arose right after we talked about being a financial blessing to someone."

The next day, Lisa had arrived at the community center a few hours early. There were several things she wanted to work on without having her staff or the students there to interrupt. Hart to Hart was not open for business until noon, which is when their GED training and Adult literacy programs began. The students for the after-school program did not usually get there until after 3:00 p.m.

After working a few hours, she had decided to see if Bartlett was online.

> **The Wonderful Mona Lisa says:** Good morning. I love you and I want to apologize again. That was definitely an instance of me regressing.
> **Brave Hart says:** I want you to take that statement back, Mrs. Hartins. Listen, I love you with all my heart! And as a matter of fact, you can even replace that statement with either of the following choices:
> **Brave Hart says:** A) Psalm 37:23, "The steps of a good man are ordered by the LORD: and he delighteth in his way." So, technically I'm progressing.
> **Brave Hart says:** B) Romans 8:28, "And we know that all things work together for good to them that love God, to them who are the called according to His purpose", so technically I'm progressing.
> **Brave Hart says:** Uh!
> **Brave Hart says:** C) I wish I had more money to sow as seeds.

Lisa waited patiently as he continued.

> **Brave Hart says:** D) I wish I had more money to shop with. (SMILE)

Brave Hart says: Uh!
Brave Hart says: E) A B and C. (SMILE)
The Wonderful Mona Lisa says: You're silly!
Brave Hart says: F) Choices A and D.
Brave Hart says: G) Choices A and B.
Brave Hart says: H) All of the above.
Brave Hart says: Those are your choices, Mrs. Hartins. You have the mic, so what's it gonna be?
The Wonderful Mona Lisa says: You sicken me! (SMILE) You make me want to do better even when I don't want to put forth the effort! A & B it is!!!

Lisa loved Bartlett much more than she had ever allowed herself to love anyone. Previously when she had decided to love someone, she feared loving and trusting them completely and unconditionally, and was constantly suspicious of their motives towards her—that they would only abuse and misuse her, or walk away after they had already reeled her in.

There was a time she felt she could not be loved the way God wanted to love her. Yet He had shown her that in order to progress she had to stop reviving her hurts and wounds. So, she vowed to not be a contentious woman—spending her life making others pay for what they had done to her. Her God was not that petty and she did not want to be either.

She had never been quite sure how to totally give of herself in any relationship. However, she realized she could no longer fear giving or receiving such wonderful love. After all, she had read in 1 John 4:18 that perfect love casts out fear. "There is no fear in love; because fear hath torment; he that feareth is not made perfect in love." She knew that fear did not come from God. It was not a necessary element in His world. The recipe for perfect love is spelled out in 1 Corinthians 13—Love chooses to suffer for a long time, and is kind about the suffering it endures. Love cannot afford to entertain jealousy. Love would rather uplift another, than itself. Love is never boastful. Love is not conceited. Love is unselfish. Love does not thrive on the edge—waiting for a reason to be pushed over. Love does not focus on others' mistakes. Love dismisses the wrongdoing of others. Love is not happy about the demise of another, even if it is justified. Love does not look for something in return. Love looks for a reason to forgive. Love embraces the truth. Love gives the benefit of the doubt. Love cannot be weakened, thus Love never fails. Love is a choice. Love is God. God is Love.

Lisa thought about the perfect love she had grown to share with Christ. It had unveiled wonderfully. *There are very few examples of real love out there,* she thought. Christ exemplified true love, not only by His death, but by His resurrection, and His return for a people who could never truly deserve His love. She would never leave Him. He had proven Himself over and over, and earned her trust. And He was so worthy of all of her praise and adoration.

Lisa was finally becoming at peace with herself regarding love. Looking to others to supply love and happiness had been a bad habit. She found freedom and peace of mind in loving without expecting anything in return. It was an all new mind set, yet she not only had Christ, but Bartlett to continuously teach her the lesson of love. *I'm finally embracing my goal of being the person I've always wanted to be, and loving the way I've always wanted to love.*

She knew there would be times when Christ and Bartlett would disappoint her, and she would disappoint them, but she did not mind as long as they all stayed together. Lisa thanked God for being a specialist at using regular, ordinary people, like herself, and placing the miracle of love in their hearts, along with spiritual gifts to help establish and sustain them.

"What are you afraid of now?" David had asked her some months ago. Back then she was afraid that she would never find love. It was truly a miracle to be able to love imperfect people, and to be imperfect and yet be loved. She thanked God for His Love, with the prayer that the unconditional love He gave her, would extend into the love she had for His people, and especially for Bartlett—perfectly, forever and beyond eternity.

Lisa stopped writing in her Psalms booklet when Bartlett awoke. She fixed his lunch, and gave him his "morning loving" and send off. Then she sat a while longer, capturing her thoughts in her journal, before preparing for another fulfilling afternoon at Hart to Hart.

Being in Love as One

An abundance of mercy...
An abundance of pain…
An abundance of tears…
An abundance of forgiveness,
with no questions asked—without looking back.

An abundance of laughter…
An abundance of mistakes…
An abundance of wounds…
An abundance of healing,
by overlooking imperfections;
by constantly moving forward.

Even when you afflict me,
I simply think of the things you've whispered into my spirit,
and my heart is refreshed.
Immediate gratification is wrought by immediate remembrance
of our love which cannot be removed or shaken,
because I trust in you.
I have hope in our eternal love,
because your compassions never fail.

This love is real.
This love is spiritual.
Because fear is cast out,
This love is perfect.

An abundance of rewards…
An abundance of risk…
Yet what matters is that in the end,
you and I are still ONE…

Printed in the United States
32180LVS00006B/73-306

9 781413 766080